Dedalus European Classics
General Editor: Graham Anderson

A WOMAN'S AFFAIR

Liane de Pougy

A
Woman's
Affair

translated by
Graham Anderson

Dedalus

Published in the UK by Dedalus Limited
24-26, St Judith's Lane, Sawtry, Cambs, PE28 5XE
email: info@dedalusbooks.com
www.dedalusbooks.com

ISBN printed book 978 1 912868 48 3
ISBN ebook 978 1 912868 55 1

Dedalus is distributed in the USA & Canada by SCB Distributors,15608 South New Century Drive, Gardena, CA 90248
email: info@scbdistributors.com www.scbdistributors.com

Dedalus is distributed in Australia by Peribo Pty Ltd
58, Beaumont Road, Mount Kuring-gai, N.S.W. 2080
email: info@peribo.com.au www.peribo.com.au

First published by Dedalus in 2021
Reprinted in 2026

A Woman's Affair copyright © Graham Anderson 2021
The right of Graham Anderson to be identified as the translator of this work has been asserted by him in accordance with the Copyright, Designs and Patents Act, 1988.

Printed and bound in the UK by Clays Elcograf S.p.A.
Typeset by Marie Lane

This book is sold subject to the condition that it shall not, by way of trade or otherwise, be lent, resold, hired out or otherwise circulated without the publisher's prior consent in any form of binding or cover other than that in which it is published and without a similar condition including this condition being imposed on the subsequent purchaser.

A C.I.P. listing for this book is available on request.

The Translator

Graham Anderson was born in London. After reading French and Italian at Cambridge, he worked on the books pages of *City Limits* and reviewed fiction for *The Independent* and *The Sunday Telegraph*. As a translator, he has developed versions of French plays, both classic and contemporary, for the NT and the Gate Theatre, with performances both here and in the USA. Publications include *The Figaro Plays* (Beaumarchais) and *A Flea in Her Ear* (Feydeau).

His translations for Dedalus include, from French: *Sappho* by Alphonse Daudet, *Chasing the Dream* and *A Woman's Affair* by Liane de Pougy, *This was the Man* (*Lui*) by Louise Colet and *This Woman, This Man* (*Elle et Lui*) and *Lucrezia Floriani* by George Sand, *The Innocent Libertine* and *The Soldier's Hat* (*and other stories*) by Colette. From Italian he has translated: Grazia Deledda's short story collections *The Queen of Darkness* and *The Christmas Present*, and her novel *Marianna Sirca*, *The Celestial City* by Diego Marani, *The Ridiculolus Age* by Margherita Giacobino and *Bloodlines* by Francesco Aloia.

Graham's own short fiction has won or been shortlisted for three literary prizes. He is married and lives in Oxfordshire.

Introduction

Liane de Pougy was a high-profile courtesan in the Paris of the 1890s. Her picture appeared in the popular papers, on souvenir postcards, on flyers and advertisements for theatrical entertainments. She performed as a dancer, in tableaux and as an occasional actor at a number of theatres, notably the Folies Bergère. She attracted the attention of a series of wealthy lovers and within a few years she had acquired celebrity status among the fashionable women of the demi-monde. When still in her mid-twenties, and possibly in imitation of her friend and mentor, Valtesse de la Bigne, who had written a fictionalised account of a courtesan's life, *Isola*, in 1876, Liane de Pougy embarked on her own similar project.

A minor sub-genre of 'courtesan novels' had existed throughout the nineteenth century. The high-class prostitute's life sometimes became a subject for mainstream writers, attended by a degree of public outrage and plentiful sales. They seemed to be either heavy-handed or salacious, and rarely written from first-hand experience, in the view of Liane de Pougy. She had a poor opinion of Zola's *Nana* (1880) for instance, and had little good to say about Colette, who,

Introduction

according to Pougy, 'appeals to her readers' latent sensuality, she titillates sex... tries to intoxicate, is well aware of the vulnerable spots and flavours her salad accordingly. It works; it works with everyone; not with me.' (*Les cahiers bleus*). An element of professional jealousy is at work here. The two women were of nearly the same age (and each lived to the same age, 81) but it was Liane who made her own career, as celebrity courtesan, 'actor' and then writer, whilst Colette, as it appeared, had achieved nothing of her own. The early 1900s saw the publication of Colette's *Claudine* novels, under the name of her husband Willy, and also most of Liane de Pougy's works. Colette's real fame came with *Chéri* (1920) and *Le blé en herbe* (1923), when both women were in their middle age. Colette might have been a good writer, as Liane acknowledged, but she felt that her own work was fresher, more genuine, more *vécu*, lived.

In 1898, Liane de Pougy published her first novel, *L'insaisissable*, which she had begun in about 1895 while fulfilling professional engagements in St Petersburg. Its courtesan heroine, Josiane de Valneige, recounts to an old flame her many adventures and misadventures. At one level her stories paint a vivid and glamorous picture of life in the demi-monde, for Josiane is hedonistic, energetic and ambitious. Yet disappointment and regret always lie beneath the surface if one wishes, in such a world, to find fulfilment in true love. In the second half of the novel, a newly chaste and idealistic Josiane pursues the path of love with an unworldly younger man only to have her hopes cruelly dashed. There is nothing out of the ordinary, in *L'insaisissable*, in terms of theme or plot; what does emerge is the author's distinctive voice. Her protagonist's verve, contrariness and optimism reflect the character of a woman who both embraced and stood out from the stereotype of the *belle époque* courtesan.

Liane de Pougy was born in 1869, not in Paris but in La Flèche, a small town some forty miles from Tours. Her name was Anne-Marie Chassaigne. Her convent education ended at the age of sixteen, when she became pregnant by a naval officer called Armand Pourpe. Their son, Marc, was born in 1887. The family moved to Marseille, following Armand's posting, but the marriage was not a success. When the naval man reacted with violence to discovering his wife with a lover, Anne-Marie Pourpe ran away to Paris, leaving her son to be looked after by his paternal grandparents. Some hard months followed, financed by small parts on stage and by prostitution, which are briefly referred to in her most significant novel, *Idylle saphique*. Her bold character and unusual looks soon promoted her advancement in life. At a time when female beauties tended to the opulent and statuesque, Liane de Pougy was different.

'Shall I draw my physical portrait?' she asks in *Mes cahiers bleus*. 'Tall, and looking even more so: 1.68 metres, 56 kilos in my clothes. I run to length – long neck, face a full oval but elongated, pretty well perfect; long arms, long legs. Complexion pale and matt, skin very fine... My nose? They say it's the marvel of marvels... Hair thick and very fine, incredibly fine, a pretty chestnut brown.'

And of her character: 'Am I vain? At bottom, yes. Not outwardly. I am aware of my beauty, naturally enough – the nation's Liane could hardly have remained unaware of it... I have a persistently naïve side which makes my first reaction

Introduction

to anything one of delighted amazement, whether it's a dress, a painting, a house, a piece of furniture, a book, a poem, a gesture, a face. On second thoughts I return to reality. So I seem very changeable and in fact I *am* changeable, oh dear yes, tremendously so. I'm always turning coats completely, and doing it with the utmost sincerity.'

Liane de Pougy's new name came to her in two parts: Liane she adopted for herself on arrival in Paris; de Pougy she borrowed from one of her early aristocratic lovers. She was to have many others. In 1899 she met the American adventuress and writer Natalie Clifford Barney and began an impassioned if short-lived affair (although the two women remained close friends for most of their lives). Liane's attraction to women was natural: if anything, she preferred them to men. It was just that the money and power lay in men's hands and her courtesan's livelihood depended on the one sex while her heart found more fulfilment with the other. *Idylle saphique*, written in 1899 and 1900, and which was something of a *succès de scandale* on publication in 1901, is a novel based on real life. Jean Chalon, Natalie Barney's biographer, writes (in his introduction to the 1987 reprint by *des Femmes*):

'My friend (Natalie) made me a present of her copy of *Idylle saphique*... She enjoyed giving me the keys to the characters. Yes, she was Flossie as she was then, under the same name as the Flossie in the *Claudine* novels of Colette. Yes, Annhine de Lys was Liane de Pougy. Altesse is that famous Valtesse de la Bigne who was one of the models Zola used for his *Nana*. Beneath the name Jack Dalsace it is easy enough to recognise Jean Lorrain. As for Annhine de Lys's official lover, "head of a major bank", Maurice de Rothschild was the man who, along with the king of Portugal and a few other powerful individuals, enjoyed the privilege of counting among Liane's protectors.'

Idylle saphique is a more accomplished piece of work than the debut novella *L'insaisissable*, although its heroine has the same blue eyes and golden curls as the earlier work's, the same impetuosity, love of luxury and yearning for fulfilment. But in this book, both more cynical and more idealistic, women, it is suggested, can be self-sufficient, at least in the emotional and spiritual spheres, while men are at best a necessary evil. Instead of amusing her readers with a parade of unreliable men, as in *L'insaisissable*, Liane de Pougy broadens the canvas, from the high society of an artists' ball to the low life of Montmartre, from Sarah Bernhardt at the *Comédie Française* (in a chapter largely provided by Natalie Barney) to destitute actors starving in garrets and broadsides against the patriarchal system. There are abrupt changes of tone and scene – Liane de Pougy's 'changeability' – comic fantasies, mystical reveries and underlying it all, the sense of a struggle towards some greater good, some fairer world, which may or may not be '*saisissable*', graspable, but which is the driving force of life.

In 1910, now forty, Liane de Pougy married a minor Romanian aristocrat, Prince Georges Ghika. He was many years younger, and sometimes a difficult man, but the marriage lasted more or less intact until his death in 1945.

In December 1914, Marc Pourpe, Liane's son and now an aviator, was killed in an air crash in the early phases of the Great War. His death plunged Liane into deeper retrospection about her past life, inclining her to seek atonement, or answers,

Introduction

in religion.

On a car journey in Savoy in 1928, Liane and Georges Ghika stopped by chance at a convent which, when investigated, proved to be the Asylum of Saint Agnes, a home for children with birth defects. Profoundly moved by the children's plight and the nuns' devotion, Princess Ghika became a life-long supporter of the asylum, seeking donations from her wide circle of wealthy friends and making frequent visits in person.

When the Second World War arrived, Liane de Pougy was seventy. She and Georges had escaped the worsening situation two years before by establishing themselves in Lausanne, where she remained based for the last decade of her life. Following her husband's death, she sought admission to the order of Saint Dominic as a tertiary. She died in December 1950 as Sister Anne-Marie de la Pénitence and was buried in the grounds of the Saint Agnes Asylum.

Liane de Pougy's published works:

L'insaisissable 1898
La mauvaise part: Myrhille 1899
L'enlisement (play) 1900
Idylle saphique 1901
Ecce homo! D'ici et de là (short stories) 1903
Les sensations de Mlle de la Bringue 1904
Yvée Lester 1906
Yvée Jourdan 1908

Mes cahier bleus 1977

Introduction

Mes cahiers bleus, Liane de Pougy's diaries, written between 1919 and 1941, were posthumously published in France in 1977, and translated as *My Blue Notebooks* by Diana Athill in 1979.

L'insaisissable (*Chasing the Dream*), Liane de Pougy's first novel, is now available from Dedalus Books, who also publish Jean Lorrain's best known novel, *Monsieur de Phocas*.

I

'Oh, Tesse, I'm so bored... My life is a desert! The programme never changes: the Bois, the races, fittings at the couturier's. Then, to end an insipid day, dinner, and what an occasion that is...! Imprisoned in a fashionable restaurant so cramped for space you can't breathe, and the air usually foul with cooking smells and tobacco fug... in the company of various friends. And what friends, too – if you can call them that, the thousand and one acquaintances of greater or lesser interest that chance throws our way...! Then the evening ends with... well, what a way to end it... oh! Now, this evening, I say: bother the lot of them! I've had as much as I can take, I want to stay here at home, just with you. They can all go hang...! Ernesta! Don't put out any clothes for me, give me my old dressing gown, the pink flannel, you know, my monk's robe with a hood and waist cord. No ribbons or laces! Enough of all these frills, they're getting on my nerves! Today I want to pare myself down to the essential me. Ah, Tesse, Tesse, I'm so tired of life! I'm so bored! And tonight, you see, it's just too much. Oh...! Here we are in the middle of Paris with all its distractions, the envy of Europe, and ten thousand times over I'd rather be alone here, with you and my dog, my pretty Princess...! Princess, come here! Isn't she pretty! Here, quick, a kiss... a kiss for her mummy! Off you go now, my funny little sweet-heart, as Maindron says in *Saint-Cendre*... Have you read it, Tesse...? It's charming... Is everything ready? Good, I'm going to take these things off. Won't it be lovely, Tesse, dear, to be alone together, woman to woman, able to relax over dinner and gossip, elbows on the table, free of corsets and, especially, of irritating people...! This life of ours is so witless and silly! It brings no satisfaction to the soul or the mind and, most of the time, has nothing to offer but a level of materialism I find both tiresome and disconcerting! I promise you, Tesse, if I didn't have – fortunately, and to a very high degree, exaggeratedly even – the sensual impulse that marks out real women from the others, I wouldn't be able to bear it. You see, when I shrink back inside myself, privately and silently, in those rare moments when the whirlwind allows me a little respite, what a void...! What banality, what disgust and sadness at the same time...! Then I consider myself a poor little thing, much to be pitied, for my soul is very good and very upright. You know that, Tesse, you know the sort of person I am. I'm a child, I have a huge need for tenderness, advice, protection, and I find myself surrounded by feelings of every sort except the ones that would be so dear to me! I bitterly regret feeling alive... I'd like to exist as nothing but a doll, a brute being, everything

I appear to be and everything that I am not, alas! With nothing good ahead of me, time slips past in the same old ways... every hour brings some disappointment and a sense of fatigue, and I ask myself why...? Why...? Why all this...?'

Carried away by her outburst, the delicate creature threw herself into her friend's arms and began to heave great sighs.

'Come now, come now, Annhine, such a pretty thing! I don't recognise you any more! What's brought on this sudden attack of misery, there must be a reason, surely? You're not explaining yourself clearly... Has something gone wrong...? Has someone said you can't have something you wanted?'

'No... no...' And the enervated Annhine shook her head. 'No, Tesse, you don't understand! This is a special moment for me. I'm giving you a glimpse into a hidden corner of my heart, where everything is bitterness and disgust... I'm speaking frankly... intimately... I'm suffering from this life we lead...'

'And that's where you're wrong, Nhinon-the-beautiful. Because a courtesan must never cry, must never suffer. A courtesan is not allowed to be like other women and feel the way they do! She must stifle sentimentality of any kind and play out her heroic and unrelenting part, in order to devote her life, her youth above all, to laughter, to joyous times, to every possible pleasure! You are wrong, Nhinon, look at me: I have a soul of iron, unbending, I want nothing out of life except beauty and pleasure, I am not minded to tolerate the slightest obstacle in my way... If it is simply a case of exercising one's will, then I will with all my energy, believe me. So don't be so sensitive, Nhinette, fight, you'll turn your pawn into a queen the same as I shall... Nothing easily throws me, and the day I'm no longer strong and capable, because everything comes to pass in the end, well, that's the day I'll smash myself to smithereens and everything will be over...'

Her agitated friend replied, her voice choking: 'Oh, my darling Tesse, how I envy you! You are so wise, so masterful in the way you think! You're so lucky! But me...!'

'I am lucky because I want to be, because the day I decided to be a courtesan I erased from my life every memory, every attachment, any sense of obligation. I abdicated all claims to having what people call a soul. For me duties no longer exist, nor any responsibility except to myself and my desire! What independence! What intoxicating freedom! Annhine, just think: no more principles, no more morality, no more religion... A courtesan can do anything she likes without hiding it under a veil... without pretence, without hypocrisy, without fearing the least criticism or blame, for nothing touches her...! She is on the outside of society and its many pettinesses... Fingers pointed at her? Once upon a time, perhaps, but not these days! The rebel is victorious...! Away with you, Lady of the Camellias, and long live the Aspasias and the Imperias...! You're made of such tender stuff, my little courtesan. There's an impish spirit abroad in this house whispering things in your ear and you must drag her back down to earth before she leads you astray! Do you not have gold in your hair? In your coffers...? And gold is our sun, for people like us... an adorable and all-powerful sun that we can put aside or scatter about as we wish! Do you not have a touch of heaven in your eyes? Pearls at your neck and behind your rosy lips...? You are delicious in your monk's dressing gown... I think your androgyny is the thing that charms me most of all about you... Enough of the philosophy of life, let's play! Pull the hood over your head... you're exquisite like that, Annhine... a real gem... an eighteenth century friar in miniature, all fresh complexion and curly hair! Annhine! Laugh, then! Raise your eyes to heaven and look like someone inspired while you give me your blessing... No, no, we don't want stockings or mules, Ernesta, you'll spoil everything... Bare feet on the white carpet, that's wonderful, your pale little feet with their long toes and transparent nails. Curse it, that's certainly a clever manicurist you've got, you handsome little Franciscan...! Come here, let me hug you...! And next...' Her voice suddenly turned grave. 'Father, I wish to make confession...'

She slid to her knees before the pretty monk who sat down and assumed an attentive pose, severe and contemplative.

'Begin, my daughter, and hide nothing from me!'

'Father, my sin... is love.'

'Ah! Good, or rather bad, for it is bad, very bad, to give way to this harmful inclination... and you have a lover, no doubt, you have...'

'I have several, Father!'

'Oh!'

'Why, yes...! The first is a useful lover, I'll even say necessary; he is old, rich, generous. I am attached to him through habit, need, a sort of affectionate friendship, a sort of duty... He is, so to speak, my lover number one, or my husband if you prefer, anyway something very nearly legitimate!'

'Ah, good...! I understand... Next...?'

'Next comes the second: young, kind, vigorous. Oh, above all vigorous...! He gives me what the first can no longer offer. Oh, Father, what amazing pleasures with my Raoul! For nearly five years now our life together has consisted solely of moving from chaise-longue to bed! He is my lover number two, the one who really loves me, this one... my sin, my...'

'Continue, continue... After him...?'

'After him come the minor ones, the occasionals: a pleasant occasion, a useful occasion, an occasion I've been looking out for, an occasion I hadn't expected, an occasion flattering to my self-esteem. I have the temperament for excess, you see, Father. I need love, sensual pleasure! I am a woman who burns... Oh, but I know what a courtesan owes to herself and I never forget that... I enjoy myself, but only while accumulating riches, for I always make sure the pleasure I give attracts the highest possible fees, although at the supreme moment when I gasp: "I love you", I am always sincere... or nearly always.'

'In that case you may go in peace, my child. Great will be the forgiveness if you have greatly loved...'

Nhine sniggered as she held out her hands.

Altesse stood up, in gales of laughter.

'It's true, fundamentally, everything I've just said. Oh, how I wish you were the sort of person I am! More literal, more lively, more resolute, therefore more happy! Strange little flower that you are, going pale under the sun's too-hot rays and expiring from the very thing that makes everyone else alive: the earth! Could your soul have its roots, then, on some distant and ethereal planet...? And could you be suffering from that infinitely mysterious ailment called exile, living as you do down here where all is mere time and desires?'

'You're being terribly sweet and indulgent, Tesse, my darling, though you exaggerate. Give me something new, is all

I ask. Something new! For the love of God, something new...! I can't carry on like this! My life needs to be turned upside down, it's essential! I need a change! Something new! New! New!'

And she beat her tiny feet feverishly on the magnificent tiger skin that covered the floor, repeating in the voice of a supplicant chanting prayers her refrain of satiety and boredom.

A ring at the doorbell interrupted her, a faint sound, only just reaching them. It was as if the stranger at the door had neither the courage nor the strength to activate the little jangling mechanism with any vigour, not daring and not wishing to disturb the courtesan's dreams of sweetness and joy.

'Listen, that was someone ringing...! What do you bring me, timid bell? A basket of flowers probably, or an invitation or even something in a jeweller's box? What a little ring, so discreet... perhaps it's nothing at all.'

'Perhaps it's this "something new" you've just been demanding so loudly,' Tesse prophesied in grave tones.

'Or more likely some imbecile come to disturb us! That must be it... I can sense it, I bet it is. And just as I'm really enjoying being with you this evening, trusting each other like this and sharing confidences! Ah! No! I won't have it! Ernesta! Ernesta...!'

Ernesta came back in.

'Madame, it's a letter.'

'I shan't read it today!'

'Madame, the person is waiting for a reply.'

'Too bad. Tell them to come back another time, say I'm busy with something important, say I'm...'

'Don't be silly!' Tesse interrupted. 'Let me have it then.

It's a pretty paper, delicate pearl grey, a washed-out shade like the colour of your thoughts today; it seems elegant and well-intentioned at the same time. Pass it over…'

'You want to…? Very well, let's see…'

And the wilful child ripped open the envelope and began to read aloud:

> '*For Annhine de Lys… my heart's dream.*
> If you are not tired
> By love that's expired
> And the dream's still in sight,
> Receive me tonight!

'It's signed: *A woman unknown to you, alas! And who wishes not to remain so.*'

She burst out laughing.

'It's weird…! What a joke…! Into the fire!'

'No, Annhine… Does it really say that? Show me…!'

'Here you are. See?'

'And who brought this thing, Ernesta?'

'Madame, the person is down in the vestibule. It's a girl, pretty, very blond, fresh, blushing, she looks a bit emotional, she refused to go into the drawing room. She says she's waiting only for a yes or a no from madame. I think she must be an English girl.'

'What do you say, Tesse? I think it's rather funny. We can agree to see her, it'll make a nice distraction.'

'Is she well turned out?'

'Madame, I didn't examine her too closely, but she seemed quite smartly dressed to me: a long beige fitted coat, a large black hat with feathers and a magnificent boa, sable, I think.'

'Let's see her, shall we?'

'We must! Life isn't as silly as all that, you see, spoilt child!'

'Yes, but...' And Annhine giggled. 'I have an idea... wait... You stretch out on my chaise longue among the cushions and ermine rugs and pretend to be all languid and weary, and you receive her, yes you, saying you're Annhine de Lys. Oh, yes! This will make us laugh! And I shall be hidden... there, behind the side panels of the glass doors... I'll leave one half open and that way I shall hear and see everything. It'll be so funny! Will you do it...? Come on, then! There, lie down, full length... head tilted back a bit more. Keep still, let me arrange your hair... Hold your handkerchief in your hand... that looks right now, that's it! Mind you play your part well! Cough occasionally and make your voice drag a bit...! Bye, bye, Nhine, Nhinette, Nhinon! Send the young miss in, Ernesta... let the blue double curtains down, light the lamp at the end of the room, that's right... stage well set, and warn that bold young person that Mme de Lys is a little indisposed! I'll creep into my hiding place and the show can begin...! Let's make it a good one...!'

This whole scene was taking place in the coquettish boudoir of Annhine de Lys, a delicious retreat in the form of a rotunda, with a décor of white and blue in which the snowy lacquers, the Louis XV trinkets, the pale silks, the fur rugs, and the Meissen and Sèvres and the gold and crystal and the flowers formed an exquisite setting for the diaphanous fairness of the adorable little mistress of this interior, a creature already famous in the demi-monde and in society at large for her eccentricities and through the very public and fascinated attention given to her slightest act and whim. Annhine was at this time about twenty-three but appeared no more than twenty. Long-boned and delicate, with her great blue eyes, dark and deep, at once innocent and perverse, with her blond hair framing her fine features in radiantly light and looping curls, she looked like a virgin on a missal, wearing a cherub's wig, or at times like one of those châtelaines from the Middle Ages, a dream creature, brought to perfection by the glimpse of pearly whiteness behind the elongated oval of the lips, frequently parted by her enchanting laughter.

Where did she spring from...? No one quite knew. She liked to tell a story of being found at the side of a road, in Italy, by some simple souls, on a night white with frost and mortally cold. A love child, no doubt, abandoned by a guilty mother, probably a great lady – her linen had been of the finest, and decorated with lace of rare quality... she had a little gold medallion at her neck... she was wrapped in a rich goat skin from Mongolia, white and silky – a great lady most certainly. For from whom could Annhine have inherited that proud and majestic deportment, that admirable and noble way of carrying her head, those princess-like traits, so refined and spirited, or indeed her ideas on life and the beyond, so mysterious, as if they had been vague reminiscences and distant memories of some kind that came back to her: from whom could she have inherited all this if she had really been the daughter of those country people who watched over her young childhood...?

Around the age of fifteen, Nhinon had come to seek whatever fortune might lie in store in the great city, and after the inevitable trials, setbacks and obscurity of any beginning she now found herself one of the leading lights among that world of hedonists on whom the Public Eye so avidly gazes. Never missing a party or celebration, she was acclaimed by all of Paris. Poets sang her beauty, theatres fought each other for her services. Her crowning apotheosis was to catch the fancy of a great aristocrat of fabulous wealth. Queen of every realm, of joy, of beauty, of extravagance, of love, she seemed to pass through life, heedless, joyous, in accordance with her whimsical motto – *As I please!* – without a thought for anything else. But, alas! Annhine had a soul, which was the source of these painful periods of sudden despair! Unbalanced, said those who knew her. No, this was the seat of her trouble: Annhine had a little soul that sat ill with her body! She thought, she analysed, she had a vivid imagination and a clear mind, remarkably acute in its observations, gifts which were all useless, harmful, emotionally burdensome above all in the turbulent and bejewelled path on which her prettiness and an imperious need for luxury had launched her with such success.

Her name she had chosen from the works of Dumas… and its echoes spread from the moment she made her debut, which resulted in her having scarcely any friends among the women who felt jealous of her good luck and silently held it against her. Just one, however, stood by her: Altesse, a courtesan herself and a woman of noticeably higher intellect. They became very close. Altesse admired Annhine greatly, and, with no ulterior motive, liked the fluidity of her character, the brilliance of her chosen circle as well as her strange way of life. She helped her with her advice and was at times a salutary influence.

Altesse was then at the height of her powers, a woman

whose bloom might be about to fade but whose charms, as Balzac so widely celebrates, are never more delightfully appreciated. Her fiery head of hair, its long locks flecked with flame and stippled with gold like a wild animal's pelt, had been immortalised in a sensational novel: *The Red-Headed Beauty*. Her eyes were blue... very pale, with an incomparable sparkle... her small mouth, finely arched in ironic wit, brought Leonardo da Vinci's Mona Lisa to mind. Her expression was thoughtful and determined, her features had a regular, cold beauty that confirmed the poet's verse:

> *I hate all movement that disturbs a line,*
> *And never do I weep, nor ever laugh.*

And further on:

> *To tame my docile lovers I have these*
> *Pure mirrors that make all more beautiful.*
> *My eyes, wide eyes, their shining eternal.*[1]

Endowed with rare intelligence, as well as great strength of character and will, and extremely attractive, Altesse had attained a prominent position among the high-living set of Paris at a very early age. Surrounded with every imaginable luxury, she coldly lived the true courtesan's life. Paris followed her affairs closely, her least acts noted, her witticisms quoted. 'How charming of you to acknowledge your descent,' she said one day to a great lady of dubious title, princess Koniarowska, who had the bad taste to lean heavily on affectations of noble

---

1 Baudelaire, *La beauté*.

birth. 'When personally all I have to offer is my rise.' Her motto was: *Ego*, and it summed her up perfectly. She was a highness indeed, aloof and without weakness.

Once, when the census lists were being drawn up, she saw that all the women of the demi-monde had timidly entered themselves, in the space where they declared their professions, as 'of private means' or 'property owner'. Shamelessly, she inscribed the simple description: 'courtesan'.

Her town house was a veritable museum; she collected the finest paintings in Paris. She had a marvellous garden in the heart of the Monceau district, and the teams of horses that drew her carriages were held to be the best turned-out. In the summer she withdrew to her château in Ville-d'Avray, where she gave splendid receptions. In the winter, she spent the very cold months in a ravishing villa, all marble and whiteness, which she had had built on the sunlit shores of the blue Mediterranean, amongst the sumptuous gardens of Monte Carlo.

Her exceptional situation distinguished her from the others and placed her above the crowd. At once, she took a particularly strong liking to Annhine, and almost every day, at the hour when elegant and worldly women withdraw to prepare themselves for the evening, around half past six, Altesse came over to chat a little with her favourite friend. They exchanged confidences, impressions, sought each other's advice, and often they would pick up their conversation again when the dinner party or theatre visit was over.

This evening, Altesse was already feeling affected by Annhine's desolation. So it was with pleasure and with charming grace that she lent herself to her friend's malicious fantasy, happy that her impish and capricious spirit should now be distracted, however childishly, by whatever this unexpected visit might turn out to be, coming so conveniently to provide a diversion.

She asked, keeping her voice low: 'All right, I'm all set, Nhinon. Do you think it could work?'

'Very well… very well… But hush, here she comes…!'

II

Indeed the door swung open at that very moment and as Ernesta was announcing in bold tones: 'Miss Temple-Bradfford,' our two mischief-makers had the delightful floating vision of a ravishing young girl of twenty coming towards them, with halting steps and lowered eyes. Clasped in her arms was a whole garden of pale chrysanthemums and lilies with long bright gold pistils, among which a few gleaming dark red roses inserted their own graver notes. Such was her emotion that the feathers on her hat trembled and her fingers, taut with nerves, crushed the bouquet held close to her heart.

On reaching the chaise longue, she knelt and seized the white hand of Altesse, covering it with kisses. The flowers scattered in a tumble of colour and scent. Blushing, confused, she spoke in a rapid murmur, keeping her head down: 'Thank you, Annhine, for being so good to me... It was no mistake, when I first saw you, so beautiful... Oh, I don't want to say boring things but, you see, I'm so dazzled I can't even muster the hymn of thanksgiving I intended, to thank you with due fervour for receiving me here in your home... Thank you!'

'But tell me, strange child...' Altesse restrained with difficulty a powerful urge to laugh. 'Do you actually know who I am?'

'You are the one woman in all the world who draws me to you.'

'Where did you see me?'

'I could say: in my dreams, in the ecstasy of my frustrated desire... ever since I knew you existed!'

'And how long is that?'

'For ever! But your presence in real life was revealed to me for the first time the other evening... You were in a box at the Folies-Bergère and I recognised you. I divined you straight away even though I had never seen you before, and your picture on the little cards they sell everywhere gives no idea of your divine beauty, my beautiful white rose. As you appeared to me, you were so lovely, so luminously white in your light muslin dress, pearls at your neck... you seemed so childlike, so pure... you were wearing on your breast a simple diamond cross that completed the angelic illusion perfectly!'

'And so?'

'And so I felt an irresistible desire to see you, to speak to you, to be close to you... and I came... without a moment's hesitation... Annhine! Such joy! You have received me... you are good... thank you...! I know,' she said, and once more began to kiss and stroke with delicate fingers Altesse's pale hand and slender wrist, 'I know it means nothing to you...'

'No... Yes, it does! Tell me who you are.'

'You know my name. For the rest, you can put me down as crazy, but that's all to the good... Mad people have much more ravishing dreams than sensible people...!'

'Where do you come from, mysterious passer-by?'

'From a distant land in America. From the land of gold and liberty: San Francisco!'

'The land of gold and liberty,' sighed Tesse. 'You mean Cythera isn't the only one? And you were bold enough to leave it behind! Why?'

'So that I might come close to you... closer to another civilisation that was more refined, more morbid... to live a little in the burning and febrile atmosphere of Sodom and Gomorrah... closer to the place where the divine couplings of the lascivious fauns of modern times may take place virtually at liberty.'

'I see... So that's it...! You're...'

'Oh, be merciful. Don't tarnish with a name the feeling which has always had hold of me ever since I felt myself capable of feeling, which overpowers me here and now, beside you, Annhine! Don't you know that there can be an aspect of the sublime in anything? And it seems to me that right now... at your feet... in this boudoir where everything, for me, breathes desire, the mystery of enchantment and sensuality... the scent of the flowers, all this airy silk and transparent lace... it seems to me, you see, I'm at the high altar of...'

Carried away by the feverish excitement of her own words, the strange child had little by little levelled her enamelled blue gaze, forgetting the embarrassment of her first entrance. Now she was staring at Altesse in a posture of ecstatic adoration...

Suddenly her look changed, to one of surprise at first, then of consternation... and finally disappointment. Her head fell back on the cushion of flowers and she murmured, through a sob: 'Ah! I have been tricked! It isn't you! It isn't you! It isn't you!'

'Whatever do you mean?' asked Tesse, amused.

'No, no! It isn't you, Annhine! Where am I? Why have I been tricked? Have pity... have pity on me!'

As she begged, great tears rolled from her eyes.

'There now, little miss, don't cry. Come along, it's not as terrible as all that.' And with a charming gesture, Altesse sat up and drew towards her the girl's tear-stained face. 'You mustn't cry, you are too nice for that.'

'No, miss, don't cry. Here I am.'

And Annhine suddenly appeared from her hiding place.

The hat of the young visitor had, in her woe, come adrift... her head of silvery hair had come undone and it was through a veil as fine and floating as gossamer that she looked upon Annhine, the real one, bending over her in confusion and alarm at the unfortunate result of her teasing. As soon as the girl saw her, her face lit up.

'Oh! Yes! It's you... you're the one I wanted to see! Wicked woman...! You're the one...!' And with religious devotion she prostrated herself before Annhine, then lifted the hem of her dressing gown to her lips.

'My poor little miss...! To start with, you must sit down...' And she tried to guide her towards a small love seat that stood at the end of the chaise longue.

'No... at your feet... cruel woman...!' Her body shook with great sighs of emotion. 'And if you will allow me...'

A Woman's Affair

In a single movement she shrugged off her long woollen coat and stood before them dressed, deliciously, as a Florentine pageboy, grey silk tights exquisitely moulding themselves to her shapely legs, her body admirably set off by a short dalmatic of pale green brocade decorated with foliage worked in precious stones. On the swelling part of the chest was embroidered a lily, in pearls and silver, a large water lily on its moist and greenish stalk: the flower that was Annhine's emblem. The sleeves and collar of the shirt underneath were in finely pleated white lawn, its puffed elbows and shoulders of a velvet whose sheen reflected the dusty blue of lavender.

'Isn't she a pretty sight,' Altesse said. 'Look, Nhine, fate's pampered favourite, look at the handsome page destiny has sent you!'

'It is Sappho who has sent me... Do you want me? Do you accept me, to serve you? Nhine, I adore you: let me feel it is possible to realise my dreams, my hopes. Don't reject me...!'

And she set herself at Annhine's feet.

'Oh! What a wild little creature...!' The slender fingers of Annhine played among the girl's blond curls... 'But tell me, how did you have the courage to come to my door? Weren't you afraid? Your family... your reputation... and then, what about me? After all, I could easily have given you a difficult reception, being the sort of woman I am!'

'Oh, Nhinon!' Jumping lightly to her feet she took a step towards Annhine and stopped her mouth by gracefully putting her lips to it... 'Don't utter such blasphemies! I'd divined everything about you!'

'And then,' Annhine said, disengaging herself, 'think about it... another thing, and the most important... perhaps I don't share your tastes and your ideas, what about that?'

'May I point out that you said perhaps!' observed Altesse maliciously, delighted by this unexpected entertainment.

'Nhinon, Nhinon! I'll convert you... And anyway, all I'm asking is for you to let yourself be loved... adored... admired. Nothing else, my Nhinon, only to accept me as your page... your fervent little pageboy of love. Will you? Will you let me employ my time – as much time as my family, for I have one here with me, alas, in Paris, and the demands of society allow (and it will give me pleasure to curtail their claims) – by coming to be with you and by telling you things in words as soft as caresses, things to distract you from the banality of your existence, or try to at any rate... and be intoxicated by your diaphanous and disturbing beauty... Tell me, Nhine... will you? Madame...' She turned towards Altesse. 'Madame, ask her too. Plead with me, to make up for your cruel trick just now... Tell me then... will you?'

'Agreed, miss... I will!... I accept you as my page, slavish servant to my beauty... my beauty, which is itself servile, alas!'

'Have you thought about this properly, where it might lead you?' asked Tesse, a vague feeling of worry crossing her mind.

'Like the holy martyrs, I shall bravely go forward even unto death for the glory of my religion... and my religion is Nhinon! Nhine! Annhine de Lys!'

She stretched her hand in front of her as if to swear a solemn oath... as if she were a mystic, an ecstatic.

Annhine rose, full of joy, and went to stand in front of her mirror, near a dressing table in white lacquer on which were scattered the gold trinkets, sweet perfumes, flasks, powders and paints designed to bring her startling beauty to life.

'Come with me, then, page! Lie on the floor just there, against the tiger's head, and admire me at your leisure! I want to hear your story. Tell me your name... your given name...'

'I no longer have any story to tell... At this blessed moment I abdicate personality entirely. I am nothing except your page, the page of Annhine de Lys...' And drunk with joy, the child crawled across the thick carpets and on to the piled furs. 'Oh! Your pretty bare foot! Oh, Nhinon... Seeing you sets my heart pounding.' And she pressed her lips to the provocative pink flesh.

'Isn't he sweet, Tesse, my page? Isn't he sweet...!' Bending down, she cupped her hand under the girl's chin and lifted her head, then examined her, full of curiosity. 'Isn't he sweet! Oh, those pretty eyes, and that mauve eye-shadow underneath... Oh, oh, pretty hair... you'd think a moonbeam had landed on it! Tell me, what's your baptismal name?'

'My...?'

'Yes, when you were christened, the name you're normally called!'

'Ah! Yes, it's Emily.'

'Oh, that's a terrible name for you. I once had a wicked chambermaid called that, and she betrayed me.'

'I have a second name: Florence... Flossie for short.'

'No... I don't want any of that sort of thing... I shall call you Moon-Beam! Altesse – she is my best friend, my only one, you must love her as well – Tesse sometimes calls me her "sun beam". You shall be my "moon beam", Moon-Beam. It's glorious! And it suits you... Show me your teeth: very white, very beautiful, very beautiful, they frighten me, the mouth of a vicious child. Moon-Beam, you have a vicious mouth... it's plain to see. Here, Tesse, look: her lips are very sensual, slightly thick, her jawline's very strong, a bit brutal. Oh, Mademoiselle, this is very promising! Your complexion is pale, but you blush easily... Your eyes are blue, but not like mine, or Altesse's... they're an indefinable sort of blue-grey and the pupils are enormous, dilated, devouring... Your nose...'

'Ah, Nhine, and you, you're just so beautiful...!' And the child, drunk with pleasure, swooned under the intoxicating effect of having Annhine leaning so closely over her.

'Don't interrupt... Your nose is finely sculpted, it turns up a little, a vicious nose as well... All in all, you're very cute. Not as beautiful as Altesse, or as me, and worse maybe! I forbid you to look at me with those eyes! Be so good as to lower them! What do you think of all this, Altesse, my darling Minerva? Stand up, Moon-Beam. A nice figure... no bosom to speak of, same as me, a trifle boyish. Tesse will love us... Your hips are wider than mine... Tesse, speak up, you haven't said a word! Have I done well to take on a little page looking like this?'

'Anything you find pleasing is well done,' Tesse replied seriously, and without the slightest hesitation.

The enchanted Moon-Beam interrupted: 'Yes, anything you find pleasing is well done, Annhine... and for the first time in my life I give thanks to those who made me for making me like this, to your taste... I give blessings for your indulgence... Nhinon, Altesse, I feel so deeply and deliciously moved, I want to cry... to weep long, hot, sweet tears of joy!'

She picked at the flowers on the floor.

A Woman's Affair

'Nhine... These flowers were meant for you. I'd chosen all the whitest and most virginal ones I could find, in your likeness. These crimson roses, they are my heart's blood, which beats only for you... a banal image, but a faithful one, and exact... Oh, I'm so happy! I would deliver a whole litany of love if I could, my Nhine, my beauty... and I have to... I have to go away from you...'

In two seconds she had gathered her floating fair hair, put on her hat, her coat and was standing in the doorway... sending her parting look... her parting kiss towards Annhine... Her voice was a low murmur, almost breaking in a wave of regret: 'Don't move, don't speak, beloved women. I must fly, until tomorrow. I carry you away with me in my heart and in all my being. I am going to live on this exquisite vision of the two of you. And tomorrow, towards the third hour, may I...? Yes, I shall return...! Until tomorrow then, until tomorrow, I bid you... farewell!'

She stood motionless, in a pose of frozen contemplation, as if unable to tear herself away from the poignant sweetness of her own emotion. Then she made a sweeping gesture, like someone throwing a last kiss to people departing on a long sea voyage... an abrupt swirl of the body that caused her to vanish into the penumbra of the dusky drawing room.

III

The next morning Annhine woke up in a very bad mood. She had spent a disturbed night, almost a sleepless one, following an evening much interrupted by telephone calls and by a slight argument with Tesse, who did not entirely share her enthusiasm for Miss Florence.

'You mustn't rush at things like this, my lovely,' her wise friend had said. 'Treat it as a little fun. Let her call, but keep your eyes wide open! You're on public view, you have people all round you, you're in the business of accumulating wealth: this young girl suddenly turns up at your house without rhyme or reason, basically. Who knows what she might want from you? To observe you, probably, then copy you. Or for the novelty and spice of a flirtation with the beautiful Nhinon. Perhaps she's part of a pick-pocketing gang!'

And when Annhine, indignant, called her a cynic, a faultfinder, a spoil-sport, Tesse went on: 'Being a lesbian, to my mind, would be the least of her faults. So what? You are not very strong, darling Annhinette, you tire easily. Think, every time you have any sort of theatre engagement to fulfil, you need to rest afterwards, you need looking after. You haven't the powers of resistance to take on this sort of relationship. That little creature – you said so yourself, rightly – has noticeably prominent incisors, an animal's mouth. Think about that fresh look of yours, Nhine, think about your lovers! Why complicate your life? And then, she strikes me as being an intelligent woman, which only makes her more dangerous. I'm willing to believe she hasn't been telling us lies, but what is she actually going to add to your existence? Your friends will begin to drift away if she gets her hooks into you, she'll be a drain on your time and you know my thoughts on that subject. Your job is to become very rich, Annhine, and to put yourself beyond reach of the vagaries of fate. Squeeze every profit you can from your years of beauty and don't get tangled up with a young miss however seductive she might be. Don't give away your secrets, the perfume you use, where you get your massages, who makes your make-up, who your lovers are, believe me; and don't give her any more of yourself than you have to. Call her when you feel bored, nothing more; and let her be a mystery to anyone and everyone.

'Are you sulking...? Look at you! Are you cross with me, wicked woman...? Right, I won't say any more... But you know, Nhine, she isn't as pretty as all that, this new fancy of yours; and as for me, I'm jealous because she's already creating a distance between us and keeping me apart from your thoughts.'

She leaned towards the spoilt and wilful child and placed a tender kiss on her blond tresses.

'And now, enough, let's talk about something else…!'

But however hard she tried, Annhine could not find a brighter mood for the rest of the evening. She invented a slight indisposition and went to bed early.

The following morning, when Ernesta tiptoed into the bedroom around half past nine and opened the shutters, she was still in the same state of agitated confusion.

'Pull those blinds down, quick. Really! The sun's dazzling,' Annhine muttered, her voice troubled. 'It's ridiculous, sunshine in Paris in the middle of November. How can anyone be expected to know where they are when the seasons don't?'

And she pulled the fine linens sullenly round her and thrust her legs beneath the silky warmth of the pink satin bedspread. Princess came to disturb her and wanted to play, as was her custom.

'Leave me be, naughty dog. Go to sleep… go to sleep.'

She could barely manage to give the animal a distracted kiss, and that a mere brush of the lips.

'Does Madame wish to take her bath? Everything is ready. I've made it eucalyptus this morning.'

'No, no! I don't want that! I hate eucalyptus, it smells of the chemist's! Change it! I won't have it, understand? I want almond milk mixed with verbena, you know that perfectly well but you're just going out of your way to upset me…'

She fell back on the beribboned cushions and closed her eyes, pleased with and somewhat assuaged by her little outburst. Three minutes later, her sense of who she was gradually returning, she called, in tones of resignation: 'Ernesta, Ernesta!

If it's eucalyptus already, I'll have it like that. I don't want to have to wait... Give me my mirror.'

And looking at herself in the charming gilt mirror her maid passed her, its handle inlaid with rubies and fat baroque pearls, Annhine smiled back at her seductive reflection, happy to find herself pretty.

'There! I don't look too awful. Tesse is silly to tell me I'm such a fragile thing. I'll bury the lot of them.'

'Madame is a fresh as a rose,' Ernesta ventured.

'Quiet, you, I don't care for flatterers. This, look, this...' and she brandished the slender mirror, 'this never lies. And the day I'm old and ugly, well, I'll do as la Castiglione did... I'll shroud them all in thick black gauze. The uncompromising, the cruel, the truthful little mirrors who never speak a word but who have more to say, and more genuinely, than... Listen! I heard someone ringing, already. Go and see who it is.' She turned to Princess and began to fondle her. 'Who's the pretty one, who's the beautiful one? Yes, we'll cover the mirrors to punish them for not lying, and we'll go and live far away in the country in a fine castle with our dog, our little doggie-woggie.'

She rolled the animal on its side, kissed it, nibbled its tummy... Princess, charmed, ecstatic, emitted little groans and yelps of joy.

'Madame, it's the little Miss from yesterday with a handsome bouquet. Simon said he wasn't altogether sure Madame was awake, he'd go and see... She's waiting.'

Annhine arranged herself properly in bed.

'Send her in. Ernesta, do I look good like this?'

She let her head fall back and laid her bare arms over the white sheets, her eyes half closed, in a pose that mingled nonchalant ease with semi-slumber.

'Madame is ravishing!'

'Just as I thought! Ah, what I'd give to be told one day my nose was crooked! Fine! Quick, send her in and take Princess away.'

'It is I, Nhine. Apologies for daring to remind you so soon of the dreadful outside world, but I couldn't help myself.' And Moon-Beam stood in the doorway, entranced and excited at the sight of this bedroom, all pink and white and gold panelling, illuminated by brilliant shafts of sunlight. Made sunny, too, by Annhine's radiant hair, its owner's tousled head emerging smiling and seductive from the depths of the vast Louis XV bed, a rare copy, unique in its gilt and garlanded roses, of a famous bed that had once belonged to the mistress of the Great King. 'I shall never see anything as beautiful as this again!' the girl murmured.

'They woke me up for you,' Annhine lied sweetly, in a mournful voice. 'And the sun's blinding me!'

'Oh, no, Nhine. It's for these poor little things. They were fading away, being kept so far from you, and I took pity on them.'

And Moon-Beam, stepping gravely into the room, began to strew its floor with her floral tribute. Her armful of flowers became a carpet for the dainty feet of her beloved.

'Listen to what they're telling you: Accept us; let us die near to you; we have but a tiny life here on earth, but we shall not have lived in vain since we have been permitted to know you and to love you... Would that I were able, like them, to die for love at your feet, Nhinon!'

'When you think about it, flowers and women, they're

sort of sisters!'

'They know more, because they haven't learnt anything.'

'They have great wisdom: they live in order to love; they don't love in order to live.'

'That way, they catch a little happiness while waiting for the great.'

'Ah, happiness…! Happiness!'

'Where is it? And what is it?'

'A puff of wind!'

'A wisp of cloud!'

'A myth!'

'A butterfly with brilliant multi-coloured wings that flits and flees before us, and we chase after it, attracted, wanting to catch it and hold it. And in our fingers what remains is a smudge of gleaming dust… a few ashes… crumbs… nothing left… nothing!'

'Happiness doesn't exist.'

'Yes, with you. Oh, if my thoughts could speak out loud, and reach you, and touch you!'

They fell silent.

'But you're meant to be taking your bath, I heard… Come on, I can be your servant, what do you think?'

'Yes, that will be nice.'

And Nhinon, amused, comforted, tossing blankets and sheets away from her, stepped cheerfully towards the bathroom that adjoined her bedroom.

'Leave us, Ernesta, and don't disturb us for any reason.'

The bathroom was a little marvel in itself, all white stucco and purest Louis XV style like the rest of the house. It was an octagonal room, surprisingly large from side to side, lit by a high-set window made from lots of small, square, bevelled panes and veiled by a curtain of pale blue silk. The window was reached, as in the old days, by four or five steps in light polished oak. The walls were hung all round with mirrors of Venetian glass, which drew a shimmering, jealous circle about the frail nudity of Venus-Annhine-Dyomene!

A single watercolour portrait interrupted the flickering reflections: a naked woman, Altesse, in a pose glorifying the human form. This was the work of her lover, an unusual whim on his part, for he was a famous painter, celebrated for his military scenes, battles, charges, cavalcades. He had wished, one day, to capture her in the full splendour of her mother-of-pearl flesh, the wild gold of her hair tumbling majestically over that shapely perfection – which the artist's fancy had enhanced by clothing it in a pair of long blue stockings. Then, on the floor, a carpet from the Savonnerie, unique of its kind, very thick, its colours faded, on top of which was spread a bearskin rug, white and silky; a boat-shaped sofa covered in rich and gleaming otter; a low chair upholstered in antique silk; dozens of silk cushions in pastel tones, scattered randomly everywhere. In front of the Carrara marble fireplace, with its cheerful little blaze, stood a small table overloaded with those indispensable English boxes and stands containing port, biscuits and coca-leaf infusions for restorative purposes. No paintings or porcelain pieces, but, in a corner, leaning gracefully and symbolically over her white and winged wheel, Franceschi's statue of Fortune, her mischievous foot at a provocative angle, her attitude proud and fickle. Tall muslin curtains, embroidered and lacy, hanging against a background of sky-blue silk, completed the elegant effect of these dreamy furnishings. Then, finally, mounted on golden feet, made of crystal drawn into spirals and inlaid with pale turquoises, the bath itself appeared at the far side of the room, illuminated by a hundred lights, like a precious and transparent chalice destined to contain the fragile, pearly flower of Annhine's blonde and delicate slenderness.

Penetrating this disturbing sanctuary of intimate repose, Flossie was overcome with emotion. She stood for a moment as if uncertain, but the thrilling sight of Annhine rising naked from the folds and frills of the chemise she let fall gave her back her courage. With a lover's sudden surge of daring, she threw herself at the pretty creature's feet and, lacing her arms round her, planted kisses of devotion on ankles, knees, legs, thighs... lost all control... murmured broken words, turning to moans of adoration, of prayer... trembled in every limb... wild... feverish... delirious. Annhine, impassive, let her continue for a while, smiling... Then, escaping with a sudden bound, she plunged into the perfumed water, sending a shower of droplets cascading over her still kneeling little page.

'There, you impertinent Moon-Beam! Your job is to serve me, not to bother me. I am in a bad mood, you know. Besides, you must love me without saying so, and with less embracing. I don't love you, Flossie: I allow myself to be loved by you, which is a different thing altogether. Put my hair up... there, on your left, in that Sèvres dish, use that tortoiseshell pin. You're so clumsy! You don't know anything, fool!' And snatching the pin, she triumphantly thrust it into the mass of golden curls piled on top of her head. 'See, I look like a clown!'

'You are beautiful... Tyrannical...' the child stammered.

'Not at all. I am no tyrant.' And standing up in the bath,

she began to soap herself all over, the opaline water and the creamy suds giving her the fluffy appearance of a white cloud. 'Come here and embrace me like this. Ah! Ow! Stop... that tickles, Moon-Beam! She's so bold... You look like the cat that's got the cream.' Her voice became severe. 'Enough, enough. That's enough, I said!' Losing patience, she plunged her hands in the water and gave the enraptured page a good splashing. 'No, really, I'm sorry, I'm all nerves... The bath will calm me. I know what! Take your things off, get in, get in with me, we'll have a bath together! Yes, get in, I said so, Moon-Beam... it's what I want! Aha! It doesn't take you long to get your clothes off, does it? Two shakes of a lamb's tail, as they say. No corset or petticoats... a pink chemise decorated with periwinkles and morning glory, that's nice, with those mauve ribbons... a bit tarty, my dear, but artistic... In you get... but you're going to be good... I shall like you very much, page. We'll play, we'll have as much fun as we can, but nothing dirty. Oh, no, definitely not. I've had enough of that... Sick to death of it... And it's my living too, worse luck!'

'Annhine, for pity's sake...!' And the child, bare, and pink and white and sad, her long hair flying, leaned over and placed a finger on her lips. 'Don't speak. What I love you for, my gentle Madonna, is the sadness and bitterness I sense in you from the life you have to lead. What I thought I wanted to be close to was just a woman – the prettiest, sweetest of women – and I have discovered a soul I want to understand, through learning everything that you are... Yes, Nhine, we shall love each other, and we shall have fun!'

'Then come here, Moon-Beam, come in with me. And let's talk about you. I want to learn about you, too. Introduce yourself. Behold: Miss Florence Temple…'

'Bradfford,' Florence interrupted gaily. 'Twenty, happy at this moment in your bath-tub, playing water lilies with you, living most of the time in San Francisco with a mother, a father, strait-laced and bourgeois, and two artistic brothers, one paints, the other acts. As for me, I love beauty! Form is my religion, what pleases the eye, and I am drawn to the mystical, the supernatural, and irresistibly I was drawn to you… Nhine.'

'What are you doing in Paris? I want to know everything.'

'Ah, yes! Visiting Paris with my mother, one of my brothers and my fiancé, staying on until the end of the Great Exhibition…'

Dumbfounded, Annhine leant forward to look at her closely.

'Your fiancé!' she exclaimed.

'Of course…! Sadly, one has to submit to the ordinary and natural rule of life. I have a fiancé, Nhine, which gives me the relative freedom that I am this very moment enjoying, since it allows me to come and imbibe your aura, my sweet flower. Where I come from, in America – don't you know, darling (as we say) – young women have considerable freedom. I go out with my fiancé, we visit the museums, the races, we go shopping, we go to the theatre, in fact everywhere a young woman can go. A fiancé, you see, is as necessary to me as food, drink and sleep, that's all. I really had to have a fiancé, my Nhine. And mine is kind, very kind, I'd say. Good-natured, accommodating… his eyes are the green of ripe grape pips… he knows me through and through…'

'Through and through?'

And Annhine, incredulous, stared at her questioningly.

'Why, yes. And through... The proof is that he is at this very moment waiting for me in a hackney cab outside your door... He adores me, he...'

'No! This is too bad!' And without listening to another word, Nhine leapt from the bath and in two strides was up at the high window, from where, tip-toe on her little bare feet, she finally managed to look down into the street. 'I can see, I can see, wait... He's got down from the cab and he's walking up and down on the pavement. I can see him clearly... dark hair, quite long, slicked down... big frock-coat. Very pale skin, no beard, looks sad and thoughtful.'

'Yes... he's suffering... If you let him come in one day, he won't suffer as much. Or maybe he'll suffer more!'

'What...? Ah, now! He's staring... he's looking up. Ah! Bother your fiancé! This is a fine state of affairs, Moon-Beam! Come over here... let's sit on the bearskin, in front of the fire. Rub me down with my white towel, and I'll rub you, my dear! It's funny, the thought of that fiancé is quite exciting. I like it. I'll tell Altesse, she'll die...'

'Poor Will,' the perverse child sighed ingenuously, as she stretched out on the floor beside Nhine. 'Just think how amusing you'd find it if you could understand the beauty of Annhine de Lys, like me, and see me touching and worshipping such marvels!'

'Here, Moon-Beam! I'm all ready.' Nhine was voluptuously splaying her arms and legs in a pose of abandon, like an offering. 'Rub me, my page... hard... really hard, don't be afraid... harder...! That's good, now my back... good, good... Ah, no! You know that's not allowed, Floss... Flossie, stop it... No, no.' She squirmed away. 'No kisses on the back of my neck, you're annoying me now, I'll shout... and I won't let you come here again... never ever. My turn now!'

And she began to rub the child, who lay passively at full length, tickling her, giving her tiny smacks, furtive caresses...

'There...! Now tea... Serve me, Flossie, American misses should know how to do that better than us, it's their speciality...'

And she lounged like a waiting sphinx, legs stretched out behind her, elbows on the carpet and head propped on her two hands, breasts lifted by the arching of her back.

Flossie's eyes devoured her.

'I obey, oh sovereign of my fantasy!'

And she served her, on bended knee before her, in adoration, in thraldom... offering up the dishes... the little cakes, the sugar, pouring into a charming white and gold Sèvres cup the delicious brew.

'Wonderful, Moon-Beam... Here, drink from my cup!'

'From your mouth!' Flossie begged.

Annhine laughed, then, taking some of the perfumed water into her mouth, leaned towards her and, careful not to breathe, joined her lips to the girl's. The child closed her eyes reverently, slowly and joyfully drinking in the golden liquid... They repeated the ceremony several times.

'Oh, Annhine, you are so good...! Annhine,' and she abandoned her French for English: 'I love you so.'

She came closer... their breasts pressed together, they played a game, touching their nipples against each other, firm and pink and swelling. Flossie quivered, her eyes drowning in a dream.

'This is nice, Moon-Beam. Let's say hallo to each other

everywhere. Let's make our acquaintance all over. Your feet on mine, because I'm taller. Wrap your legs round mine. Squeeze me as hard as you can. I like being crushed. Our bodies are warming each other, see. Now, my hands on your hands, then your mouth, your teeth, our eyelashes... that's nice! Our noses, like the Chinese... Let me go now, no more... I forbid you to do that... no, no, Flossie, go away!'

She escaped, pushing her away and putting the width of the table between them as a defence.

'You'll kill me! Nhine, you're driving me mad.'

'Go now, page! The duties of my profession call me and your fiancé is waiting for you. Put your clothes back on... I have to go to the Bois.'

'I shall go as well, to catch sight of you... And when shall I see you again in these pretty rooms that shelter you?'

'Well, tomorrow, Sunday. It's the one day I am relatively free. If you like, I'll get a box for us at some theatre, we can be like small children and go to the matinee. The Folies if we just want distraction, or better, go and shiver at Sarah in Hamlet, it's one of the final days of the run.'

'Nhine, let Willy get it for you, let him do it, will you?'

'In your name? I don't mind. But he is not to come as well. He's only allowed to see us from a distance. I have no wish to know him, he looks like a clergyman and he is necessary to you. I have a repugnance for useful things. Tell him so... no, not that, but about tomorrow. There's almost no one of note at matinees, you know, it can't compromise you to go with me. Ready already? Goodbye, my page, I like you; I love your hair and your cast of mind.'

'I'm mad about your voice, Annhine, it's soft yet compelling, with a tender musical ring… it's so lovely, that slow voice of yours, my Nhine!'

'Yours is nice, very soft as well, and the slight accent gives it an extra charm. We go well together… Tell me, Moon-Beam, just a tiny thing: do you have a heart?'

'"Seek my heart no more, the beasts have eaten it."'

'Already! In any event, heart or not, you have a quick wit, some education, a good memory and you know Baudelaire! I adore him, but he has caused me pain. I definitely find you most pleasing, little miss! Goodbye, monster! It is kind of you to want to cheer me up. Look, my bad mood has disappeared, thanks to your visit. Until tomorrow. Come and collect me here around two, exactly…'

'Very well, Tyrant… And then, shall I see you shortly, in the Bois, for you promised to come and charm the last leaves of autumn, and your Flossie too…?'

'Yes… agreed… goodbye.'

"A very amusing young woman, certainly not ordinary, and she's good fun… If it doesn't give rise to complications, the adventure will make a charming pastime," Nhine reflected as her maid helped her dress and did her hair. "Something in my life at last! An innocent platonic love, because I do want it platonic… It's strange, nice, unexpected… It suits me to perfection! I'll keep out of Tesse's way, though, I got the impression she was a bit jealous, and I love my Tesse so much. She's so good! So certain and so, so sensible! I don't want to hurt her feelings. And what you don't know can't hurt. It's just too bad."

A new idea suddenly struck her. She'd go and see Tesse

and forget the Bois, the American girl and the fiancé. She began to laugh. She liked the idea of being waited for... and think how keenly...! and by whom...! and not going... And then, she could surprise Altesse, who wasn't expecting her... "That's what I'll do, yes..." The capricious lady spent an eternity getting herself ready... in no hurry at all.

'Everything red, Ernesta... My Callot dress, the tailored one, and that little embroidered bolero with the high collar that fastens at the front. Pass me my rope of pearls... then my coronet brooch for the collar... my walking cane, since I shall go on foot, the carriage can follow me. And I want my tricorne hat from Lewis's, the red felt with the black rosette. I'm lunching at Paillard's with Monsieur... if anything turns up, telephone me there. I'll be going on to the theatre afterwards, and then to visit Mulcar, who is ill. Put my sable cape in the carriage. Quick, my hat veil, my gloves.'

She leant towards the mirror, renewed the red of her lips, applied powder, squeezed the atomiser at random, sending wafts of perfume everywhere, then departed having stuck one of her page's roses in the narrow black belt of her elegant costume.

'See you later, my Princess, until this evening, my pretty... Be good, and I'll come and fetch you for a walk in the Bois around five... See you later, my darling little dog!'

IV

'At your feet, Nhine... Let me sit on the floor and that way no one will be able to see me in the box and I can look at you as much as I like... watch you, if it doesn't put you off, enjoy your reactions.'

And Flossie slid into the dark recesses of the box, close to the stage, making herself invisible to the inquisitive eyes of the audience, who, intrigued and curious, peered closely into this sheltered corner whose half-raised screens mysteriously revealed only the vaguest pink and blond hints of Annhine's provocative beauty.

'Put your feet in my hands. I'll be your foot-rest.' And she briskly pushed aside the little wooden stool provided by an eager and smiling usherette.

'But you won't see anything like that, Moon-Beam!'

'I'll be studying you, and then I'll be hearing the golden

voice of the great Sarah as she picks over those bitter, ironic reflections given to Hamlet. You know, Nhinon, we should protect my reputation as a young lady for a little while yet. I can serve you better if I sustain the hypocrisy of the world I live in, for I want to serve you in everything and every way.'

Annhine, serious, bent her head towards her page.

'Serve me?' she questioned. 'Poor little thing!' A deep sigh underlined her words. 'Do I even know what I want?'

'Of course!' The child's voice came muffled and intense. 'I know exactly what you want. You want independence, Nhinon, and only a fortune can give you that. You enslave your beauty, your grace and your charms to the whims of one man and another, almost always without pleasure or desire, in order to profit – forgive me for using such terms – to profit from your years of youth and beauty, amass as much money as possible and become a rich woman. Ah, Nhine!' Moved, the child gazed up at her in grieving affection. 'Well then, I can help achieve that goal. I want to, to prove my love for you. Oh, don't say anything, don't protest... I can see into you, yes, and I can see all the good that's there inside you. It comes through in everything you say, in your every gesture, in the look on your angelic face! Listen, my Nhine, unlike the men who admire you and claim to love you, who find you exquisite and take their pleasure without thinking further than their own first impulses... without thinking, I mean, of the winter of life, I want to help you all the time and beyond any fleeting desire! You'll see, Nhine, you'll see. I have great plans. Like today, when it is so delightful and strange to step out of the too glaring daylight of a too noisy Paris and be transported with you to another century and another place, in tune with the deep harmonies and vibrations that move between... But hush! Here's Sarah!'

Indeed, the divine Bernhardt made her appearance, in the character and costume of Hamlet; and so sublimely transfigured by her art that she seemed to be nothing other than a morbid, tormented being, at the mercy of a hundred warring fancies. This person interested you, attracted you, yet was bizarre and incomprehensible, so entirely did the actor immerse herself, not in a stage role, but in the identity of a blazingly felt real life.

Seeing that Annhine had turned her attention to the play, Flossie set herself to study her beloved's features, curious to read in them her innermost feelings. Annhine listened, with only half an ear when Sarah first arrived on stage, then with proper attention, and when Hamlet said to the ghost: *Be thou a spirit of health or goblin damn'd*, her interest focussed fully, intensified. She experienced emotions that were powerful and many-layered; and when the curtains closed at the end of the first act, her voice trembled with enthusiasm as she asserted: 'That was art, not artifice!' It was with minds coloured by such bitter philosophy that they returned to the prison of themselves, and Flossie resumed: 'I have the aspirations and the morbid scepticism of a Hamlet without the distracting compensation of a vengeance to be enacted! No ghost comes along to tell me the path to action. All is struggle and confusion in the chaos of my brain... it will send me mad! Mad with rage when I look at myself and consider how powerless I am in the face of the prejudice-riddled mass. To raise your fist against a villain who usurps the rights of an honest king, now there's a worthy task for a prince bound by birth to uphold justice and defend a kingdom.

'But for me, what is there? What is there for women who feel storms and fevers raging inside them, when pitiless Destiny holds them in chains of iron hardened by centuries of blindness, if not betrayal? Destiny decided to make us women in an age where the law of man is the only law recognised and heeded. Destiny says to me ironically: "Go on then, little woman, hurl yourself against the unmovable object, break your fists against everything that oppresses and crushes you; or else follow the current, fall back, let it all go. And the spirit that makes you bow your head and not fight will carry you away, humiliated, reduced, enslaved. You are useless; at least be peaceful." I see too clearly. Hamlet fills my soul with nostalgia! I shall not succumb as he does in a glorious fight for my ideal. My hands drop, exhausted. I am only a woman. I can only weep...'

'Yes, that is the only comfort left to us,' said Annhine, on whom these words had left a sorry impression. 'That is the theatre's mission: it will be the temple of the future, for it melts the ice of our self-centredness and reduces us to tears, awakes us to noble emotions, raises us above ourselves by making us capable of entertaining higher desires... only for a moment, perhaps, but...'

'But,' Flossie interrupted, 'you think it's all in vain, then? All lost?'

'Lost? No, my sweet. Nothing that is great is lost. Flossie, I have an idea, more than an idea, a belief, that somewhere, in another sphere far away and beyond this one, everything that was once a noble thought, everything that has ever made us feel intensely, if only for the duration of a lightning flash, will flower again. And in some ultimate paradise-world we shall pick the fruits of what we have sown here in our passage through this earthly test. Everything that was art, light, enthusiasm, vigour, in this earth-bound past, will become immortal... in another place!'

Flossie smiled and said: 'Ah, what a gift imagination is! If the fairies had offered me one treasure at my baptism, that's the one I would have chosen before all others. I'm not laughing at you, darling, far from it, but I will say, with an element of truth, that fantasies, which always have a tendency to soar beyond the realm of possibility...'

'Spare them, Moon-Beam. They've had their wings cruelly clipped often enough. Never bind to earth by the weight of fact a thing that wishes to soar! We should confound what we know as fact in order to preserve the appearance of an illusion. Any person who wants to seize any joy and hold on to it must first take Truth by the throat and wring its neck. What gratitude we owe to those who are able to lie skilfully! The novelists, not the faithful historians!'

'It's true... Did you know,' Flossie was struck by a memory, 'did you know that the Hamlet Shakespeare portrays, sad and delicate, was in reality a warrior with the coarsest of natures, nearly a savage? Instead of sending Ophelia to the convent he had his pleasure of her brutally in a wood and sent her packing, and then, prosaically and wisely, he married a princess in England, where he'd been exiled to, as in our version, because the guilty king feared the wisdom of his follies. Finally he took another wife, Hermathrude of Scotland, a scornful Brunnhilde whom he conquered by cunning not by dashing deeds. Accompanied by his two wives, he returned to Denmark, where they were celebrating the false news of his death. The murderous king who had stolen the throne recognised him, but before anyone could devise a way of getting rid of him, Hamlet set fire to the castle. All his powerful enemies died, as if by magic, and the people, always ready for a change – the people, alas, are the same in any place or time – the people acclaimed him. Hero! Saviour! King! It needed a man with the imagination and genius of Shakespeare to find our image of Hamlet in this selfish, scheming and barbaric character. But there he comes now, reading... We should be quiet and listen, even to his pauses... and savour them!'

At that moment Hamlet was bowing low to Ophelia. Silent and still, they followed the drama, drawn together in the same absorption, moved and thrilled. The intervals between the acts became for them a space for meditation, they exchanged ideas, little pieces of analysis and philosophy, in slow, thoughtful murmurs, feeling a need for this communion of souls.

'Ophelia is definitely not the simple young girl that Mellot is giving us,' said Flossie. 'Her virtue isn't ignorance and her purity isn't because she's immature. An Ophelia like the one we're seeing wouldn't be capable of going mad. The real one has a big soul, passionate and impressionable, which knows things... Her origins in a northern country and her Anglo-Saxon character prevent her from being a lover in the Juliet manner, but her life at court, even in Denmark, shapes her and she's a long way from the unreasoning innocence of a Marguerite. People always insist on making young girls out to be silly. It's a misleading and bad habit, especially when it's applied to Ophelia. A brother isn't going to say to a blissfully naïve girl that Hamlet's love is unlikely to last. *The perfume and suppliance of a minute; no more... think it no more*, etc. And equally, from her own replies, you can tell that she's no longer protected by the frail armour of ignorance.

'Hamlet is not a man in a particular state of mind, a stage in a person's life. He's an emblematic soul, representing everything that is aware of its own fact of living. Human beings are changeable things. It is a common failing to see them in only one light. The simple-minded put them down as being like this or like that, and force of habit makes the judgement definitive. Sarah is portraying for us the human spirit in its widest terms: stable but ephemeral, strong, weak, without energy, full of fervour, in other words changing with events. Her creation is not a dummy, an artificial man designed to embody some moral point. She shows us with great clarity human sensibility and the outcomes that result from it. It's magnificent... Hamlet turns everything on its head... Here she is again... Let's pay attention... This is the end...'

When the play was over, they woke as if from a spell.

'Ah, what a masterpiece! What an amazing artist!' Annhine murmured, enraptured. 'I'm still quite stunned! My dear, that was wonderful! But quick! Let's get away... We'll slip out through these crowds and you must come with me. You can hide from sight in my coupé and we'll go and get some fresh air in the Bois. It's dry and fine – would you like to?'

And Nhine hurried them away, wrapping her long woollen coat round Flossie and putting on her own heavy fur cape. They left arm in arm and while they were waiting at the door for the footman to summon their carriage they came across Willy, the respectful fiancé, escorting them out, a few paces behind, in mournful and worried attendance. She squeezed Florence's hand.

'I say, look, there's your Will... He looks sad and anxious.'

'Oh! Yes, Nhine, I'll have to speak to him. He was here, and you made me forget all about him. He was in the stalls and we didn't even give him the charity of a glance... It was the sight of your pretty feet, and the disturbing effect of feeling your warmth beside me, and Shakespeare's intoxicating language that drove everything else from my mind. You don't mind, do you? Would you like me to introduce him to you?'

'I don't know why, but I've not the slightest wish to, on the contrary. Go and talk to him, Floss, go quickly, the carriage is here and I'll be in it, waiting for you.'

'Wicked, cruel Nhine! But your will shall be done...!'

And the child detached herself for a moment whilst Annhine made her way towards the carriage. She sat by the door, lowered the window glass, took the little mirror from her elegant gold vanity case and gazed at herself, arranging a curl of hair, applying rice powder and lipstick with little pretty gestures full of grace. Some children had gathered round, admiring her from a distance; a murmur was already rising among this Sunday throng: "Look, it's the beautiful Annhine de Lys." Irritated and flattered at the same time, her face passed through several rapid changes of expression, from careless to burdened, while she reread her programme. She loosened her sable, rosy-complexioned beneath her curly fleece of hair, charming and simple in an embroidered sheath dress of grey wool that moulded itself to her body. Losing patience, she leaned forward and caught sight of Miss Florence, apparently having a vigorous argument with her fiancé. The man had his head down and was speaking very rapidly, holding her thin wrist in a tight grip and emphasising his remarks with nervous, unconscious gestures which caused the frail creature's body to jerk all over. Flossie seemed able neither to meet his eye nor turn away, but stared instead at the wall, her replies inaudible. After a little while she made a gesture of rebellion and wrenched her hand free, then, in dignified fashion and paying no further heed to her companion, leaving him pale and beside himself with fury, she made her way back towards Nhinon and smiled sweetly as she came up to the carriage. Nhine pulled her in and settled her in its depths. The fiancé, stupefied, had not moved. His wits returning, he was about to rush towards them when the coupé moved off at a swift trot, drawn by the courtesan's famous high-stepping team.

'Nhine, I still want my favourite place at your feet.' And Flossie let herself slide down to the carpeted floor of the coupé. 'It is my refuge, my own little corner, the page's corner. Will is jealous of you, furious you should welcome me and push him aside, so he's having his revenge by making scenes!'

'A good thing too,' replied her capricious mistress. 'Yes, it is…' And she went on: 'It's a good thing, because it's only right you should suffer for my sake a little, Moon-Beam. And what was the gentleman saying to you? He looked ridiculous, and you did too, the pair of you, huddled against the wall like that! He was the very image of the outraged lover!'

'Quite right! Imagine this: he was saying – and he'd already started last night on account of this box at the theatre – he was saying that you're so well-known, so famous, that this folly of mine would end up compromising me and if that happened he wouldn't be able to marry me. Well, that set me thinking, Nhine, and I thought: Will is very rich. He has five or six million dollars, his father is one of the biggest engineers back home, he builds railroads. I'd chosen Will because he is over-sensitive and intellectual and not a brute like the majority of my compatriots. My family, practical like every other family, was happy with my choice because of his fortune, because they're well enough off to live comfortably, but nothing more, and there are three of us children. So I made Will fall madly in love with me, then I sanctioned his declaring himself my fiancé, meaning to take advantage of the situation to do what I wanted. I've always dreamed of Paris, not feeling at all at ease in the overcrowded, work-obsessed turbulence of my own country. I suggested this voyage. When I explored deeper inside Will, I discovered a soul that could perhaps be made to accommodate mine. And one radiant evening, when night's uncertain and troubling veils were gradually enfolding us, and the moon was gently illuminating the dark blue vault over our heads and looking down conspiratorially on us; and a little on edge and excited after a reading of Swinburne, Sappho's words to Anactoria... well, leaning shoulder to shoulder, looking over the parapet, searching for the stars' reflections in the vast depths of the water one finds so mysteriously attractive, and when it seemed the little touches we had been exchanging, and my warm breath, had stirred him to fever pitch, then feeling the urge to share secret things and find a mutuality of lustfulness, I revealed to him my real self. He saw another Florence, the true one, the only one, the pagan one! And each evening, from that time on, I have been advancing my work of initiation!'

'Your work of perversion!'

'No, of conversion! Because I converted him to the charms of perverse love, by making him admire its beauties whilst erasing the inevitable brutalities, showing him above all those two divine functions so well described by Pierre Louÿs: the Caress and the Kiss. I evoked visions of pretty women, long hair tumbling over perfect white breasts, delights of form, profferings of lips, stifled moans, incomparable shudders of pleasure. In short, I made him a different sort of man, and as soon as we arrived in Paris we set out in search of those adorable instruments of pleasure that can only be found in your country. You try a horse before you buy it! Well, I tried Willy! I led him wherever my whim happened to take me. I made love to women in front of him: he had given me his solemn promise never to take me. He promised that his pleasures would only ever be chaste and cerebral. I tested him to the point of martyrdom sometimes. He kept his word, relieving himself afterwards in the beds of pretty slaves often chosen by me and who submitted to his desires dutifully if not joyously.'

'So why this sudden anger because of me?'

'You'll see, Nhine. Always, after these sensual feasts, he would become closer to me. His nerves would be shredded, his soul full of woe, and we would weep together. And he would say: "Flossie, dear, I will cherish any suffering you cause me, I will die smiling for your pleasure, I will tolerate your most outrageous fantasies, the tortures you inflict, I will never be jealous of your body. But I want all of your soul: never give it, Flossie, to those beautiful strangers you love in so material a way and with such wild passion. Keep your soul for your Will..." I was moved; I said yes, I squeezed his hand in mine and gave him my lips. He was trembling from head to toe. "I want all of your little soul, my Flossie, my fiancée, and your complete trust as well. I promise to respect you always, to be content with what you are prepared to give me, but if one day you were to elude me, if you were to deceive me morally, if you were to lie to me, Flossie, ah!, I think I would go mad...! I'd go wild...! I'd harm you...! I'd rather leave."'

'That doesn't explain why...'

'It does, Nhine, it does... Up to now, I have always approached women who were not you, and who used to let him into their boudoirs as willingly as they let me... I enjoyed them swiftly and usually with no aftermath. I would feel sickened, and find myself closer than ever to him, only to go off again in search of new conquests... I was a real butterfly. Only one relationship – since I'm telling you everything – the last one, with a married woman, very young, an amazing brunette, very passionate, lasted a little longer. He wasn't jealous of that one, being a witness of our perversities, but discreet and gratified by the pleasure... That relationship would still be going on... but since I came to know you, so beautiful and so fair, I have abruptly broken it off. Jane – that is her name – has not seen me since. They find their consolation together!'

Excited by her own confidences, the child pressed ever closer against Annhine, inhaled her scented aura, raised the hem of her dress and pushed her tiny hand among the frilled satin and lace underskirts whose snowy, perfumed cascades almost covered her, made her all the more agitated.

'Stop it, Flossie... You know I don't want that.'

And kicking at the girl's bold and burrowing hands with her little feet, Nhine repeated: 'You know what was agreed... I don't want that... I don't want that.'

She flattened down her dress and spoke severely: 'All right, enough…'

'And that's the reason… that's the reason why Will is jealous! The others gave themselves to my caresses straight away, either out of excitement or curiosity, they responded when I got carried away, they gave me an illusion of love! But you, you make me want you, you exasperate me, you drive me wild… and you won't let him through your door!'

'That's the last thing I'd do,' Nhine muttered sullenly, slumping crossly back in her seat. 'Oh no, absolutely not. I have never been a lover of women, and if I ever… if that ever happened, well, in the first place I don't know if it would be with you, and then in any case, there'd be no one discreetly watching. That's evil, that is, it's debauched, revolting! It's dirty, it's what we call troilism, or there's another very ugly term that I don't want to say!'

'Oh, I know… voyeurism…' and Flossie pronounced the foul word, unashamed and unalarmed, with her delightful trace of a foreign accent.

'Oh, Miss, you scandalise me…!' Nhine assumed a prim expression, then burst out laughing. 'So Will is angry with me because I won't let him play the little voyeur?'

'Yes, but not just because of that… You see, it's a matter of heart and soul for us, even in our most dreadful adventures. He's suffering, because it's the first time we've been separated. He's very aware he's already losing something of me to you, Annhine. He's afraid of what's to come, he has a presentiment, he's frightened I'm slipping away from him… He's completely wrong!' The girl threw her head back and began to laugh. 'I'm turning into a courtesan for the love of Nhinon! Yes, I am!

Can't you see what's happening...? Look, I adore you, in the end I'll make you love me just a little bit, I'm marrying Will and I'm making my adored mistress – you – rich, rich and independent at a single stroke. I'm showing you a new world, I'm giving you a new set of bearings, I'm saving you from ever having to consider the dreary matter of your profession, which I find so disheartening, and I'm handing you the freedom to go wherever your imperious and triumphant caprices dictate. Henceforth you are the sole director of your own life!'

'Idiot!' said Annhine, tenderly. 'Do you really believe everything happens the way we want it to?'

'And why not? You'll see, my love will be stronger than anything in its way, it will overcome any obstacle that life and the stupid laws of morality can put between us.'

'And if I never do love you?'

'Too bad! I vow to devote my life to your happiness all the same, Annhine, and I have a will of iron... a tenacity that nothing can deflect... And after that, being loved would be just a bonus! To love, actively to love: that is everything. One day, my Nhine, you will be happy in spite of yourself, through me!'

'All right, yes! Why should I have doubts, when all's said and done? Anything is possible! What does it matter? It would be quite funny and certainly out of the ordinary to achieve through a woman what men fail to provide... I accept! But I don't want to love you just because of that and I don't want to have to pretend a love I may not actually feel! I also want to put heart and soul into my most hardened vices. Make me love you, Flossie...' And in an access of emotion, Annhine, softening, drew the young woman to her and held her tenderly.

'Make me love you,' she murmured, 'and I shall bless

you. You are so sweet to me, you speak to me in a language no one has ever used before. You open me up to things I never knew, you show me infinite possibilities, Flossie. Make me love you...!'

The girl was transported by a surge of joy, of ineffable delight.

'Oh, Nhine! Nhine! Yes, love me! Let's love each other! Such heavenly delights, you'll see! I'll be more loving than ever! Don't say any more, you will love me, I feel it, since you accept my lifelong homage, the giving of my whole self. I sense, at your side, things I have never yet suspected... You'll see, you'll see...!' She could no longer prevent tears from flowing. 'I shall be your friend, your sister, your page. I shall draw you towards me, slowly but surely, the whole you! And the rest of the world won't count for us any more.'

She leaned her head on Annhine's shoulder. Annhine, in some turmoil, put her arms round her in an affectionate embrace and held her closely, overcome by an unexpected rush of tender feelings.

'Oh, Flossie, you're an extraordinary girl!'

They remained like that for a long time, leaning against each other, not speaking, lost in that first glow of intimate togetherness. The coupé drove noiselessly on through the deserted heart of the woods, while the light faded and dusk approached. A pale precocious moon of white crystal appeared through the leafless trees. From time to time, a rare walker broke the calm and solitude of this dark and silent scene.

Nhine felt the need for activity: 'Let's walk for a bit. Do you mind?'

She gave a signal. The carriage halted.

Wanting to escape her troubled mood, she jumped nimbly to the ground and Flossie followed. They walked hand in hand, like two children, not speaking, unwilling to break the spell, straight ahead. They went a long way, not thinking about the time. Guided by the same inclination, they plunged between the trees, along small paths. They felt a coolness touch their skin, their hearts seemed to beat in unison. They found this momentary impression full of charm... Languid and tired, they dreamed in silence, lost in a sweet sensation of peace; all thoughts about anything had evaporated, and it seemed to them that in the whole world, at this precise moment, not a soul existed who wasn't also dreaming! It was Miss Flossie who broke the silence first... in a small, constrained voice: she should be getting home... Her parents... Will would have got there already perhaps, before her. But tomorrow... Ah, tomorrow! Perhaps... Her tone took on a note of entreaty. Perhaps she could come over, renew this happiness?

'It's such a shame to have to part!' And Nhine sighed, half won over.

But then, if it had to be...! And she began to run back towards the carriage, followed by the child, who caught up with her where the little covered path rejoined the main avenue, just as she was about to climb back into the coupé. Laughing and out of breath, they sat very close to one another and Flossie covered her with tiny kisses, on her neck, under her hair, behind her ear, like a woman possessed, unwilling to desist, while they drove at top speed back towards Paris, towards life and the coming day. At the park gates, Flossie got down. She summoned a cab to take her home, following the dark shape of Annhine's vehicle for as long as she could with a sad eye, in which, however, there gleamed a vague hope of the joys to come.

V

'You look like a little flax flower, this afternoon, Flossie, in your blue clothes!'

'Pick me then!'

'Come here, let me smell you. A sweet scent, sharp at the same time. You smell nice, Flossie!'

'And you too, my Nhine! The intoxicating, spicy smell of a flower that unsettles, incites desire, won't gratify it...'

'What a hateful planet! I'm ill, Floss, I've got the vapours, as they would have said two centuries ago, and apart from that, I'm extremely put out. I saw two marvellous pieces at Lalique's: an exquisite little ring, pale greeny gold with enamelling round the central diamond, a big one, olive-shaped, and the whole thing made to look like one of those little field grasshoppers... unique, I'm telling you. And then a silver brooch in the shape of a fern ... genius, a real miniature masterpiece… it had brilliant chips of emerald at the tips of its delicate leaves. Well, my lord and master came, I mentioned these objects, making clear my desire to have them, and he refused me. Yes, Floss, you can see how wretched I am! As Altesse so rightly says, the only purpose of my sad existence is to gratify my every whim…'

And, upset at this trivial disappointment, Nhinon pouted, wrinkling up her pretty mouth and frowning, which gave her an adorable expression of mutiny and revolt. She continued: 'So I am sulking, suffering, I'm in a foul mood. It's true that he's just settled a very large bill at Callot's and he brought me this pretty rope of black pearls with a ruby fastening. Well, I'd rather have had my fern and my grasshopper. Ah, Moon-Beam, what a wasteland my slavery is! That I should have to ask those men whose mistress I am for everything, the irony of it! Everything, from the innocent little ribbons on my chemises to the two white horses that pull my carriage…! Which reminds me, they are outside… Lets' go for a ride, would you like that, dear child? It might put me in a better frame of mind!'

'Whatever you like, my Nhine. But don't be miserable over such a little thing!'

'Such a little thing! But my life consists of nothing else! Where do you see any great things? I have nothing to do, Flossie, but powder my nose, waggle my hips and show myself in public, like a doll. Enough, I don't want to think about all of that. It's splendid weather, in stark contrast to my mental torments today: I want to enjoy it! Come on, let's go. We'll make for Ville-d'Avray by going through Saint-Cloud park. It's chilly but dry. Ernesta! Ernesta! Give me my short cycling skirt, the black wool, because we'll be running about a bit... a short blue blouse and my tie with the white spots... that's it... and over it, my big single-breasted china-blue coat that does up, with its velvet hood. Then my cerise hat... What about you, Moon-Beam? Look, you're wearing a short skirt too!'

'Yes, I thought it might rain.'

'I hope it does. It'll calm me down. We can run about in it, like two horses turned loose. Right, that's me ready, let's go, let's put these sad surroundings behind us. The idea of escaping like this makes me feel quite playful! I don't know what time I'll be back, Ernesta.'

'And if Monsieur were to call...?' the maid wanted to know.

'If Monsieur were to call...? Well, tell him anything you like. All right?'

And she bustled out, pulling her friend after her. As they went, she spoke her thoughts aloud.

'Those things, you know, I will have them. He'll give them to me. But why annoy me by refusing to begin with, they won't give me as much pleasure now! Men really have no idea about female sensitivity! I detest them... Besides which, I can't love something if it's a thing I need; it's the way I am. Do you understand his stupidity, Flossie? Bringing me sixty thousand francs worth of pearls, no skimping there, yet unwilling to make me madly happy by getting me two bits of trash hardly worth four hundred louis!'

'Yes, that's what they're like! Exactly so in my judgement and by my reckoning,' Flossie replied, her mind running off on its own thoughts. 'I remember – and this goes back to when I was just a child – I was very small, I was just losing my milk teeth. One of my uncles came to our house, my mother's brother. I was a delicate and fearful child. He laughed at my weakness, and promptly got his fingers round one of my little teeth that was very wobbly and pulled it out. I fainted from fright. The next day he wanted to make it up to me for having been too rough, so he took me to a patisserie and stuffed me full of cakes and candies, so much so that I had terrible indigestion and I was ill for several days. You wouldn't think it, Nhine, but in my little girl's brain, which was already quite sharp, I analysed and connected those two actions, and I formed a judgment about men, the beginnings of a contempt that only increased as I grew older…'

She interrupted herself.

'Nhine, my sweetness, forgive me: I have to set up my alibi, for I want to stay with you for as long as you'll allow. So, might you have a bit of shopping to do? Oh, just for half an hour, that's all I need, and I'll meet you outside the gates at the Bois de Boulogne.'

'Of course, my darling. Yes, I'll go and see Altesse. You've rather made me neglect her. Then I'll come and collect you. I understand about managing things, making arrangements. All too necessary. It's still very early anyway. Off you go then, my radiant Moon-Beam, off you go…'

They quickly parted. Flossie was pensive; she walked away and briskly turned the corner, while Annhine arranged herself in the victoria and gave her coachman Altesse's address.

Her visit was brief. She found her friend attended by the hairdresser and the manicurist. An old admirer was there too. Nhine was relieved to see them, as it avoided the danger of giving away her inner thoughts. As it was, she confined herself to mundane matters… they made plans for a dinner party.

'I haven't seen much of you these last few days, my lovely,' Altesse said with a hint of regret.

'I'm feeling sad and I've been in a disagreeable mood. You haven't missed anything, honestly.' And Nhine kissed the floating locks of burnished gold. 'You're making yourself look very beautiful.'

'We're going to see Hamlet this evening… Have you seen it? Do you want to come?'

In spite of herself, Nhine was overwhelmed by a sudden memory. She became distracted and struggled to reply.

'Now listen, my darling, when you're sad like that, it's a mistake to stop doing things, you ought to get more involved with other people. If you can't enjoy their happiness, then look in another direction, at people who are suffering. You'll forget your own troubles for a while by helping them in theirs.' Altesse was a very charitable woman. 'There's a sad case I've recently heard about, for instance: a poor comedy actor from somewhere in the provinces who came to Paris in search of fame and fortune. He's starving to death in a little attic, right at the top of one of those narrow alleys on the Butte de Montmartre, with a kid of seven left behind by its mother, a poor girl who died from misery and want of care. Take the address; I pass them over to you.'

'Oh, darling, thank you! I'll go… You're as good as you are beautiful! Good to everyone… Ah, you don't know! I haven't told you…'

She lowered her voice and related her misadventure, the disappointment over the jewels… Altesse laughed and teased her.

'Oh, you poor thing, deprived of a grasshopper and a fern.

I'm so sorry for you! Silly woman, look, telephone them and tell them to send them both round. Buy your present yourself, and in compensation for all the bother, request an extra ten thousand francs from your friend next time he's feeling generous. All done!'

'That's an idea!' Annhine ran to the telephone in the little sitting room next door. After protracted inquiries, she returned looking even more out of sorts.

'No luck! Nothing I do turns out well. You wouldn't believe, those two things…? Sold, my dear, both of them sold, five minutes ago. It's infuriating!'

'Both of them? Sold to him, no doubt?'

'No, to a lady!'

'Poor darling! Really, you are out of luck!'

'That's what I told you! And all you could do was mock! No, I can see you're ready to laugh now! Oh, don't bother, it doesn't matter…' And Annhine turned away to the window, ready to dissolve into tears. 'Perfect, I was wanting to go out… get away from Paris to where I can breathe a bit, and now it's raining! Right, I'm going anyway, I feel I'm about to burst, it's all I can do to hold myself in check and not quarrel with you… Farewell, Altesse!'

And she dashed away as if carried off by a whirlwind.

She had herself driven to the Porte Dauphine. There she found Miss Florence waiting in a cab, which cheered her up a little. She explained what had happened.

'Do you see what I mean, darling? Oh, he'll pay for this, the wretch. And I have the address of these unfortunate people. Let's go there straight away, they may be hungry, I've got some money on me. Then I don't want to go back to my own hovel this evening, I'd like to have dinner with you, out in the country. If that's all right with you, we'll take the whole evening over it, and come back very late…'

'Yes, darling, I'd like nothing better; I'm free until midnight at least. Willy is getting ready to return to America. He's leaving in three days' time, stricken with grief and jealousy, to wait until I come back to him. It won't be as easy as before, with him not there, to stay away from my family, but I've found a new excuse: my pretext is an abandoned woman, just fancy! Yes, I saw her again this morning, that poor Jane, terribly attractive in her despair. She's agreed to help me out, doubtless in the hope of getting me back. She visits my family from time to time. So, thanks to her, I can carry on being your companion without causing ructions… Let's go and see these poor people, yes…!'

Nhine gave the address and the carriage made off in the direction of Montmartre. Climbing the slope of rue des Martyrs, the roadway was so slippery they had to step down from the carriage and follow on foot along the pavement. A number of people gathered round them and the handsome team. Some workers shouted insults. They drew close together.

'You see, Flossie, how wicked and unfair the world is. We're on our way to do good works and we get called names.'

'Get the carriage to stop here and let's go on by ourselves, what do you say? It'll be better, I think.'

In this fashion they reached rue des Trois-Frères, and in a miserable building let out as furnished rooms came face to face, right at the top, beneath the eaves, with a dreadful spectacle. The luckless performer, wearing next to nothing, was lying on a straw mattress, with his child beside him. In a corner, a little stove was filling the narrow attic with billows of thick and acrid smoke that caught in the throat. It was difficult to see. Daylight came in through a skylight whose glass, broken in places, also let in the rain... Some old rags of clothing, a lump of hard, shapeless bread, a chipped basin where some tattered underclothes were soaking, a sliver of scratched mirror glass hanging on the wall, then a woman's portrait, the dead mother no doubt: a cold and sad image, beneath a sprig of consecrated boxwood from Palm Sunday.

The sudden apparition of these two petite figures, all blond and diaphanous, caused the man to rear up, startled. He thought he was dreaming...

'I'm a fellow artiste who has come to see you.' Annhine spoke very fast and held out her hand. 'I was told things were difficult just now. I had to be in this part of town and it occurred to me to come over and help you out a bit, if you didn't mind.'

She was interrupted by a fit of coughing that broke from the child, hollow and harsh, racking its chest. Flossie, aghast, took a step back, pulling her friend towards the door.

'Please,' she began again, 'we don't want to disturb you. Is this your baby?'

Peering towards the wretched bed, she made out, in the dirty straw, a ravishing little face: two big black eyes, made bigger by fever, the skin around them mauve and blotched; the small face long and pale, pinched, its little puckered mouth aflame, all red; and red hair sticking clammily to its temples in an unhealthy sweat.

'But he's ill! Poor darling!'

She bent forward and kissed him on the forehead.

'Here, take this, my friend, there's a hundred francs...'

And she held out five gold louis.

'Have you got some change for everyday things?' asked Flossie, more confident now and composed. 'No, I expect? Well, here's a little...!' And she emptied her purse into the child's hand, making it laugh at the sight of the small silver coins.

'You really must get something to eat,' Annhine said. 'And see a doctor... You look as if you're suffering too, monsieur?' she added inquiringly.

'Suffering?' And the stricken man, recovering from his surprise, sat up painfully. 'Am I suffering? My dear fine ladies, I am dying... Ah, I know who you are, I recognise you, madame de Lys... Thank you...! Thank you...! But honestly, I think it would be better to leave us to die! To join the one who's gone before...!'

And his anguished gaze fell on the little portrait fixed to the wall.

'No, no!' Nhine insisted. 'Your duty is to this child, who will be a great man, perhaps, in future years... You must start by looking after yourselves properly, the two of you... Drink some good broth, eat eggs... I'll make it my business, and when you are better, we'll organise a benefit matinee of some sort for you, since you're a performer. That way you'll have some money to start you off with and you'll see good times return. Now listen, I'm leaving, but I'll be back in three of four days and I want to find you both better. I'll give you my address in case you need it.'

She took a gold pencil from her bag and looked for a scrap of paper.

'Oh, well, never mind, I'll write it on the wall. Right,

baby, kiss us goodbye!'

She whispered in Flossie's ear: 'He can be our child, would you like that?'

'Kiss the ladies,' said the poor father, already half restored, encouraged by the prospect of health and work that Annhine's kind words opened before him. 'Kiss these two angels that the good Lord has sent you, Guillaume…'

'He will be our little protégé,' Nhine repeated, 'but he must get better quickly. Don't move, he mustn't be left on his own… it's raining and it's going to be cold, this evening. I'm going down to see the manager. You're going to change rooms. The maid will come, she'll go out and fetch you some broth. Hide the gold away, just take out a few francs. Tomorrow you'll be moving… and you don't want anyone to see your money. I'll go myself and call on my doctor and he'll come and see you some time in the evening. You must wait for him and listen to what he says, he will send you some medicines… Right then, farewell, dear comrade; you see, one should never give way to discouragement.'

'May God bless you and repay you in kind, madame. Thank you, thank you…!'

And the poor man wept warm tears as he kissed the beautiful slender hands, ungloved as they were for the offering.

'Goodbye, Guillaume, goodbye, my sweet… he's so pretty! See you soon…'

And the vision disappeared before the eyes of the unfortunate pair, who would have said it had been an hallucination if they did not hold in their hands the pieces of gold and the silver coins.

An hour afterwards, our two friends were driving through

the park of Saint-Cloud.

'How close I feel to you, my pretty Nhine, my dear, fragile treasure... What a terrible spectacle of misery!'

'True! I'm not thinking about my grasshopper any more, nor my fern... But I'm sad, Flossie. Life is sad, cruel. Look at those poor people... I feel quite moved, I had my days of poverty too. It doesn't mean much when you're young... It's much worse now. Materially, I don't need anything, but the poverty of my heart is terrible... my life is so empty...'

'I'm here to fill it from now on...' And Florence, with tears in her eyes, huddled close against her side.

'And look at those great big leafless trees. They make me sad. They're like giant ghosts with elongated limbs, all withered... Those mossy banks remind me of tombs. Oh, Flossie, let's go home, I'm shivering, I feel like crying, crying for ever, my nerves are stretched to breaking point, they're a tangled mess... Oh, I wish I could go far, far away, to the ends of the world... I wish I could die.'

'And I fear I'm too much your soul-sister to do you any good... I understand you too well to be able to console you. We need to be shaken out of it, Annhine, let's try to step outside our normal selves altogether. When you're sad, a good cure is to lose the sense of your own individuality. It's like a short death, better than sleep and more interesting. This desire of yours to travel or to die, all it means is that you're tired of yourself and need a change of scene or people. It's easily done and no trouble. Oh, if only you lived with me all the time!'

'God, what am I to do, what am I to do? My soul is a bottomless well of distress. Ah, this rain, this misery, all this horribleness everywhere around me. Flossie, Flossie, help me…' Tears slowly fell. 'To go away, to die… to sleep a deep sleep, if nothing else.'

'No… Let's leave those "vile potions" and opiums aside, they're for people without spirit, spirits without resources. We should plunge into life, wander about in it like vagabonds, make ourselves more receptive to the things that surround us. Sometimes it's the things that are closest to us that we know least about, that are the strangest. For instance, Nhinon, this rainy night, look at the way the dull light of the lamp-posts throws pallid reflections on the road surface just as we come into this little village at the edge of the woods… it makes them gleam like the watery streets of Venice. Your carriage is suddenly a gondola and we two are lovers from the days of old. You smile at that. Stop the carriage and let's run about in the open country, like two artless little girls in our short skirts, hand in hand and our feet on the wet grass. Come with me, we'll walk away together, leaving everyone behind, forgetting everything that drove us into exile. Like two children, like two young girls, we shall be amazed by everything we see, and enamoured of nothing… All of nature will be our friend, we will revel in the sensation of our hearts beating healthily.'

They jumped down from the carriage, taken up in their new fantasy, and began to walk. Attracted by a light, they entered a small farm to beg hospitality. While fresh milk was being sent for, they sat in the corner of a high-backed bench, observing and talking in whispers.

'As expected, Nhinon, all the grown-ups are busy eating soup while the little ones are sleeping like beasts, mouths gaping, as if the weight of their disgustingly fat and healthy cheeks had split them open.'

A Woman's Affair

'Look... the mother's expecting – it wouldn't do to waste time, her last one's a year old already!'

'I find that woman repulsive, Nhine, with her gross stomach. Everything about her puts me off, it's all so functional and ugly. There's no avoiding the fact that honesty and bourgeois respectability are designed to nauseate. And to avoid it, let's leave and look elsewhere.'

They settled up, were given change, which they left for the children, and walked on further. The rain had stopped, little lakes of muddy water were everywhere. Nhine was struck by the transparent reflections of the sky in one of these impure mirrors, and Flossie gave her a pretty explanation for it.

'When love comes down from another world, all azure, and lights on my soul, it lends me a little of its dazzling beauty, but at all other moments, my Nhine, I am mere mud. It shouldn't surprise you therefore that my one desire is always to love you and to devote my every act to your service. It restores me to normality, by stabilising all my conscious and unnatural perversity in the quest for some higher goal...'

'Look, there's a proper den of vice, a tavern...' And Annhine pushed her inside.

Here, the only sentient thing in the whole degraded place appeared to be the ceiling as it throbbed and re-echoed over a tumult of coarse laughter. Men in smocks were playing nap with greasy cards and grubby hands, while the smoke from their pipes tried and failed to obscure a bevy of tarts, dead drunk amid a waste of smashed bottles and piles of dirty plates. Our two explorers, in horror and fright, clung to each other's arms and ordered a peppermint cordial which they paid for but didn't dare touch. Eyes turned their way, probing, malevolent.

A Woman's Affair

They left without further ado.

Nhine could only gasp, beseechingly: 'Floss! Oh, it's even worse! Why is this earth so horrific?'

'Close your eyes, my sweetness, and let me guide you.'

They proceeded some way in this manner. Then all at once a musty, damp smell caught at Nhine's throat. She opened her eyes. She found herself in a little church, in an unwholesome atmosphere of mildew and holy water, with a suspicion of spiders lurking in the corners... On the high altar a small lamp had just consumed the last of its oil and expired, leaving a faint ribbon of smoke coiling above it. In the partial darkness, Florence spoke at length on vaguely gothic subjects. They felt haunted by the strangeness of the hour and the place.

'You can see the grotesque gargoyles making faces at us, Nhine, and all around the air is impregnated with religious signs. The Christ looks as if he's getting bored, up there on his cross. Look, he's slowly climbing down and limping towards us. His hands are clasped together and he's murmuring prayers in a tone of lamentation... then he's speaking to us, his voice sounds very sincere, his words not so muffled... Nhine! He says he deeply regrets robbing the world of all its beauty, he weeps for the lost joie de vivre of the ancients. He says he has been a poor replacement for the sunlit gods of Greece, with the pallor of his livid face, its weeping and suffering; but he has been poorly interpreted too, not understood... his disciples have deformed his religion. And in doing so they have rendered the earth barren of beauties and void of flowers. If it pleases him to approach you now, it is in memory of Mary Magdalene. He is becoming a figure of pathos and making us even sadder. Why has he come to disturb us? We should leave here him in his house where only hypocrites listen to him any more. His century of glory is fading, as it does for any Saviour. There are no religions fitted for all eternity, except the religion of beauty! All changes, all passes with time. Our age is dark, we are in the night-time of belief, and the dawn of a new hope has not yet come.'

Disconcerted, they turned to face one another.

Florence murmured: 'You are everything to me: my belief, my hope, my soul and my life!'

Annhine replied: 'I do not love you in the way you wish, but you are sweet and I feel you are mine...'

They clung to each other in a sudden, passionate embrace and left the holy place, continuing their wandering course.

They stopped on the bank of a broad stretch of water. This limpid mirror of the preening stars set their imaginations roaming.

'Those water-lily leaves, Nhine, see? They are women, waving their arms to annoy these reeds, which are fauns. They know they are out of reach, they laugh, they mock, they huddle together. When you look at them, doesn't love between women seem a fine thing?'

'Ah, Floss, hush...! Be quiet, don't talk of that.'

'Yes, I understand you. Love of any sort causes you pain, because the past is always present. I know that without your having to tell me...'

And they walked slowly away from the great lake.

'It's growing late. We should go... return to the carriage... our gondola! Ah, Nhine, I want your lips.'

'I feel different. You make me see so many things I'd never even suspected...'

A Woman's Affair

She sang softly to herself to dispel the impression of morbidity: *We'll go home by the light of the moon!*

'The moon...! The Soul of the Night! See how white she is this evening, how serene... She's escaped the clouds and is floating on high, giving us a feeling of peace, a calm and cold spectator of our earthly struggles. Listen to her, Nhine, she'll tell you the secrets of my heart, the illusion that comes in my dreams. I tell her about it sometimes at night, when she slides her beams through my window to pay me a visit and bathe me in her light out of pity for my troubles. She lies, and promises me a thousand delights... Ah! Nhinon!'

'You say such pretty things, Flossie, little satyr, little siren... you make my head spin. Let's go home, I'm shivering. I'm afraid of everything, of your words, of the moon, the dark, the shining waters, the trees... of your caresses... of you...!'

She dashed on ahead and eventually came to her carriage. Flossie climbed up beside her. They drove back without saying a word.

At her door: 'I'm tired, Flossie, very tired. I live in an imaginary world, unreal. I don't know who I am any more or where I am. Goodbye!'

And Flossie: 'A plea, Nhine: go to bed, go to sleep, but I beg you to grant me the favour of watching over you while you do.'

Annhine hesitated for a second, then suddenly made her mind up: 'Yes...! Come in with me...! I'm frightened of being on my own. My head is full of ghosts... Come in, Flossie!'

She rang, and that simple little act brought reality back...

'And then we must have some supper, since we didn't eat dinner.'

They went in together.

'Ernesta! Find us something to eat, because we haven't had anything all evening.'

As soon as they entered her boudoir, she hurried to take off her coat, unhook her dress, and stood in a little underskirt, lacy and palest blue, attached to the slender satin corset.

'Clearly, blue is your colour.'

'Yes, Moon-Beam, I now think blue is the prettiest there is. Before, I used to like pink, nothing but pink. It was right for my age and cast of mind at the time, full of illusions. Pink means joy, hope, gaiety. Blue is a more settled colour, gentler too, restful. Blue is definitely the colour that a blonde twenty-three year old like me should prefer, wiser and calmer after learning the lessons of life. Blue is tender, it's affectionate and good. Later on... soon, perhaps, it will be mauve. Pink and blue together suggest experience, roundedness, and mauve expresses that.'

'You are a delight, Nhinon, you bring soul even into the choice of colours you wear.'

'Then,' continued Nhine, pulling on a transparent muslin dressing-gown trimmed with lace, 'after that comes grey, indicating matter consumed, fires burnt out, ashes cooled and purified: a sort of remote mourning for griefs now forgotten. Then, most significant of all, white: beginning and end... the new-born's swaddling clothes and the winding sheet of the dead, future and past. I love white, Flossie. For a brunette, a woman with presence, generous in form and ardent in feeling, I see red, yellow, black... green too if it suits her temperament... Colours are full of symbolism, Moon-Beam... You, you're like me, white, blue. You are virginal, you could still wear pink... green too, very delicate, almond or eau de nil. Just those. Nothing overpowering or that shouts.'

Ernesta arrived, bearing a tray loaded with all manner of things.

'Here you are, madame. I've found some consommé, cold. It's already half past eleven and everyone in the house is asleep, but looking round the kitchen I managed to come up with some cold chicken as well... then there's some grapes, apples and biscuits. I've opened some champagne... that's everything. If the ladies would care for eggs, I can prepare some?'

'No, thank you, this is quite enough.'

'A salad, perhaps?'

'This is fine. You may go now, I can prepare for bed by myself.'

Ernesta disappeared.

'Here, Floss, come and eat something. Sadly prosaic, but necessary.'

'Ah, Nhine, I'm not hungry!'

'I want you to eat something. Or drink... have some bouillon.'

It had been poured out in two cups. She offered her one.

'Nhine,' the child said, 'I'll only eat or drink anything if you let me have it the special way we drank our tea the other morning.'

'No, no, you can have your dessert like that, if you've eaten a proper supper. You must earn your reward, Moon-Beam!'

Florence slid to the floor, obedient and well-behaved. When they had finished: 'Now?' she implored.

A Woman's Affair

From a bowl filled with sweets, dates, chocolate-coated almonds, Nhine picked out a selection... She put them in her mouth, holding them lightly between her teeth, and bit gently to break them. Then, as Flossie crawled over to her, radiant, she presented them to her. Flossie, lips half open, teeth ready to bite, took the sweets by pressing her mouth to Annhine's. It was a game that ended as a kiss.

'Oh, your lips, Nhine,' she murmured. 'You don't know how wonderful they are! What would I do if you refused them? But even then there's something I value still more. You yourself, your pleasure, your happiness! I want you to understand me. You don't know what you are to me! The word everything doesn't say enough.'

She led Annhine towards her bedroom, made her sit on the wide bed, took off her stockings, kissed her feet and undressed her completely.

'To see you, to look after you, to learn how to serve you, love you... closely, distantly, any way you wish... the whole time... infinitely, absolutely and still more! To be the staff you lean on, the slave you smile on, to weep for your troubles, laugh for your joys...! That is my goal, my destiny, my happiness from now on...'

She spoke to her in a hushed, slow whisper. Nhine listened, dizzy, lost. She saw herself, naked beneath the child's roaming gaze and fingers.

'Ah! What are you doing...?' she said. 'No, Flossie, don't take advantage of me. I don't know what it is, everything feels unreal and far away, I'm in the grip of some strange terror, I could all too easily fall into your arms, and it wouldn't be fair... Put me to bed, send me to sleep.'

Flossie came to her senses.

'Yes... yes... you're right, I was overcome... I was overwhelmed... All I want is to devote myself to you. Here...'

She drew from a pink and perfumed satin envelope Nhine's chemise and slipped it over her, the white nightdress emphasising the length of her slender frame. She might have been a painting by Greuze, with her fair hair tumbling in wild curls around her pale and delicate little head. Flossie tied the blue ribbon at the embroidered neck.

'You need one for your hair.'

Like a baby, Nhine surrendered to her ministrations. She slipped into the coolness of the bed and let her head fall back on the pillows, closing her eyes, languid, arms spread, hands dangling, in a pose of adorable abandon.

'Sleep, my love... Sleep, my pretty one, sleep, my angel, close your eyes until tomorrow and may your soul fly to the land of dreams on the softest of wings, may your dreams restore you and bring you joy. Sleep... Sleep.'

Then, in silent and contemplative worship, Miss Florence absorbed, watched over, feasted her delighted eyes on the sweet and aery vision of the sleeping Nhinon.

VI

When Annhine first woke and opened her eyes, she could remember nothing and her head was muddled. She quickly closed them again, sighed, and stretched lazily, with the voluptuous weariness that comes from having slept too well... An unexpected contact with something hard woke her up again. Some object had a tight grip on her finger... it felt like a ring... she must have forgotten... it was odd, normally she took them all off at night before going to bed. Hard luck, she was much too tired, maybe she could still get back to sleep again. Turning over in the vast bed, she had the sensation of something pricking her, there, under the end of the sky-blue ribbon, just above her right breast. She put her hand to the place, gropingly, it was there, yes. She sat up suddenly, opened her eyes fully and kept them open this time... and gave a cry of joy.

'My grasshopper! My fern…! Oh! What fairy has come and granted my wish while I was sleeping…?'

Whisperings, a door opening gently, gently, as if someone was keeping an eye on the sleeping beauty: 'Ah! You're awake, my Nhinon! Good morning!'

And Miss Florence walked in.

'What? You…? You…! And where did you sleep last night…? I don't understand. Am I really awake? It seems as if I'm still dreaming…! These jewels? How did they get here? How did you…? Daylight! Reality! Ernesta, open the curtains, raise the blinds!'

And Nhine, puzzled, turned to face the brightness…

'Ah! I've guessed! It was you, Flossie: the lady who bought the two objects I was longing to have. Oh, that's so sweet of you… But tell me, how do you come to be here?'

'It's very simple, my gentle queen, I returned home very late and I left home very early. The jewels were here when we got back yesterday evening and you've been wearing them all night. I'm so happy to have been able to give you pleasure! I am rewarded, more than rewarded, by your lovely smile.'

She made an adorable little figure: her long overcoat hung open over a very short pair of black culottes that clung to her thighs, with a white shirt, cut like a man's, covering her neatly rounded breast, big yellow boots up to her calves, whilst on her head perched a grey felt hat with a broad brim, as if riding on the rebellious, silvery hair.

'What a sight you are, Moon-Beam, in that outfit! You look like a cowboy… Where can you be off to?'

'I have assumed the spirit and costume of a young ragamuffin from back home today, to amuse you and serve you... I shall be your valet and you will command me as you think fit, would you like that?'

'Oh, you're completely mad, but so kind...! Listen, no...' She drew her on to the bed and began to stroke her. 'No, Flossie, I can't accept these beautiful things.'

'Why not...? You were very keen to have them from your lover, why not from me?'

'But you, Flossie, it's not the same thing. You're a woman, a new friend, I really can't...'

'And you, Nhinon, aren't you my idol? I want to buy you things... I want to set up altars to you. Oh, the things I want, the things I want...! Lying here next to you like this, still warm from the soft heat of your sleeping flesh... Oh, all my wild desires come flooding back...' And Flossie stretched out sensually on the white bedclothes. 'My idol! I want to drench you in jewels! I want to transport you to some vast and ethereal realm! With a moon-beam for our swift steed. I shall pluck the little stars and make them into magnificent jewels to hang round your neck... The steep cliffs that frame the ocean will make a halo for your angel's head, your frail feet will make a carpet of my heart... it will beat very gently so as not to make you trip... A clear lake for your mirror, for your garden the whole world, where all will be a perpetual flowering of springtime... your one and only love a soul which understands your own... and the focal point of all that is beautiful: yourself!'

Carried away on the flights of fancy conjured by her outpourings, Flossie had caught Annhine in her arms, laid her whole body over hers... The scent of her skin finally drove her to excess, she covered her in a frenzy of kisses, trembling all over, heart pounding loudly in her chest. She kissed her mouth with such passion it was almost a bite. Their teeth clashed and blood was drawn. Then she completely lost her head, and in an act of rashness clawed at the body of her beloved, throwing the sheets aside, tearing off the delicate muslin nightdress and hurling herself violently towards new and terrible delights with a groan of ecstasy.

'Flossie, this is wrong, I don't want to...'

And Nhine fought to get free.

'I want it...' the girl shouted, 'I want you!'

'No! Ah! It's wrong...! But it's true that you have bought me things...' And falling passive, not struggling any more, Nhine uttered the chilling words: 'I can't refuse you what you've paid for...'

Flossie reared back... beside herself and her eyes wild...

'No, this is wrong! This is wrong! How can you say things like that? You profane everything, Annhine! You're a cruel woman! All right, I'm leaving, I'm going away! I'm not a man, but I'm still flesh and blood! Goodbye!'

'Flossie...!'

'No, goodbye...!'

And through her tears she groped towards the door...

'Flossie! Floss...! Come and talk to me.'

The child was still stumbling away, not replying.

'Come back, I tell you, I want you to, you have to listen to me... you must! You can't know, but what I want to say is something you'll be truly glad to hear. Come back!'

Then, when she was by the bedside again, Annhine spoke to her very rapidly, in a low voice: 'You must understand me, Flossie. I am a very simple person, basically, although I am famous and well known everywhere; and, I swear to you, I have never yet trifled with the vice that possesses you, never! You do not know me, my darling, I have no wish to play the flirt with you, still less to exacerbate your desires by rejecting them. So, if you demand my acquiescence, I am yours, have me. It will be the painful continuation of what I have submitted to for eight years... One more or one fewer, it makes no difference.'

Flossie made an abrupt movement, as if to pull away.

'No, no, hear me out to the end, I want to talk to you frankly, once and for all... You have come into my life at a moment of disgust and disillusionment when I was looking for something: something, good, true, above all new! So, Flossie, you interested me. At first I laughed at you, then I was attracted by your charm... Your perversity frightens me and repels me... It comes too close to the things I do for a living. You have widened my horizons... it seemed that you understood what is happening inside me. I love you with a kindly love, my darling, that has nothing destructive in it... Your words give me a strange sense of comfort. In the sense that I am at all your lover, I am more so, and a much better one, the way we are rather than the other way... and then, as you see, I am here... Do as your wishes tell you, I shall not try to defend myself any more; but don't debase the feeling of tenderness I have for you. I'm not lying to you, Flossie...' There were tears in the child's eyes. 'Any kind of love that is bestial just kills it for me. You don't understand what I mean...? Does that put you off? Yet there I was, all ready to believe in you! Make me love you, take me wherever you want to go. Yes, you promised you would... you mustn't shock me, you mustn't demand my obedience. I want to be sincere and spontaneous with you, Flossie, and not submissive or false as I am every day with all the others!'

Flossie continued to weep, saying nothing. She rested her head on Annhine's shoulder in a mingling of the two women's grief. When she was able to speak, amid the sighs and tears: 'Oh, Nhinon, my Nhinon! I can only love you all the more for the treasure you've given me... I am at your mercy, do what you want with me. Always and for ever I will be your friend, your soul-sister... But this past that keeps coming back...! Shall I ever be able to forgive you for doing yourself so much damage...? And all the dangers the future brings...? Swear to me, yes, swear, Nhine, that when I come to you again, free and rich, to offer you independence and escape from your hateful bondage, swear that nothing in the world will put a distance between us!'

Convinced by the child's solemn and prophetic tone, Nhine replied: 'I swear!'

Flossie, in a state of exultation, went on: 'And as for me, I swear to devote my every effort, and if necessary my whole life, to saving you!'

Her voice trembling, Nhine said again: 'Be my rescue and my cure, Flossie, don't drag me any deeper into evil things. Oh, if you mean me to be yours, it is the only way!'

She suddenly went pale and clasped her hand to her heart.

'What's the matter...?'

And Flossie, anxious, bent over her.

'Nothing... a twinge... a touch of dizziness. I'm a fragile plant, you know, you've blown me about too much! See, I'm shaking... It isn't anything... I feel giddy, I'll get up, it will soon pass.'

Unsteadily, she tried a few steps round the bedroom.

'My head's going round… Flossie, hold me… It's gone… You're not angry with me any more? You'd kill me, you know.'

'Lean on me, my pretty darling, my sweetness…! You've gone quite white!'

'Yes, you see, I've scarcely any strength and I need it to live, because men's love is murderous.'

'And they love you so much!'

Ernesta brought in the mail.

'Do you want me to read you your letters?'

'No, it's going now, look…!'

Indeed, the pinkness was returning to her cheeks and lips.

'A little rest… something to eat, and I'll feel quite normal again. Don't worry about me.'

'In that case, while you're reading, allow me to slip away to your bathroom for a moment. I need a glass of cold water, my throat's parched, I'm terribly thirsty…'

Flossie, very concerned, hastily joined Ernesta. The maid answered her questions in a manner only moderately reassuring. Madame was not at all strong. She hardly slept at night, and heavens, sleep is the main thing! Then she was spoilt and capricious, never taking care of herself as she ought. For instance, for months and months now no one had been able to persuade her to touch meat. On top of that she read a lot and thought too much. Some people only have to put their heads on the pillow and they're away, but her, oh, not her! Sometimes at night, very late, Ernesta would see a light still burning, tip-toe in and find her mistress awake, eyes wide open, contemplating who knows what! And on top of that, so highly-strung! Her nerves were eating her up!

'But her friends?'

'Ah, yes, her friends! Mme Altesse is the only one of them who gives her good advice… and all of them, they all whisk her off here, there and everywhere… dinners, suppers, theatre. It's all very well paying for her, letting her do anything she pleases, they're killing her by inches. Madame is delicate, she can't keep on like this for long, and such a good soul too… it's a real shame…'

And the good maid shook her head.

"I need to get her out of this. I'll lose her unless this way of life stops," Flossie told herself as she returned to the bedroom. "I must think about what to do, and as soon as possible."

'Look, Moon-Beam, an invitation, the day after tomorrow. It's a ball, masks and costumes, at the Continental, given by a number of successful writers for the acting community. They're celebrating hundredth performances at three different theatres. All Paris is going to be there, Sarah, Réjane, Granier. Look…!'

She handed her a richly illuminated card printed in several colours on a background of apricot yellow.

'It sounds such fun, what a clever idea,' she went on. 'We can go together – yes? – since everyone will be in masks. We'll disguise ourselves, you can come and get dressed here, make sure you're free, we'll have dinner wearing our costumes. I'm going to go as a priest, I've got a brilliant abbot's outfit in purple velvet with embroidery… What about you? You should go as a man too, it's easier for dancing… You can teach me what to do and we can make advances to all the women. Let's think, what sort of person would suit you best…?'

She pondered the question.

'But Nhine, what time is this ball?'

'Midnight, darling. Oh, you absolutely must come!'

'I'll come if you really want me to but, but... it'll be tiring! Why don't we stay here? That crowd of people, the heat, all that dancing, supper...'

'What's got into you, Moon-Beam? Honestly...!' And Annhine, at this objection, stamped her foot. 'We're going! There! I've also got a costume for a Louis XV marquis, small size: it would fit you like a glove. It's white, with little brocade roses, and you'll have a sword! Come on, Moon-Beam, you can't turn down the chance to wear a sword!'

And captivated with her new idea, Annhine ran to call Ernesta, telling her to go up into the attic and search through her theatrical trunks and bring down the two costumes.

'Don't forget the tricorne hats... the sword and the wigs, because we'll need those as well.'

Won over by her childish delight, Flossie gave way: 'All right then. You have such lovely ideas, it's impossible to resist! Yes, we'll go! It's the day Willy departs, just to make life difficult! I'll invent some excuse, a sick friend. Listen, I'll leave you now, I'm going to begin my quest for a convincing alibi... I'll see you this afternoon, my adorable sovereign, my little blonde fairy... A kiss, calm, candid, in loving friendship and fraternity... I'll see the costumes when they've been smoothed out and tidied up, that'll be better. I'll be on my way.'

And she disappeared, just as Annhine's breakfast was being brought in.

Outside the front door she bumped into a man who was

just about to ring. Her heart lurched and she went pale. She turned round quickly: he was striding in like the master of the house, without waiting to be announced. He was a tall, dark-haired man, quite good-looking, with deep eyes and a slender moustache. Annhine's lover, no doubt, she recognised him now. She seemed to have seen that face in the photographs on the furniture in her drawing room. It was him...! Ah! She felt faint. She wanted to turn back and follow him inside... she restrained the impulse... thought of the future, of the momentous purpose she hoped to achieve, the duty she had imposed on herself. She continued on her way, saddened, but resolute, merely murmuring these simple words: 'What a shame! So I shall always see my shining treasure through a film of mud!'

She was out in the street already. She sighed, then hailed a cab and drove away without looking back, but fearful... fearful that if she did, she would see their outlines behind the mystery of the veiled windows. She gave the coachman the address of Lachaume. At the corner of the street she noticed a figure that seemed to be trying to keep out of sight. She leant forward and recognised Jane, the woman she had abandoned, apparently keeping watch outside Annhine's building. Her thoughts elsewhere, she attached little importance to it. She waved the sight away with a distracted gesture and sat back in the cab, hoping she hadn't been seen. At the florist's she selected a spray of chrysanthemums, whiter than snow, added a large bunch of dark, strong-scented violets, then asked for a card, on which she wrote these words: *Half an hour after leaving you, feeling close to you still, and so sad to send you something as commonplace as the flowers that anyone can send.*

She signed it by drawing a crescent moon and had the whole thing dispatched to boulevard Malherbes: "For Mme de Lys."

VII

Annhine's very rich and very dull lover found her in her dressing gown, finishing her breakfast. He was just dropping in for a moment. The previous day they had parted on bad terms. Then, in the evening, he had telephoned several times, invariably to be told by Ernesta that Madame had gone out in an agitated state and without giving any orders. He was worried, fearful of losing her, since after all he was very much in love with her; his anxiety had been intolerable, and after a sleepless night, he absolutely had to come round this morning to see her for a minute and explain himself. For the three years he had known her he had encouraged one extravagance after another, never refusing her anything: this sumptuous townhouse, those white horses, a recent whim of his pretty mistress, some beautiful jewellery boxes, always happy to satisfy instantly whatever new and costly caprice. His fortune was enormous, it was true, but not as vast as people liked to say. And then he was a married man, with a family to support, and head of a major banking house; his life-style may have been almost princely, but he had no choice, alas…! She must try to understand… try to be a bit more reasonable… He adored her, giving her pleasure was a joy to him, but he was exceeding his means. He had been doing some calculations: over the past three years nearly four million francs had slipped through the slender little fingers of his darling little woman… She was intelligent, she could follow his thinking, couldn't she, could put a check on her desires… slow down a little… oh, just the tiniest bit!… If she could put some order into things, that was all he would ask… And her clothes… God, the fantastic sums that disappeared on clothes! If only she could introduce a little bit of sense into that pretty head of hers…!

And as Annhine continued to sit there, listening, sulking, not even interrupting with some sally of her own, as she usually did: well, on this occasion he would give way again, she wanted those jewels so badly, she would have them. He looked at his watch: before mid-day he would drop in at rue Thérèse and have them sent over immediately… Along with some flowers, he hastened to add… and then a large box of chocolates from Boissier, because he knew she was childlike and highly sensitive in these little matters. She was his spoilt girl… his very own little darling. He leant towards her to hold her and kiss her. She resisted a little, then, staring evenly at him from under her long lashes, she said, her voice full of ironic mockery: 'Goodness me! What a tirade, my friend, what a tirade…! This horrible haggling over everything connected with me, I've absolutely had enough of it! And anyway, those things, I couldn't care less about them now!'

Astonished and confused, he was reduced to stuttering: couldn't care less...? What was this? They were two little marvels... she was going to have them... Come now...! He became tender, ingratiating... He had not meant to hurt her feelings, she was misinterpreting him, he was speaking honestly and out of affection. It was for her own good... he was only thinking of her. He wanted their relationship to go on for ever, with no worries and no obstacles.

'Everything comes to an end,' she interrupted again.

She stood up. Taking a step towards him, a sardonic expression on her face, she pointed a triumphant finger at the silver fern still pinned to her nightdress, visible in the opening of her dressing gown, whilst maliciously spreading before him the fingers of her ring-encrusted other hand.

He recognised the famous grasshopper and turned scarlet: 'What does this mean, Nhine...?' he demanded harshly. 'You were out all day yesterday, and today here you are in possession of the things I said I wouldn't buy...?'

'Ah, listen to him! If you're going to speak to me unpleasantly I won't tell you anything...

'But I want to know... it is my right to... to demand an explanation.'

'Ta... ta... ta...' she jeered, relishing her teasing of him. 'You have no right to tell me: I want... any more than I have, it would appear, since you behaved so unfeelingly yesterday. Put it down to a fairy, assume...'

'I do not want to put anything down and I do not want to assume anything. Nhine, my darling, please... I beg you, tell me the truth. You can see how on edge I am, how upset;

my imagination is running riot, I know the sort of things you might do... and you mean everything to me, everything!'

Nhine took pity on him in his desperation, having gained the satisfaction of her little victory and suddenly mindful of Tesse's advice. She told him: 'Ah, ah, you wicked villain, now you see what comes of resisting your Nhine's desires. Say you won't do it again.' She assumed a cajoling tone, approaching him with all the sorcery of her seductive smile. 'Say... say this, quickly, quickly: My Nhinon, I will always do everything you wish!'

Docilely, he repeated: 'My Nhinon, I will always do everything you wish.'

'Well, silly man! It was me who went to Lalique's and bought these jewels. In fact they aren't paid for yet, and you've said you'll get them for me. Come here and let me thank you with a kiss, although I ought not to, to punish you for your hesitation in the first place.'

He breathed a sigh of relief.

'Oh, the merest little hesitation, twenty-four hours, if that! You did the right thing, Nhinette...!' He pulled her to him, full of desire. 'And I deserve an extra kiss, for being nice...'

She extricated herself.

'Ah, no! One kiss is already too many, you know, since you virtually kept me waiting.'

'By the way, I was forgetting... Tell me, Nhine, I met a peculiar-looking person leaving the house just as I was coming in. No doubt you did not receive this early-morning visitor? She seemed strange and was very oddly attired. She stared at me. A funny little woman with a pink face and hair shooting out madly in all directions.'

A Woman's Affair

Annhine lied boldly: 'She's no one! One of Tesse's protégées, she sells flowers... artificial flowers...' And making a swift transition: 'Oh, and do you know, I've got a little protégé of my own now...'

And she began to tell the tale of her visit the previous day to the rue des Trois-Frères.

But as time and the Stock Exchange wait for no man, he was obliged to be on his way very soon afterwards.

As soon as he had gone she rang for Ernesta and sent her to telephone immediately to the jeweller's, who needed to be informed that someone would be calling on behalf of Mme de Lys and paying them a second time for the items sent to boulevard Malherbes the day before.

'Tell them to send the money round to me,' she called. 'Oh, God, constantly forced to lie... always play-acting... accepting limp, unwanted kisses...!' Nhine let out a sigh and collapsed, exhausted already, on the heap of bright little silk cushions that occupied one end of her familiar divan. 'I've had enough! And I have faith in Flossie... yes... I'm drawn to her, that child... she is good, and she is quite different from anything else I've come across...'

Her mind moved on to another tack: 'Ernesta, fetch Princess for me.'

'Madame, she went out with the servant.'

'Have you prepared the costumes?'

'They're airing in the linen room, madame. I intend to brush them later, this afternoon, and do some small repairs.'

'That's fine, I'll look at them tomorrow when they're ready. Pass me a book, the *Second Book of Jungle Stories*... There's a ring at the door; see who it is... What can she be doing? She should have come back by now. I'm always in such a hurry to know who might be calling! It's as if I was desperate for something unexpected and nice to happen.' And the impatient creature wriggled against the satins and laces of her chaise longue. 'I expect it's a tradesman. Ah, there you are at last! Well?'

'Madame, it's a lady... she wouldn't give her name, so I told her Madame did not receive unannounced callers. She insisted, insisted, then in the end she asked for something to write with.'

'Show me, quick!'

And Nhine plucked the piece of paper from her hands.

The note simply said:

> *Madame Jane d'Espant,*
> *wishing to see you about miss Bradfford.*

'Well, well!' said Annhine, intrigued. 'Old? Young? Well-dressed?'

'Soberly, madame, in black, a tailored morning dress... quite a good-looking person.'

'Show her in and let's see what happens...! All the same, I wonder what this woman wants? Ah, I've got it now, I've got it... She must be the...'

She had no time to pursue her interior monologue further: the stranger entered.

'Do sit down, Madame,' said Nhine. 'Ernesta, go and see to the disguises and when Princess is back, don't forget to send her along.'

Turning to the visitor: 'To what do I owe the honour,

madame, of this unusual approach?'

'Ah, madame...! Madame...! Forgive me, such rashness, yes. I can't help myself... Miss Bradfford comes here, I know, she told me, then I saw her leaving the house just now! So I wanted to see you, speak to you, tell you. Let me collect myself! I'm distraught, on edge... excuse me a moment... it's all terrible, terrible... I've had some dreadful times these last few days, awful attacks...'

Wild with misery, she rubbed at her forehead as if to erase her inner turmoil.

'Compose yourself, madame,' Annhine told her gently, looking at her closely and with a degree of admiration, for the poor creature was extremely beautiful. Very white, beneath a wonderful mane of wavy black hair that threw a dark and emphatic frame round her striking pale face. Her deep sorrowful eyes seemed to look into some distant world; there was a contained suffering in them, so that they seemed to be dying even as they shone with brilliance. Her straight nose flared curiously at the nostrils. Her mother-of-pearl teeth gleamed through her parted lips, which, twisted with emotion, were so intensely and improbably red they looked like a freshly opened wound... No tear came to her eyes, no sob choked her throat, but her chest rose and fell rapidly and her expression was wild... Moved by pity, Annhine went over and drew her gently against her shoulder, murmuring: 'I know, I know, I can guess. You are her friend, her special friend that she loved very much and now she's deserting you in favour of me... Poor little thing! I feel sorry for you! But... what do you want from me?'

'From you...? From you...? Ah! You know! Ah! You can

guess...!' And like some fierce and magnificent animal, Jane stood up, tall and terrible. 'So I was right...!' She prowled up and down the room, teeth clenched in fury, beside herself... 'She comes here every day! All the time...! You're the one she loves! You're the one she's left me for... She's put me on the rack because of you...!'

In a rage, she grabbed Nhine by the wrists.

'You're beautiful...! Oh yes, that's true! That's well known! And seeing you close to, you're pretty, slim, delicate... But me! I'm beautiful too! And maybe more beautiful than you! More alive, more full of bloom... You, you seem frail, incomplete...'

She lifted her head proudly, flaring her nostrils, giving each word separate emphasis. Her hair, shaken by a brusque movement, came undone and tumbled down her back, releasing a musky perfume.

'It's true! You are beautiful, you are magnificently beautiful,' cried Annhine in spite of herself. 'But let me go! Is it my fault...? Did I go to her of my own accord? Did I set myself up against your pernicious form of love...? I, for a start, am not the same sort of person! Let me go, I will explain...'

'Explain!' the woman roared. 'Ah, there's nothing you need explain! Not the same sort! As if I didn't know Flossie and her sweet ways and tender perversities...! She comes along and sidles up to you, and deludes you with troubling talk, she leads you on, spins a web round you, and eventually takes possession of you completely, of your deepest being...' Overwrought in the immensity of her suffering, she began to shake Annhine violently. 'Then one day she vanishes, suddenly called away by some new fancy... and there you remain, ruined, shattered, finished, frantic with regret and thrown into eternal despair... No! No!' she shouted, staring at Annhine. 'I rebel against it with all my power! I want her...!' She fell on her knees, begging, stretching her hands out towards the terrified Annhine. 'Madame, give her back to me! I'm asking you for her! You are loved wherever you go... what will you do with her? Give her back to me! Tell her, send her away... break with her... then perhaps she'll come back to me... Give her back! Give her back...! I beg you... give her back!'

Half-maddened in her distress, oblivious to all else, she reiterated her urgent prayer in a hoarse and rasping voice, distraught, beseeching Nhine with a stare that contained the full force of her soul.

'Poor little thing!' And Nhine stroked her brow with light fingers. 'Poor little widow...!'

Jane started back as if touched by a red-hot iron. She swayed and fell back, broken, on the carpet, incoherent... Reaction set in. Prolonged sobs came to her relief, words of less bitterness rose on her lips, whilst great sighs shook her whole body. Little by little she calmed down. Keeping her voice low, Nhine spoke softly and kindly, urging resignation: 'You are married, Jane, you have children, I expect?'

The unhappy woman shook her head.

'No? That is a great pity! But you have a duty to the man whose name you bear, to yourself, your family... Oh, a family!' she exclaimed with regret. 'Think how lucky you are to have a family; and how I envy you, I who am alone in the world. It is sad, I can tell you, to be a foundling! One has nothing... no little corner of the world, however humble, to say where you come from or provide a retreat when one feels the need... Nothing! Just whatever fancy is temporarily in fashion, debased and mercenary love affairs... I'm the unlucky one...'

She talked for some time about her own life, her disgust with it, her sadness and weariness.

'You are going through a crisis. Stand up tall again and look at life below you...'

With her delicate intuition, Annhine found words of consolation, words that entered the poor creature's heart like a healing balm. She knew that one began to suffer less once one appreciated the suffering of others. We are made that way: other people's troubles and griefs have a softening effect on ours and make them feel smaller.

Jane slowly raised her ruined face and Nhine wiped away its tears.

'Poor little thing...! Truly, anyone would think you were mourning a death, in your black clothes! And then, you know, it's very wrong, all that. Religion forbids it, and morality, and nature too!'

Astonished to find such tact, such kindness, in a woman of her sort, Jane calmed down... She got up from the floor and let herself be led to an armchair.

The atmosphere eased, her rancour had melted away. She became simply sad and melancholic, watching Nhine, surprised to find herself here, with this notorious figure from the demi-monde, the topic of much gossip... in this house, at this hour, and for such an extraordinary reason!

Nhine continued: 'So is there nothing you believe in...? Yes, there is... Lift up your eyes, then, and say a prayer. You are rich, married, respected, and you're weeping for a vice that has packed its bags and left! Ah, you don't know your own good fortune!'

She told her about her own life, its resentments and disappointments... Jane, persuaded, recovered her composure. She felt comforted, a new sense of calm slowly came over her, the way quietness is restored after a storm. She dried her eyes and thought about repairing her disordered hair.

'Powder?' Annhine passed her the gold and crystal box.

'Thank you. Oh, how good you are! Thank you...' She clasped Nhine in a powerful embrace. She was a woman of strong feelings, a passionate woman, excessive in all she did. She held her in her arms hard enough to hurt. 'It's easy to see why people love you, truly! So sweet...! Such a pure little courtesan, deep down, not a trace of unnatural vices... a truly nice soul! I want to be your friend! And there I was, thinking you were... Oh, no, let's not dwell on that...! I want to prevent you from falling into the disorder resulting from this vice you have no experience of... because you wouldn't lie to me, would you...?'

Seized by resurgent doubts, she grew restless again, fixing Nhine with a suddenly darkened and inquisitive eye.

'Hush, hush! Calm down,' Nhine told her, fearful once more. 'Yes, of course, everything I told you is perfectly true. Listen, this is the entire story...' As plainly as she could, she recounted the full history of her idyll with Flossie. 'It's very brief, as you can see, and amounts to very little: a meeting of souls, that's all!'

'Ah, how I envy you though!' said Jane, who had been trembling as she listened to the courtesan. 'How I envy you, my dear!'

A Woman's Affair

Her voice had become harder, no longer the plaintive, imploring tone of before, but something with a masculine edge, almost imperious.

'I want to protect you, to keep you safe. Ah, you don't know the voluptuous pleasure of women's embraces, the passions roused by a lesbian's caresses... the dreamy sweetness of forbidden kisses, the fevered wakings and renewed desires... the little bites that set your skin on fire, the slow climaxes that kill you, the cries and spasms of two loving women oblivious of anything else! *Each wears the other out, revives, devours; – We kill, we pity, hate the other; yet – Not one of us can part from what is ours.* A poet said that, and I have lived it! Ah, we mortals are only too ready to be woken into dreams of love...! Forget? Yes, but it isn't possible. My blood is still on fire! To forget, I'd have to die! Ah, Annhine, sweet child... pure... yes, pure compared to us, whatever your disorderly public life may say... Yes, I envy you and I bow my knee before your innocence... There are so many girls who fall prey to Florence's voracious vice! I pray she spares you, though! I want to see her... speak with her... we can be three women united by love... united by you, pale and gentle little flower, beautiful lily of whiteness that has grown, proud and radiant, on the dung-heap of life. What trash we are, the hypocrites, hiding behind our make-up and our veils! You are far less to blame, a lovely little thing who had no one to support you and guide you through life's dangers, and who has succumbed gently and with no sense of pleasure... in order to live! And so beautiful as well! Oh, you poor thing! Listen... somewhere in this panting, bleeding, torn-up heart of mine a new feeling is growing, sweet and profound, a feeling of affection for you.

It could be the one thing that will help me forget! Could you wish, Nhine, could you wish to have a friend? To have what remains of my heart?'

'Well, let it be so...' And Nhine smiled, won over by the spontaneous energy of the woman's feelings, pitching herself thus into Annhine's arms... into her life. 'I'm going to be happy from now on, I'm sure I am...!' She closed her eyes in hopeful contemplation of the joys to come. 'The three of us... Jane, Flossie, Nhine... Go, go and see her, let there be no jealousies between us, and come back soon, the pair of you... We'll do each other a lot of mutual good, since we're all equally to be pitied. With Altesse, I shall have three friends, and you will be loving towards me. Go, Jane, go and find Flossie again... and don't think about the brutal past any more, it's painful and full of lies.'

Just then Princess bounded in and ran towards her mistress.

'You won't be jealous, will you, little one, my pretty, promise? We were virtually alone in this whirlwind, this crowded, feverish life swirling all around us, and now we've got some friends, a whole family, my princess, my pretty...'

The little dog leapt from one to another of them, avid for attention. Ernesta, followed her in, and announced the arrival of Altesse.

'I've come to ask you to lunch. Time to get your feet back on the ground, before you become a complete stranger...' And Tesse walked in, holding out her hand and with a smile on her lips.

VIII

'Mme Jane d'Espant.' Nhine performed the introductions, disconcerted. 'Mme Altesse, my best friend... my only one.' She wasn't quite certain what face to put on things. 'I'd be delighted to have lunch with you, Tesse. It's a good idea, a very good idea... Are you going already, madame?'

Jane was standing.

'I must leave you, yes. You know what I have to do. I shall come back soon, if I can deal with my difficult situation. May I...? So, goodbye, madame.'

She shook her hand firmly, staring at her, and sighed. Annhine felt as if her hand was being crushed; she only just suppressed a squeal of pain. As she passed Altesse, Jane acknowledged her with a brief inclination of the head.

'Madame!'

Altesse returned the courtesy. When the visitor had gone:

'Who's she? A new friend? A new face, anyway. She looks fraught, hysterical, a real femme fatale. I haven't seen her here before, have I?'

'Don't I even get a kiss?' said Nhine in plaintive reproach. 'You're much more interested in a stranger than you are in me, you horrid thing.'

'True enough, darling, you're right. But it comes back to you anyway: what's wrong, my pretty? You seem pale. Is it the light in here?' She led her to the window, pushed the blind aside and studied her carefully. 'Yes, you're very pale. Your face is pinched and your eyes look tired. You're not well, Nhine.'

'I don't know. Actually, I do feel weak, I feel funny, I don't know what it is... I'm tired and on edge, I'd like to sleep the whole time.'

'You're doing too much, do you realise, Nhinette? And then,' she wagged her finger at her humorously, smiling, 'are you sure you're telling your best friend everything there is to tell?'

'Of course,' Nhine murmured feebly.

'Aha!' said Altesse, not insisting, 'I see some pretty things. The very items you were longing for yesterday. Henri did his stuff, then.'

'I followed your advice, Tesse, and look...' She came closer to show her the two objects. 'Beautiful, aren't they. Oh! And then I've something to tell you. We – I, that is – I went round to see those poor people you mentioned.'

'With Henri? You said "we" then!' And Tesse laughed. 'Oh, Nhinon, you're a very bad liar, honestly!'

'Am I? Well, all right, I'll tell you all about it. Promise

you won't scold me.'

And because her head was full to overflowing with difficult thoughts, she was glad to let them spill out. She came and sat on a low pouffe beside Altesse. She told her everything: her resistance, the attraction she nevertheless felt, how it was drawing her ever closer to Flossie, her visit to Montmartre, their mad tramp through the country lanes in the rain... and how she had woken up to find these jewels on her person.

'That's not so bad in itself,' Tesse interrupted. 'But it isn't right to tire you out. My Nhine is a fresh and delicate plant... I'm very happy for you to be amused, flattered, adored, heaped with jewels and loaded with presents. But what I do worry about, Nhinon, you see, is this vice's contagious effect. I'm afraid you might succumb, I mean genuinely fall for it. Your heart is too sensitive, everything makes such a deep impression on you. You'd be done for, excuse the expression. You don't give way at the time, but you think about it afterwards, when you're alone at night, and it's upsetting you... you may not want it to... but it's preying on your mind. It's a slippery slope, and it seems such a gentle, harmless one, just like the words and caresses of Miss Florence. Devil take her, I say. She had no business coming here and forcing herself on you. I mean, she's barely twenty but when you look at her closely her face is covered with tiny lines. I bet she uses lots of skin cream, of course she does! There's already something bitter and cynical in the way her mouth turns down at the corners. You don't have to go up close to see that, and it will only increase with time. Those women all lose their bloom very quickly and very young. By the time she's my age, she'll be old and past it, if not worse! And madness is never far away. Remember that Prélat woman you saw at my house in Ville-d'Avray and who used to play for big money at Monte-Carlo: she died in a madhouse quite recently. Then there's Diane de Croissy, paralysed in both legs and now wheeled around in a chair at the age of twenty-eight. And then there was the artist Delavagne's woman who killed herself in a fit of frenzy because some crop-haired female or other had left her in the lurch. Look at Riscogni, that Spanish dancer everyone admired and who was so beautiful: she fell into the Koniarowska woman's clutches, her beauty suddenly vanished, she grew huge, mannish, and now her face has turned into the chilling mask that symbolises her vice. Oh, Nhinon, Nhinon! I would hate to see you change the same way!'

Annhine was left reflecting, a faraway expression on her face, greatly troubled... She was telling herself it must be an extraordinarily powerful and addictive sort of pleasure if those who yielded to it did so without regretting the permanent loss of their dignity as women, their youth and their beauty.

'What are you thinking, Nhine...? Nhine?' Tesse touched her arm. 'If you were different, I'd say: so all right, give it a try... just once. Give yourself the experience of this perverted pleasure – if I knew that you'd laugh about it afterwards. But knowing as I do how you are – affectionate but vulnerable, full of imagination but too ardent and head-strong, I say: no, Nhine, be careful, it would finish you. And what about Henri, who gives you everything and guards you so jealously? Henri would be furious. He'd leave you on the spot, and then where would you be? You still need him. You have to think about all that carefully, darling!'

Nhinon was still dreaming. Tesse's wise words oppressed

her. She didn't wish to hear them any more. She stared at the wall. She preferred the caressing sound of Flossie's voice, she thought about her feline looks and ways.

'You're changing already,' Tesse went on. 'Listen to me, my dear, I have never given you bad advice, and you know how genuine my affection for you is: clear your mind of the whole subject as fast as you can... We'll go on a trip, travel somewhere, if you like. With Henri.' Nhine flinched. 'Well then, without Henri. With my old Georges, he's got a soft spot for you. I could easily be jealous, you realise? I'll talk to him... For the sake of your pretty face he'll abandon the boulevardier's life without a qualm. He'll leave his collections and his old friends and his whist parties behind to accompany us wherever our fancies take us. Would you like that? It can be arranged in no time, and I'll take it on myself to smooth things over with Henri... Which reminds me, you do remember the four of us are dining together this evening at La Maison-Dorée?'

'Yes,' said Nhine, 'but don't say anything to them yet. We'll go, later... later, I promise. Oh, but don't worry so much, Tesse!' She took hold of her hands and squeezed them gently, but not looking her in the face, confused, as if trying to hide her real thoughts. "Poor Tesse, honestly, she makes a tragedy out of everything... she's so proper," she said to herself. 'Curse it all!' she exclaimed out loud. 'Everything is so aggravating, everything! I refuse to say another word if you're going to lecture me like that!' And she burst into tears, her tension and agitation seeking release in the calming and restorative effects of giving way.

'Oh, Nhine, Nhinette!' Tesse kissed the white skin of her

neck which peeped through the lace of her dressing gown. 'But you can see, I'm right, your nerves are strained. Cry, my lovely, it'll do you good.'

And Tesse, shaking her head, looked imperturbable; but already her heart was filled with deep concern.

'I just happen to find one little thing... which amuses me and which... interests me... not the same old routine... like... everything else... and you... you scold me for it.. You want to... to prise me away... And those men... oh, there's no escape...! It's my job...! They won't... won't let me have...' And Nhine's words came out ever more jerkily, between sobs. '... the things I... actually... like... Oh...! Sh...! Sh...! Sh...!'

'My darling creature, you put me in mind of that princess in the fairy tale. She was as beautiful as a sunny sky but when she opened her mouth, out came snakes and toads and frogs and all sorts of disgusting things...'

Nhine couldn't help laughing in the midst of her tears.

'I'm sorry, Tesse darling, I don't know what's come over me.' Her fingers twisted themselves in knots. 'I haven't told you about...'

Needing to confide, she explained how Jane had arrived, and the scene that followed.

'Ah, now I understand! This was your Act Four, the one that really turns the screw. No wonder you're upset. My dear Nhinette, I won't say anything more on the subject since it disturbs you... You're a free woman, but that whole scene is a bad one, it's unhealthy, do you hear me? Just mind you watch out. Tell me then, will you be going to the ball tomorrow...? The actors' ball?'

Nhine hesitated.

'No!' she ventured, timidly.

'Good. It's going to be a terrible crush, it seems to me. I'm not either.'

Ernesta came in. She looked troubled.

'Madame, it's...'

She groped for the right words.

'Well, what?' Nhine got up and went to sit at her dressing table. 'Speak up, what's the matter?'

'Madame, there's a woman who... She's come to...'

'Ah, no! I've had enough of these surprise callers, these mysteries. Haven't we, Tesse?'

She was combing her hair vigorously, yanking its tresses into long strands, still agitated.

'Ah, yes!' said Tesse. 'Enough! Spare us!'

'Madame Altesse,' the chambermaid responded, with the air of a familiar sharing a secret, 'she's a procuress, I didn't quite know how to put it to Madame.'

Nhine was about to powder her face. She span round, brandishing the powder puff in her raised hand.

'Kick her out, at once.'

'She was so insistent, madame.'

'You heard what I said.'

'We should see what she wants,' Tesse put in, ever the wise and practical courtesan. 'Let her in for a moment, it doesn't commit you to anything. It's not unreasonable and it might be of interest to you. This is our business, after all... It might be a good opportunity... See her anyway.'

'Yes, and then she'll go round spreading the word that she only had to show her face at my door and she was warmly welcomed.'

'Not at all. These women are very discreet,' Tesse asserted. 'Professional secrets, and so on.'

'And it's very much a private matter, it appears.'

'All right, show her in, then.'

Ernesta ushered into the room an elderly woman with wavy white hair piled on her head like a crown, giving her an air of snowy respectability. She was dressed in black and seemed very proper. She kept her head lowered, not daring to meet anyone's eye, and held a small packet in her hand. She apologised straight away for her boldness, but she could not miss an opportunity of this sort: it was – and she spoke softly, mysteriously, almost whispering as if she had strayed into a church – it was a foreigner, very rich and head over heels with Mme de Lys. He had seen her in the Bois de Boulogne one day and had followed her. He had been dreaming about her ever since, he wanted her whatever it cost. Not knowing anyone who could introduce him, he had come to her to ask for help. She knew that access to Madame was extremely difficult to obtain, so – to be frank – she had tried to put him off at first, suggesting other women who were very attractive too but more open to financial persuasion... He wouldn't listen. It was Annhine de Lys he wanted. And, oh, she could see why, now that she was granted the opportunity to admire Madame in person. "Listen," she had said in the end, "I can't promise you anything for certain, but, nothing risked nothing gained, I will go and find her. But what are you prepared to offer her?" – "Anything she wants. You can go as far as twenty-five thousand francs..."

Tesse's face was alight with joy: 'What a windfall that would be, Nhine!'

'Are you quite sure...? Is this guaranteed?' asked Nhine, mistrustful.

'Madame, it's as I said, this man is crazy for you. He went quite pale when he talked about you. I swear I tried a hundred ways to put him off, but nothing doing. I didn't dare come here because I knew you're a woman who has everything she wants already. It's a very delicate matter to appear unannounced before a queen like you. I brought a little parcel, done up tightly, and presented myself as a lace-maker, then I spoke privately to your chambermaid. I said I had to see you, she tried to send me away! Just imagine! This gentleman had promised me five hundred francs of my own if I could contrive to see Madame... even without result, and two thousand francs if Madame came. He's as rich as Croesus, that's for sure! His wallet was stuffed. Perhaps he'd make Madame very rich very quickly! A man who promises twenty-five thousand francs like that! He'll deposit them with me in advance... Diamonds, of course... pearls the size of nuts... she can have anything she asks. He wants you, he wants you, he wouldn't budge an inch. Ah, we don't deserve to eat bread in our old age if we refuse offers like that. Twenty-five thousand francs for an hour or two in the afternoon... and hopes of gold...'

She would arrange the meeting for tomorrow between two and four; she was aware that Madame had ties... Oh, she knew everything in Paris! – Her voice became obsequious, her manner conspiratorial. – Especially when it concerned a woman so much in the public eye. Madame would certainly rather it was in the daytime. It would be over sooner... much less awkward...

'What do you think, Tesse?' Nhine asked, weakening.

'Goodness me, what is there to lose...? Is he good-looking?'

'A dream...! With big blue eyes... And he was so worked up! He was shaking...! He even stammered a bit too... but he spoke very good French all the same... Just a young man, thirty, no more...! Madame won't be disappointed, for sure... unless his emotion... well, bless me, gets in the way! It does happen!'

He was awaiting a reply at her house in rue Tronchet.

Nhine was still hesitant: 'You're absolutely sure he's a foreigner... and not some-one put up to it by my friend, for example, trying to catch me out?'

The woman was shocked: A trap! Ah, no, of course not! Her house was known to be an honest house, she wouldn't soil its name with that kind of affair! Go-between, madam, yes! But not Judas, oh no! Madame could rest easy on that score. He was definitely an Englishman. If Madame was dubious, she'd rather abandon the whole idea. Lend herself to such evil practices...! Oh! One thing was for sure...

She began to grow excitable, her voice loud.

'Hush,' Annhine said. '...So I can be certain of twenty-five thousand francs and absolute discretion?'

'Absolutely, madame...' Calming down, she lowered her voice: 'If Madame wishes, the chambermaid can come back to the house with me, see the gentleman and judge for herself.'

Nhine pondered.

'The idea of going to your house bothers me. I might run into someone; and at my house, it's out of the question...'

'Excuse me, madame! But no one will see you! You travel in an enclosed carriage, you wear the sober clothes of a respectable woman and a thick lace veil on your hat which will hide your face. I'll wait for you behind the door, which will be ajar. You won't have to ring, just push your way through... and you enter an empty corridor – don't bother with the cab, I'll pay it off later. When you come out you'll find another waiting at the corner of the street so as not to attract attention, and once inside you have yourself driven back here – not all the way – to within a hundred metres, say, and the thing is done: twenty-five thousand better off, and who knows anything about it...? What do you say..? Is it a deal?'

As Nhine remained silent, Tesse said: 'Yes, of course, don't you think, Nhinon? A risky adventure is all part of the trade, it could be fun, especially when it's so well paid!'

'I shall give you two thousand francs as well,' Nhine declared.

Madame was most kind, most generous. Ah, but she was known for it all over Paris... It would be a good day's work for everybody, then!

'But I want it in advance, you know. I'm not in the habit of doing this kind of thing, I'm only making an exception this time, because of the sum involved.'

'As some queen, I don't remember which, once said,' her friend remarked, "It's no laughing matter."'

'Exactly, and then since this person clearly thought nothing of coming out with a crude demand to meet him in a place like that, I'm not standing on ceremony when it comes to settling the question of money.'

Madame was very hard...! Places like that? The smartest house in the whole of Paris! Oh! Madame would see for herself tomorrow. She'd have the best room prepared for her, complete with dressing room, bath, shower, sitting room, tea...! Everything was of the highest quality! Madame would see, Madame would think very differently then! As for the rest, fair's fair, it was all arranged already: Madame would get her hands on the cash the minute the carriage dropped her off.

'And you'll get yours too. Two o'clock... I'll be there between two and two thirty.'

'Madame must be sure to be punctual... Oh, he was wild with desire! He won't be able to contain himself, I know it. Between now and tomorrow... my God!' She wouldn't want to find herself in bed with him, tonight! 'Madame mustn't keep him waiting too long – he won't be able to hold himself in check – and the whole house will be at Madame's sole disposal. There'll be no one around in the corridors, we'll have flowers placed everywhere.'

Oh, the business they'd done there, with some of the finest ladies, beautiful society women, top drawer, the grandest in the land. It had fallen away a little in recent times, because everyone now had their own little love nest, but it still happened, with foreigners especially.

'Really?'

Altesse, intrigued, wanted to know more.

The woman assumed the expression of one reluctant to betray confidences. She couldn't say too much, but for sure, heaps of them came, heaps and heaps... and not for twenty-five thousand francs either...! For a lot less than that! Oh, she'd have set out with a lighter step if she'd been calling on one of the toffs, those countesses and baronesses, instead of coming here, no doubt about it... And the poor man left waiting...!

'I'll be on my way. Goodbye, ladies... Ah, if Madame

wanted to, we could make a mint together!' Anyway, this affair first, and after that, they could see, yes? 'I must run. Until tomorrow, then. I'll drop by again about twelve… not to disturb Madame, just to check with the chambermaid and make sure… Goodbye… goodbye.'

'Goodbye, madame. Until tomorrow.'

'Until tomorrow…'

A bow and scrape, a wheel towards the door, and she took herself triumphantly off, a radiant messenger of good news.

IX

Dinner was drawing to an end in good spirits. Nhine had been remarkably happy. Altesse had not left her side all day and her wise influence had worked a calming effect on the taut nerves of her over-sensitive friend.

The getting-together of two Parisian couples in a private room at the Maison-Dorée was hardly a major event, but what made it special was the intimacy and companionship they were able for once to enjoy. They talked of their own affairs, their plans, their individual feelings, simply and without pretension, happy just to be together.

Annhine's lover, being married, found a double pleasure in this sort of outing, which it was difficult for him to arrange with any frequency. He smiled as he stared at her.

'You find our Nhinette beautiful this evening,' Tesse said nicely.

And he replied: 'More than anything else in the world! This girl, you see, she's my ray of sunshine!'

'You took the words out of my mouth, Henri...'

And it was true, Annhine was adorably beautiful that evening. She wore a very pale blue chiffon dress that floated like mist. A broad belt of dull gold, set high, emphasised her slender waist. It was decorated with white water lilies, their centres made of velvet, their long, greenish stalks weaving among the rod-like stems of fresh pink gladioli. A dragonfly with wings of transparent blue formed the buckle. From her splendid diamond necklace hung a pendant, modelled as an eel and studded with tiny emeralds. Her fingers sparkled with stones. On a whim, she had tied her hair on the top of her head with two narrow ribbons of blue satin, in Greek style. And to sit above her ear she had simply threaded a single white rose.

Meanwhile Tesse, on her advice, had chosen a straight and clinging dress of Irish guipure on a flesh-tone backing. For embellishment at the side, floating lengths of white muslin were fastened in place by small bunches of dark pink orchids, while lines of sapphires, diamonds, pearls and opals, all intermixed, traced long glittering patterns all down the lacy fabric. Nothing was more charming than the sight of two pretty women of such refined elegance, so graceful in their gestures, so captivating in their looks and smiles, seated at this flower-decked table, making friendly conversation, teasing, playful, sometimes tender... It was easy to understand the delight and mute adoration of the two men seated opposite who returned their looks and witticisms in kind.

Towards the end of the evening, Nhine grew silent. She

closed her eyes for a moment and seemed to have difficulty breathing.

The attentive Henri said: 'Is something the matter, Nhinon? You don't look quite well.'

'Oh, it's nothing... I just need a little air... Could we open the window for a minute? Do you mind, Tesse?'

He darted forward. She allowed him to lead her out on the balcony. A breath of cool air revived her.

'That's better. Leave me here, go inside and smoke. That's what it must have been, making me feel unwell... your unvarying bad habits!'

He threw his cigar into the street: 'My darling, you should have said something to me earlier!'

'Oh, well, of course! Everything has to be said to you, the whole time... Leave me alone. Give me space to breathe... Go away, will you, I find you oppressive...'

She stamped her foot, dismissing him harshly.

He returned sorrowfully to the table: 'I don't know what's got into her. She sent me away...'

'Nhine's not well, Henri...' Tesse lowered her voice to speak to him. 'You must have noticed, she's been pale and nervous for some days... she's a little bit over-tired, she's been doing too much... she had a part in Prince Azur recently which really took it out of her. You ought to get her away from Paris for a while as soon as you can, take her off somewhere, go travelling... down to the Midi, or Italy, or Spain. We would come with you, wouldn't we, Georges?'

'But you know what she's like, Altesse, she doesn't listen to me, and then I'm hardly free to do as I like...' A note of regret crept into his voice. 'All the same, though, if it was necessary I'd find a way to do what needed doing somehow. But this is nothing! She's a resilient woman, this is just a bad patch. I upset her yesterday, and again this morning.'

'What are you two plotting...?' And Nhine was coming over to them, a worrying light in her eye. 'Tell me, Georges.' She rested an arm coaxingly on the elderly scholar's shoulder. 'Tell me what scheme those two have been dreaming up to disturb my peaceful existence!'

'Oh, the siren, look how she works her charms. She's well aware Georges is defenceless against them... So all right,' Tesse said with decision, 'we were discussing the idea of a little trip... the four of us... or the three of us,' she hastily corrected.

Nhinon frowned, displeased.

'But I've already told you we... This is very strange. I mean, I'm not a child, I can act for myself... And here you are trying to control my affairs. When I want to go, I shall go... and not with you, to begin with... With you, Tesse, yes, but alone, the two of us, to find new countries, to see new faces, because I'm tired of it all, tired of everything I see around me here.'

'That's nice,' her lover said. 'Very friendly, excluding me like that, just when I was saying I'd do everything in my power...'

'To irritate me, as usual,' retorted Annhine, working herself up. 'For a start, I'm not ill, my nerves are on edge, that's all. And it's your fault. You never understand me!'

'A good thing too, maybe,' Henri interrupted, unwisely.

'Oh, so now you insult me...! You resort to crudeness! That's all I needed! I've had enough, my dear...' Her face reddened, she began to lose her temper. 'Yes, I've had it up to here and I'm going, I'm going home, now! No, don't come near me, don't say another word. I'm telling you, I've had enough!' she yelled. 'I forbid you to come with me and I forbid you to follow me... Leave me alone before I do something I'll regret...'

'Nhine, Nhine...'

And Altesse came over to her in distress.

'Oh, forgive me, my darling, forgive me... and you too, Georges... but you know what it is I want, you know what I think, and you, at least, understand me...'

'Yes, yes,' said Altesse, trying to be conciliatory while remaining perfectly calm. 'I do understand you, but that doesn't mean I always approve...'

'Well, that's just too bad for you...!'

And Nhine, blazing with anger, strode out, slamming the door behind her.

The three of them stood looking at each other in stupefaction, dumbfounded.

'I don't know what's got into her...' Henri said, hesitantly. 'I must go too...'

'Annhine is not her usual self at the moment, my friend. You'll only make her worse. My advice would be to let her quietly go home tonight, by herself... She'll spend all night working things out in her head and she'll come round of her own accord, she's such a good soul at heart. I'm going to hold back as well, and I'm convinced she'll have called to see me by this time tomorrow, full of apologies for this evening's little scene, all down to nervous stress... You should do the same, trust me, and then be very patient, very gentle. She's having a difficult time at present, emotionally, and more than anything she needs moral guidance. Keep this little trip of ours in mind: we'll carry her off by force, one day when she's in a responsive mood.'

'Yes, yes,' Georges said. 'Altesse is right. She knows our pretty little friend very well.'

'But I don't recognise her any more! She's changed. Sometimes I think she hates me...' And Henri shook his head in misery.

'No! No! She tells me everything and I know she doesn't. No, the thing is, you see, the child has spent too much time with her head in books. She thinks too much, and has to analyse everything, which isn't healthy. She's become very self-critical and though she tries to keep her bitterness hidden away in the background, one fine day, when her nerves are strained, it all comes tumbling out. Her instincts are extremely refined, and her impulses can be delightful, but she feels things too much, and at times when she's low, the emptiness of her life or rather the weight of her existence crushes her... She questions herself, undermines herself, almost kills herself.'

'The poor girl...! You're right, Altesse, but I'm suffering too, and I love her...! Ah, if I was free I wouldn't hesitate to take her off somewhere. We'd go far away and for a long time... I'd take her on distant voyages, to lands unknown... That would distract her.'

'And afterwards, what then? It would be the same thing all over again. The trouble is here...' Altesse pointed to her forehead. 'Here, in that pretty little head... She needs a goal in life, a serious occupation... something to engage her mind. We must see to her physical well-being for a while first, and then we'll definitely find a distraction of some sort, that's the way to proceed...'

'You are wonderfully good, Altesse...' And Henri, taking her hand, bestowed on it a devoted kiss. 'I'm going to do as you suggested... stay at home for twenty-four hours and wait. A brief telephone call, to see how she is. Have some flowers sent round, and that's all.'

'Too much, perhaps... Well, all right, you love-lorn boy, it's such a nice gesture I'll allow it. Goodbye, then. Georges and I are going to look in at the Comédie-Française for a while. Are you coming with us?'

'With your permission, just for an hour.'

He helped her into her long evening coat, straw-coloured velvet inlaid with lace and lined with chinchilla. She smiled at him over her shoulder and they left, comforted, and resolved to support each other in the quest for the happiness and health of the spoiled and highly-strung child they were all so fond of and whose life was going through an unexpected and painful crisis which threatened to overturn and destroy everything.

X

Annhine stepped briskly down from the cab and paused under the entrance arch. It was the wrong building... so much the better! This way the coachman wouldn't suspect anything. She imagined he had given her a strange look when she had told him the address. She retraced her steps and saw him driving away, which was a relief. She also saw, a few metres further on, the house she had been directed to. She pushed her way through the door, feeling anxious, and found herself face to face with the venerable matron.

'You stopped too far down the street,' she was told. It was nearly three and everyone was growing impatient. 'Here are the twenty-five thousand francs...' The woman handed her a bundle. 'Count them quickly and follow me, madame... He's waiting for you, he's waiting for you...!'

And she led her up a steep twisting staircase that emerged

on to a corridor.

Annhine felt ill at ease and unhappy. Unpleasant associations filled her mind. She remembered her beginnings, the hard days of her youth when, still a minor, she used to creep about furtively in this way, wary then of the police. Almost every week she would turn up at one shady address or another for squalid little appointments whose rates varied between twenty and a hundred francs, in order to have the means to feed herself. Ah, it was a different matter now; and yet she was fresher and beautiful in a very different way in those days! She counted: twenty-five thousand exactly.

'Here you are, madame. For you...'

The woman turned and held out her hand, greedily. She seized the bank notes and swiftly thrust them in her corsage.

'Thank you. Here we are, this is it.'

'Let me get my breath for a moment,' Annhine said outside the door.

She hid the money in her pocket.

'I'm a bit nervous,' she said. 'My heart's racing.'

'Come along, come along, it'll all be over in an hour. You just ring the bell and I'll come and fetch you.'

She pushed her forward and closed the door on her.

'What a fuss, I don't know... Their kind, really...' she grumbled as she went away. 'Honestly, if wasn't for the pots of money... Look at her! Acting as if she was a princess of the blood...! What a joke!'

There was no going back now. Annhine saw the foreigner at the window keeping watch, motionless and pensive. She coughed. He turned round suddenly. Where had she seen that face before? He was coming over to her, pale and trembling, not saying a word.

'Monsieur…'

'Madame…'

They were both embarrassed, clearly uncomfortable.

Wanting to break the ice, Annhine said: 'So, you were particularly anxious to see me…?'

And the man: 'Ah! Yes…!'

A great sigh escaped him, a sudden light flashed in his eye, a rasping laugh broke from his lips, while his whole face flooded with colour. The power of his emotion, she thought. She smiled at him nicely. There was something shifty and surreptitious about the way he stared back at her, taking her all in.

"What a bore!" she thought. "He's a dreadful man, I'd give anything if I could just go away."

The silence began to weigh on her.

'So, I was very happy to come… What do you want me to do?' she said, to see what would happen.

'Take your clothes off!' he coldly commanded.

She saw red. Rebellion flared inside her, she wanted to fling his money in his face and walk out…

"The fact is, he's within his rights," she reflected. "A woman who takes a man's money has to go through with it. It would be stupid of me to expect to find good manners in the sort of brute who resorts to methods of this kind to approach a woman… His coldness, ugh…! He's an Englishman all right, this one! Well then, the thing is not to care. What an idiot you are, you'll never make a good whore!"

And, her mind made up, she began to undo the bodice on her dress. The stranger's eyes glinted in delight.

"Aha, he's thawing now...! God, how aggravating this all is!"

She removed her hat. While unfastening the face-veil her fingers got in a tangle.

'Help me then,' she demanded.

He came up close. His hands trembled, inept.

"I might have known! He's even more agitated than I am. It's his English stiffness that makes him so unbearably crude... Come on, let's get it over quickly...! All you have to do, little courtesan, my dear, is laugh at the thought of the pretty blue banknotes, smile at the generous lover-by-the-hour, respond compliantly to his animal appetites, and get it firmly into your head that this is what you're here for."

Her petticoat fell to the floor. She stepped out of it in her chemise and made towards the bed in the alcove.

"It's not too bad here – the old woman was right – clean, nice linen and a white room with blue curtains... my colour!"

She prepared herself, putting on a suitable expression and getting into the right frame of mind, all the while humming to herself the tune from Blue-Beard, *We'll take whatever comes our way, but we'll always look on the bright side!*

'Naked,' he commanded, 'completely naked!'

She started up, a sulphurous look in her eyes, then she obeyed, passive.

"It's too bad! No, but he must be out of his mind, daring to speak to me like that!"

'There!' she cried.

Proud of her beauty, she angrily threw her chemise into the middle of the room... and stood there, radiant in her slender nudity, flawlessly androgynous: slim, smooth legs, body a graceful curve, hard little breasts, beautiful as the statue of a young god, her snowy whiteness brushed with rose, the prettiness of her fine, curly head carried on a shapely neck. He stood back and contemplated her with a sort of drunken fervour.

'Lie down!'

She lay on the bed, amazed, thinking she must be in a dream. He rushed from the room. She waited, raising herself on one elbow, vaguely anxious… Some minutes passed. Then the door opened again; he was not alone… a female form behind him… But… Yes…! Oh, oh! It was too much!

She leapt from the bed and was about to flee the room to call for help. A choked cry stopped her.

'Nhine!' someone was calling.

What! That woman… Was it…? Why yes, yes it was, it was Flossie…! What did this mean – she didn't understand any more – she couldn't think straight! Flossie…? Here? To take her by force? To have her… like this? As if she were the lowest of tarts? How utterly humiliating…! Why? Why?

She crumpled on the edge of the bed and waited, rigid, for she knew not what, desperately trying not to cry.

Flossie, turned to stone, was standing in the middle of the room.

'How disgraceful…! Ah…! I can't believe what you've done, Willy! It's disgusting!' she finally managed to declare.

And she tried to get past him.

He pushed her violently aside and barred the way.

'Disgusting…!' he cried in a paroxysm of fury. 'So it's disgusting to bring you face to face with your own vileness! It's a disgrace to confront you with the person you'd rather have than me, your fiancé, your lover! It's a crime to pay vast sums to bring this prostitute here to give you the benefit of her professional services! In order, precisely, to disgust you so deeply you never want to again... You must be the vilest of people, Flossie, or a total madwoman to want to sink to such depths! I thought you were blind, I wanted to open your eyes: there she is, this famous beauty, this filth! She has come to this revolting whorehouse and stripped naked because I told her to and because I gave her money to. Beautiful? Her flesh is, yes... and you may drool over it, but, ah, to sacrifice me, to drive me away for that piece of dirt, for that whore who sells herself like this to anyone that comes along, is that possible...? Is it even believable...?'

Flossie turned on him, infuriated.

'Get out, you monster...!' Her voice rose to a shout. 'Get out of my life, for ever! I order you! It's all off, it's all over between us! Get out now, or I'll kill myself!'

She opened the window and set her foot on the sill.

His anger instantly evaporated.

'Flossie, my Flossie, my fiancée, my wife! Oh! Forgive me...! I'm going mad, Flossie! No, you wouldn't be so cruel... I love you, I adore you...! I don't want to lose you, Flossie!'

And he began to sob uncontrollably.

'Get out!' she repeated.

She made a movement. He threw himself at her... grabbed hold of her.

'No! No...! Don't kill yourself...! I'll leave, I'm leaving. Ah, Flossie, Flossie, this'll be the end for me... I'm going away, goodbye for ever, you won't see me again! I can't give you the love you demand... horrible, servile, belittling... but it's the end of me... Floss... my Flossie! Don't you have the least pity...?'

'Get out!'

'Flossie, listen, there's time, you need to think. Besides, we can't possibly part here, in a place like this...!'

'Well, I'm leaving you: goodbye!'

Annhine, who had put her clothes back on, was striding coldly towards the door.

Flossie ran to her.

'I'm leaving with you, my sweet, so beautiful, so misunderstood...! I'm leaving!'

Heedless of her fiancé's dreadful agonies, she went down the gloomy staircase with Nhine. They walked away without a glance and fortunately met no one who might delay or question them. In the cab they couldn't speak but simply fell into a desperate embrace.

'However close to each other we are, we shall never be close enough!' Flossie sighed at last. 'Oh, Nhine, forgive me for being the cause of this dreadful thing that's happened to you!'

'Be quiet,' Annhine said, 'be quiet.'

When they arrived at her house: 'Go now,' she said. 'Have nothing more to do with me. Farewell. This isn't the path for you. I don't want to bring trouble into your life, poor creature. Leave me...! With my way of life, I have to expect the worst, to put up with anything. But you...!'

'No! No...! Leave you? Never! Nhine, think: if you send me away, it will make things more complicated, not less. I've lost my fiancé, I hate him now for even thinking of that despicable scheme. I shall certainly never see him again! So let me stay with you, my martyr, my beloved Nhine... You'll see... In any case, am I not your page?'

Touched, Nhine relented: 'That is true. Come in then, we'll talk...'

They entered the house, serious and thoughtful... As she was getting undressed, Annhine thought of the twenty-five thousand francs which she still had in her pocket.

'Here,' she said in all simplicity, handing her the money. 'Here, you can give him this back!'

'Nhine,' the child was trembling. 'Please keep it. You must.'

'Ah, yes! I earned it, it belongs to me!'

'No, my Nhine, that wasn't what I meant. But... keep it all the same... It's something at least... With that...' Her eyes filled with tears, she seemed to be struggling for words. 'With that... look, you know, those poor people, the sick little boy, well, we'll give it to them... You see, for them it'll be a fortune.'

She threw herself into the arms of an astonished Annhine, who burst out crying.

'All today's horrors and tears will have won them this, my sweet, don't you see? We won't have suffered for nothing... Oh, Nhine, I feel closer to you than ever, and further than ever from men – whom I hate in their entirety, in the person of one man!'

She clasped her with fierce strength and kissed her urgently.

'I don't know! I don't know!' Annhine moaned. 'After so much harsh reality how can I believe in anything? I'm frightened of finding it's just another illusion...'

'You'd listen to me though?'

'Yes, but the way you listen to music in a church, without believing in its religion, or even understanding it any more. What would you do in an existence like mine, so deeply scarred by everything that's happened that only death could remove the traces?'

'I'd do good.'

'Good? Is it still possible?'

'I'd help you first of all... and then together we'll help other people.'

Nhine saw a glimmer of hope: 'Yes, we can do good works, and that might redeem this appalling way of life, redeem today's appalling events which have suddenly brought me face to face with myself... and everything else. I feel I love you too, nothing will come between us. Ah, let's not talk about all this any more.'

She held her at arms' length and said once again: 'I wonder, Flossie, how you can possibly feel desire for a body as soiled as mine, sullied by so many degrading encounters. And that's all my life is...! Oh, I want you to have what no one else looks for, the best part of me: my soul... that's what I can give you...'

She placed a lingering kiss on the girl's lips.

'I adore you, I adore you...! You'll send me mad,' Flossie exclaimed, her head reeling. 'Yes, your soul is the only thing I want. I shall cherish your body, but it will remain sacred, until the day when you yourself...'

'That? Never...! I swear! Too sullied, too soiled. The thought of love-making gives me the horrors! You have to try to understand me – after all I've been through!'

'I love you, and I suffer with you because I understand only too well. I will be your slave and wait for you all my life…'

'If you knew, if you only knew,' Annhine went on, 'I've been terribly unhappy these last few days. I had a row with Altesse last night, just imagine. And my lover too. They haven't sent me word all day. Everybody is against me. I've been abandoned. You're the only person I have, Flossie. Love me, love me well…'

'Ah! With all my soul and for all eternity.'

A knock came at the door. It was the chambermaid.

'Madame, it's the costumes, I wanted to show them to you.'

They looked at each other, speechless.

Flossie said: 'But of course, it's tonight. Let's try them on, what do you think…? It will help us forget. Let's go to this ball.'

'I'm hardly in the mood!'

'Nhine, yes, it'll make us forget! We mustn't let other people's bad behaviour affect us.' Her face lit up in an expression of defiance. She drew herself to her full height, her manner became haughty. 'Let us walk tall among that crowd of enemies and ignoramuses, proud of ourselves and invincible! We shall always be misunderstood. Who cares? We shall trample them all beneath our feet, sustained by the sublime power of our special union. Let us go to the ball, let us laugh, let us dance, let us live our dream…!'

'Is that what you want?'

'It's what I want, and you do too, my Nhine. Want, you have to want: it's the key to everything!'

'You're right. Oh, you give me courage, Flossie. Don't ever stop giving it!'

'Ah, when I know you're with me like this, I feel something new in my heart, a force, strong enough to plunge deeper than the deepest abyss and rise again higher than the outer limit of the distant stars, and I laugh at humanity! I would like to make you love yourself the way I love you!'

'My sweet thing, I am in pieces... your words do me good. Aren't you afraid to dirty yourself by wading into the foul mud that surrounds me?'

'Don't think about it! That mud will dry out, harden in the glowing sunlight of my burning love. It will be the very foundation on which we shall rise, Nhine, my beloved.'

'For ever, then!' Annhine declared.

'For always...' Flossie replied.

XI

'Well now, Father, you look dashing in your party clothes, tasty enough to eat... You must have vast numbers of penitent ladies at your feet, looking like that; my word, I've never seen a better turned-out little vicar.'

'Ah, my lord Marquis, God has been kind enough to form me with a certain care. Indeed religion is not difficult to practise when one is young and favoured by nature... There are some beautiful ladies among my flock who are particularly assiduous in their devotions; it is dangerous for my virtue at times, but is not God's mercy infinite?'

'Father, we shall take dinner together!'

'With pleasure, Marquis!'

'And you will tell me of your little scandals.'

'Oh, Marquis...! If you knew...'

'Ta... ta... ta... Elvire! Pour us some of this ancient

foaming wine, which would loosen the tongue of a corpse, and let us take our places at table.'

And the Marquis – powdered, curled, pretty as a cherub in his white satin doublet, tight-fitting, embroidered with tea-roses, a broad sky-blue sash worn across his silver waistcoat, his calf shapely beneath its clinging silk stocking, the curve of his thighs moulded by skin-tight breeches, tricorne tucked under his arm and his hand resting on the pommel of a glittering damascened sword – skipped on light feet, shod in highly-lacquered, red-heeled dancing slippers, to show the joyous priest to the little salon where dinner had been laid out.

'A pinch of snuff, Father?'

The priest, turning round, held his nose.

'So! You wish to be mysterious! Ah, ah...! Very well, but by the time dessert is served I'll know everything.'

'And before the fourth course, Marquis, you will have told me all your sins.'

'The list would be a long one, Father. Sit opposite me.'

The dashing little priest obeyed. He cut a perfect figure in his pretty costume of purple velvet, its long skirts brilliant with sequins, the collar and white beaded bands trailing at his neck, his frosty hair coiled above his ears; a short pleated cloak hung from his shoulders like a sombre wing; his gestures suggested a contrite spirit, though the nimble, sprightly legs, encased as they were in mauve silk stockings embroidered with gold, seemed to contradict the asceticism and other-worldliness of his lowered gaze.

'You look to me like a man with many secrets to hide, Father.'

'And you, Marquis, like a terrible lecher!'

'Oho, that is my role in life!'

'And mine!'

'Well, what a funny thing, what a funny thing!'

And the Marquis roared with laughter and slapped his thigh with great vigour, while the priest looked up to the heavens, smiling beatifically.

'We must eat, Father.'

'We must drink, Marquis.'

And this, and that, and a hundred similar things... Dinner passed in high spirits. Ernesta waited on them. A comely servant was required for two such noble gentlemen. She had therefore been dressed in a silky material with a leafy design on a pink background, with an apron of blue taffeta tied with little ribbons, a black velvet choker round her neck, and, for complete period accuracy, she had been given a beauty spot on her cheek just above the mouth; and for tonight she was answering to the name of Elvire.

'She's nice, your serving girl, Marquis...'

And the priest winked, nodding at Elvire who was serving the next course, smiling, her arms half bare and the top of her dress unfastened.

'Aha, Father, I catch you at it and we haven't even reached dessert...! Wait a little, dash it; and to get us in the appropriate frame of mind, we can swap old stories from the past. I can be indiscreet with you, you aren't allowed to pass anything on. I chose this girl,' and the amorous Marquis leant his elbow on the table and propped his elegant chin on his fist, 'because she resembled my most recent passion.' A glint came into his eyes. 'The countess of Azinval. Observe: is the figure not the same? Head held in the very same way? Nose subtly turned up Roxelane-style, provocative and mean... and those blue eyes! Look, Father, aren't those the exact same blue eyes of my faithless goddess? On which subject, I shall describe the final farce the cruel, perverse creature inflicted on me. Listen carefully, Father.'

The priest shook his lace cuffs, then, pulling his chair away from the table, twirled it round and straddled it.

'I am all ears, Marquis.'

'Well, right then: you are familiar with my character and you know how easily I lose concentration, my mind wanders like no one else's. The mental wanderings of the good monsieur de La Fontaine were mere play compared to mine. So it was, then, if you can imagine it, that towards the end of my enslavement to her pretty little feet that smelled of roses and ambergris, the light of my life began to flirt...'

'Ah, no, Flossie! That word hadn't been invented in those days...' And Nhine burst out laughing.

'That's true, you're right.' She guffawed too, then collected herself: 'My mistress was secretly at dalliance with the handsome lord de Grandlieu, that ridiculously arrogant and stupid Hercules... Women! Ah, women...!'

'Ah, women...!'

And the little priest lifted his eyes to heaven.

'Quiet, Father, listen. You can sigh later! Gadzooks, this frothing wine has gone to my head, unless it be the memory of the lovely Sylvie...! As I was saying, that's how it was: she ended up falling madly in love with him, while he, for his part, was completely stuck on...'

'Ahem, ahem!'

'Ah, no...! While he was in a state of attentive thraldom

A Woman's Affair

to baroness d'Esquintes. My Sylvie wished to supplant this lady in the heart and in the arms of the fortunate nobleman who gave her to understand that he would like nothing better but that he needed a proof of her love, visible and irrefutable proof. He also told her he was not unaware she had accorded me certain rather intimate favours. She could be very determined and single-minded and he wished to be the same, so he commanded her to dismiss me without delay. All or nothing, at once or else never. We were staying at that time on the estate at Ramonlès-Tours, for a grand hunting party at which the king was due to be present. The court was there in its entirety, and in the evenings, after the beats and before supper, we would meet, a chosen few of us, the fortunate and the favoured, in a conservatory which ran round the great state rooms of the château and led on to the terraces beyond the reception rooms. We would meet there in conditions of strictest privacy. Our ladies would take their seats beneath the green palm trees and flowering medlars, with us, naturally, gathered at their feet as convention dictates, making conversation around whatever subjects their regrettably whimsical minds lit upon, tolerating their poutings and sulkings, or laughing at their pleasantries... conversation that never strayed far from matters of love and ardent requests for a secret assignation! My Sylvie then produced a diabolical piece of mischief...! You see, Father, a woman in love is capable of anything... anything! And this one's inspiration was infernal and feminine to a degree. While we were all gathered there one evening, before a grand ball – needless to say everyone was dressed for the occasion – she sat down with complete naturalness next to her rival. I approached and sought the honour of a stool beside her. "With pleasure!" she told me, giving her most charming smile. Never had she shown me such courtly politeness, nor had she seemed so adorably desirable, in her white pekin frills and furbelows covered in pink bows. Ah, I can see her still, Father...! Garlands of eglantine twined round the farthingale she wore, yards wide, bursting into flower on the artfully raised side paniers that set off her amazingly slender waist; a string of pearls wound closely round her long and sinuous neck; brilliant emeralds made a foliage of greenery atop the snowy peak of her powdered hair... With a charming gesture she indicated my place on a low seat to her side. While I was arranging myself there, she made a startled movement I can't quite describe, and leaning towards me, said, sending one of those looks that are guaranteed to make me giddy: "Oh, Adalbert...! Mercy on us... I fear you have lost your head completely, my dear beloved. Look!" And she blushed delightfully, directing my attention at something small, white and dainty that was protruding – level with the edge of her chair – from the place where my satin breeches fastened. "But it must be your shirt...! You haven't buttoned your... aperture... properly," she said, trying to shield her pretty face behind her fan to hide her laughter or confusion. "Oh, I shall die of embarrassment!" I lost my composure and hastily threw my plumed tricorne hat over the deplorable object. "Don't stop talking, speak to me, then, speak to me!" she continued, crushing my foot beneath her little heel whose smart red colour came nowhere near to matching the flush of embarrassment and annoyance now illuminating her face. And I talked... I forced out a stream of hurried remarks, lacking all understanding, never pausing, taking advantage, whenever

A Woman's Affair

I could make a gesture of explanation or wave a descriptive hand, to push the wretched shirt tail little by little back where it belonged, trying all the while not to draw attention to it. "Oh, you make me thoroughly ashamed. Look at you!" And, with magnificent lack of humanity, she walked away, leaving me to my distress and my ridiculous situation. "Your arm, duke," she said to Grandlieu. Determined in spite of everything to fight him for her, I jumped to my feet, seizing the opportunity to thrust out of sight the major portion of my disastrous mishap. Hardly anything showed now, just the merest tip, virtually invisible to all but an initiate of the incident. "Ah!" the traitress exclaimed, "I have mislaid my handkerchief... Baroness... be my saviour... Would you mind lending me yours while a new one is fetched...?" And, while the baroness was innocently searching: "Don't bother!" she said contemptuously. "I've seen the game you're playing! Your handkerchief is in monsieur's breeches...!" She was pointing at me! I understood the full measure of my ungrateful friend's cunning and perfidy. Stupefaction on the face of the unfortunate baroness! To cut a long story short, it resulted in a duel with Grandlieu, I was wounded, ridiculed and I lost my beautiful beloved. And ever since, I surround myself with pretty servant girls on whom I may gaze and who are willing to please me, but as for love, I curse it! Do you know what I love, Father? Would you like to know...?'

And Flossie made her small hands into a loud-hailer to shout at Nhine, her amused and attentive listener: 'Well! I love my sex, and my handsome little pages!'

'You're so funny, Moon-Beam! You're so funny! Where does all that come from?'

A Woman's Affair

'It comes from the fact that I love you and want to amuse you. Yes...' She assumed once more her braggart's voice. 'Yes, Father, it's splendid! I get my revenge on the beast and I am all the better for it. Ah, the world would come to a very neat and tidy end if only everyone was like me!'

The priest, scandalised, turned his head aside: 'You offend me, Marquis.'

'Zounds, Father, there's nothing to fear! Drink, drink...!' She filled his glass. 'I live life to the full, I do! I'm not stopping you from praying and mortifying yourself on my behalf when you're not in my company, but when you're at my table, you are required to laugh and be a proper rascal. Do you hear, Father?'

'Oh, if I could speak! The things I could tell you, Marquis!'

'There we are...! Well, then? Speak, scoundrel, or I'll untie your tongue by re-baptising you with a bottle of this wine from Champagne, which isn't... baptised, that is.'

'Very well! On my side, Marquis, I have a trio of exquisite beauties, great sinners before the Lord and bacchantes without peer before me. I give them absolution following their trespasses, which I enjoy each week. They are three lesbians who make love to each other in my presence... One red-gold, one pale gold and one ebony! A trinity of love, at the bidding of my desires...'

'Your desires, Father! They must be as pallid as winter moons... gentle as a doe's eye, inoffensive, timorous...'

'You can rid yourself of that mistake...!'

And the priest spoke in a whisper, looking furtively around in case some indiscreet person might overhear. First, they came to him for confession, naked, then the one who had

committed the least grave sin received the heaviest penance...
yes, that was how it worked... and the penance consisted....
he spoke ever more quietly... of doing this...

'Ah, ah!' the Marquis sniggered, 'not bad, not bad, Father!'

'And of this...'

'Better and better!'

'And then finally...'

'Ah, what can I say...! Listen, you must invite me to this contest, I'll bring my pages!'

'No, no, just the two of us, no need of recruits.'

'Silly! Don't you understand...?'

'Oh! Yes! That's right, got it...'

'Father, you're worse than I am!'

And they both laughed.

'Darling,' Flossie sighed, 'I want some pink anisette out of the wonderful cup that makes me so deliciously dizzy!'

They drank in their ritual way, and in the same fashion smoked endless cigarettes, all the while making up fantasies in the spirit of the evening...

'My head's spinning,' said Nhine. 'It was late when we sat down to dinner. Elvire! Ernesta! What's the time...? Come on, we ought to be going... Give us our masks, our coats.'

After adding the final touches to their appearance, they wrapped themselves up and left the house, keeping up their comic roles until they were in the coupé.

When they arrived in rue Rouget-de-Lisle, the way was blocked by an interminable stream of carriages coming away empty, while others drew up outside the entrance door. They had to wait. The crowd was dense, swarming eagerly to this spot in the hope of seeing the guests arrive and admiring their costumes as they went by.

'Look at those two little fellows! Aren't they sweet?' cried someone as they eventually made their way beneath the red-striped canopy.

'You hear that, Floss? They think we're sweet.'

'That's a good start...! Don't leave me, Nhine, there's such a huge crowd of people.'

'Hold my hand. It would be in period, in fact, if you did.'

They entered the first of the great rooms, which had been transformed into a cloakroom, and discarded their coats. Some people were taking off their masks, others keeping them.

'Mine's stopping me from breathing,' Nhine said. 'I'm getting rid of it.'

'I can't,' said Florence. 'I have to keep mine on like a dutiful hypocrite.'

In a corner, a Spanish woman, masked, vivacious in bearing and whose richly spangled costume seemed to radiate sparks of all colours, was carefully observing the people as they arrived, keeping watch from behind a pile of coats and discarded garments. Her eyes glittered through the velvet mask. When Annhine revealed her features, she started, took a step forward, very nearly dashed out. She quickly restrained herself: 'No, better than that...' she muttered, 'I'll follow them. It'll be amusing... or maybe much worse!'

And she darted after them.

Our two little creatures entered the ballroom, threading through the crowd that swarmed hither and thither, brilliant and rainbow-hued under the dazzle of the lights and amid the splendour of the decorations. The most beautiful actresses in Paris were there, full of joy to be the stars of the gathering;

elegant socialites had solicited invitations in order to enjoy the spectacle of all this hustle and bustle and the risqué behaviour that might go on in such crowds... They passed through every room, driven by curiosity, wanting to see everything, wanting to take stock of it all. Nhine was recognised, acclaimed, greeted. Some paid her compliments, others inclined their heads as she passed, pressing round her. They were intrigued to know who the mysterious friend might be, clinging close to her side, so pretty to the eye and so unconventional in her manners. They questioned each other animatedly, trying to guess.

XII

Among the women there was a great show of bare skin: shoulders were exposed, arms enticingly adorned with jewels and flowers; luxury, liveliness, cries, laughter… it was all very provocative. The orchestra attacked a waltz.

'My handsome Father, you look most splendid and suggestive, I will gladly make my confession to you.'

'Full and entire…?' Nhine asked maliciously.

'And why not?'

'It would scandalise me!'

'But you must surely be able to cope with anything, and give absolution for it too.'

'Faced with such enormities, a dispensation would doubtless be required.'

'A lily-livered priest, tut-tut…!'

It was Jack Dalsace who overtook them, handsome as a

demi-god in a costume of peacock-blue silk. A hind in mid-leap, picked out in gold and pearls, decorated one of its long pendant sleeves, while on the other a vast and frightening frog, traced in aquamarines, emeralds and beryls, seemed alive and ready to spring into the crowd. Mythical beasts roamed all over this fantastical costume.

'What do you represent this evening?'

'Light of Asia,' he replied with emphasis. 'Light of Asia illuminating the Jungle! Don't you recognise the turban with its crescent and gemstones?'

And he came up close to Annhine.

'Shall we dance?'

'Well, we two are staying together, so it'll have to be all three of us!'

Flinging an arm round each of them, he whirled the pair to the far end of the room.

'Stop!' Nhine begged... 'You're making me ill. We'll just walk instead.'

He followed them.

'He's Jack Dalsace, you know, the poet of sirens, fairies, delicate willowy women and hideous symbolic beasts. The morbid, the sarcastic... the writer. He's my friend.'

'I know of him,' said Florence, who was contemplating with a sort of inquisitive admiration this tall, well-built fellow with a gleam in his eye and a brow furrowed by imaginings both unhealthy and sublime.

His long and slender fingers were laden with strange, heavy rings, bizarre confections where pearls, blueish, greenish, opaque, shimmered in a single mass; or an evil eye stared, cold and ironic, specked with enamel; or sphinxes squatted enigmatically. Around his right arm, above the wrist, coiled a jade serpent veined with white.

'Those eyes shining beneath the velvet seem very beautiful, have I seen them before...?' he said.

'All lovers of the moon understand and recognise each other,' Flossie at once responded. 'That's why I admire you. You have no need to know my name. What is a name, after all? A moronically banal designation...'

'For someone who is not, I'll bet...! Annhine, your friend interests me! I shall follow you and protect you.'

And together they strolled through the great rooms.

'The pretty person over there, dancing with someone who looks like a kitchen boy got up in white satin – and completely off the beat – that's Suzanne de Blinges, the lovely Suzon. She's wonderful in that heavy dalmatic with its yellow brocade. Look at the way the lotus flowers on it have used silver thread to make those pearly calyxes in the centre. That girl has exquisite taste. And see how she's gathered the hair: she's put it up using a burnished silver pendant to hold it in place, and the pendant is carved as a medusa's head, showing those enormous greeny eyes all dilated and streaked with gold. I deplore the emotional attachment she has formed to that Janelle d'Hurat, who appears to have come as a vanilla ice cream, in that laughable travesty of Vatel.'

Annhine's hand tightened on Florence's.

'You see, Moon-Beam, Suzanne is like you, an initiate of female love...'

And a little further on: 'And here again is Madelène de Gemmes, the gentle mistress of the countess de Zirnel, a sort of mystical version of a knight's squire... Doesn't Madelène look sweet as a little marchioness, with that smiling face under the great snow-heap of her powdered wig? The countess of course has chosen a man's costume, she's a Watteau shepherd. Those white shoulders are wonderful with the Mongolian sheepskin thrown loosely across them like that, her legs are perfect and that strong head with its slightly rumpled features is very appropriate…'

'More sisters…!' Flossie murmured.

Then all at once the music changed to a lively farandole, which began in the middle of the ballroom and soon turned very wild, twisting through all the rooms, forming a dozen distant ripples and eddies. Our friends stationed themselves in a corner from where they could see it all. The orchestra had struck up a brisk galop, and, carried away by its urgent, irresistible rhythm, snaking joyfully round the room, there passed in rapid succession before their eyes visions of indiscreet white petticoats, arms linked in arms, coiffures coming adrift; processions of Hindus jangling little bells, their skins strangely afflicted as the ochreous make-up, dissolving, left pale patches; Spanish ladies with swarthy complexions, cruel in their vivid scarlet and black lace; followers of Bacchus, hung with bunches of grapes, bare-bosomed, clothes reduced to rags by their revels; bashful shepherdesses, lips a-curl, bodices loosened, cunningly provocative in their short skirts set flying by the dance; warriors of immense stature in plumes and breastplates, their boots stamping loudly… And Mujiks, Persians, Romans, fairies in gauzy veils shimmering with greenery and water droplets reflecting the colours of the daylight, the skies, the cloudless starry dark in the surface of lakes, nights of promise, nights of love…! Here and there, a comic note: an Alphonse-the-pimp, along with his Gigolette-the-tart, an unlikely but good-hearted pair. She: hair in a bun, kiss-curl at the front, flimsy skirt, cheap blouse well-filled, alert expression; he: funny trousers with extravagant floral patterns, alpaca jacket or short blue coat, red scarf at the neck and the famous three-decker cap! A married couple up from the country, sweet in their rustic ribbons, then the inevitable mass of Pierrots, Pierrettes, Harlequins, and leaping, gambolling clowns, proud and pompous King-Henri-the-Seconds, conscious of their great beauty, Chinamen ornate with embroidery, Bretons, Neapolitans, Punchinellos... Diana with her bow, in golden helmet; Venus, admirable in the universally famous and celebrated nudity of Nebbai, the little actress from the Variétés; then Mephistopheles, red with the fire of the sombre pit, violent with the flames of hell, against whose glow stood out in slender perfection her inseparable companion, Line Neurout.

'Another two!'

'Yet again!'

And Annhine squeezed Flossie's hand as she pointed out these characters.

A woman in a dainty cat costume was tickling with her furry white feathers, light as a snowy mousse, the rosy cheeks of a woman dressed as a dazzling red poppy. The flower's eyes gleamed feverishly as it leant towards the animal.

'That, over there, is Violette Turck and Rita Samuel... it's said they've been lovers for years; then here's Riscogni and la Koniarowska,' she whispered in her ear.

And Flossie saw, coming directly towards them, unaware of the looks she was attracting, a still youthful woman, dressed in, or rather closely clung to by a black satin skirt and a high bodice of the same material which covered her to the neck, over which she wore a white brocade waistcoat. Her short curly hair, topped by a dark hat, framed a face devoid of colour, expressionless and rigid, in which glittered eyes as shiny and dark as black cherries. But they were small, deep-set, red-veined and disappeared at the corners under folds of skin. The mouth, in contrast, was bright scarlet and finely drawn. She was in the company of a superb young woman who followed behind, grave and reflective, as if unable to rid her mind of some insistent thought. Her height was accentuated by a long white dress with silver lilies at its hem. A band of chased gold secured the veil of white gauze that lightly covered her pensive head, allowing a clouded glimpse of the jet-black hair beneath. She was as dark as the damp hearts of water-flowers and as white as the thick sheen of their sleeping sepals. She was coming closer, majestic and slow, like a handsome ship whose sails are yet to fill... sad and weary,... mind far away, as if deaf to the sounds of joy all round her. There she was, more absent than the furthest star.

'Oh, she's really beautiful, that Riscogni...' said Flossie. 'Look at her, Nhine!'

'Her fatigue is not so noticeable late in the evenings. In the daytime, you'd be afraid she might fall down dead, she looks so pale. What can she be thinking about in all this crowd?'

Flossie leaned closer: 'Thinking about...? Everything! About the kind of ecstasies that defy all rationality, about pleasures that are real but ephemeral. About the chasteness of the highest communion between two people when not a single idea enters your mind and even the Dream itself hardly dares to whisper in your soul...! About the sensuality that has you in its grip and consumes you, about the Love that kills you slowly and devours you... And above all, about the Beyond, which hovers all round and whose veils you only lift in the folly of complete, unthinking abandon...! Ah, Nhine! How stupid are these correct, bourgeois pairings-off! How utterly bestial are the dealings of a couple made to follow the corrupt rules of our narrow morality! And look...! It's the opposite with these women, there's a glow round them. All of them have a spark in their eye, a beauty that stirs, affects, engages you. Oh, Nhine, you wouldn't hurt a fly; so why would you be cruel to a soul like mine which goes out to you? Let yourself be loved, Nhine! Join the revolt against human laws. It will wash away all the stains of the past. Don't spoil things for yourself by telling your soul it's had its fill, even though it's not satisfied. Your soul is hungry for impossible dreams: it can achieve them! Turn your back on men, spurn them! They are pitiless butchers of gentle souls like yours that chase after illusions, for it is your soul that gives your mortal form its radiance! Men will never be capable of meeting your longing for the Beautiful, the Ideal, for satisfaction in the fullest sense, Nhine! One day, will you hear, will you feel the prayers my whole being offers up to you...? Ah! I dream of a union so complete and so sublime it would obliterate all the earthbound and human elements our sensual enslavement binds us to! My desires, my thoughts would be no more than the ecstatic adoration of you, immaterial, shimmering! Nhine! Say you'll be mine... and for ever!'

In a dream, her head turned by these intoxicating words, Annhine replied softly: 'Yes, completely...! Any way you want and as long as you want!'

Then, heedless of the people all around, they embraced, and, in one long, sweet kiss, bound themselves wholly to each other.

'Oh, Nhine, the thought of so much happiness is too much for me. Oh, Nhine, my love for you will be unique, the ideal will become a reality, and you will be the Paradise Gained of my desires! In Sadness and in Joy, through Good and Ill, by Night and by Day, in Life and in Death I shall be yours also, obedient to your every wish…! We may be cut off, we may not be understood in this arid and loveless world, we may be held up to ridicule by the mediocre, the deaf and blind, Nhine, but just think of the joys that will be our special preserve…! Let's go…! Come with me…!'

They turned round, and found Dalsace smiling at their excited confusion.

'I didn't say a word! It would have been sacrilege to interrupt Mademoiselle. I understand you completely, handsome young mask, I understand everything. You are absolutely right to love each other, it makes perfect sense! For me, female love is heightened narcissism, love of the self pushed to extremes through the contemplation and adoration of one's own image in that of the other. And what ensues is something as sweet as a kiss one flower might give another, as one wreath of mist mingling with another, as the intangibility of snow alighting and melting into the shimmering water of great ponds, something as graceful as two doves' wings skimming under a blue sky, as morbid as the sigh that softens tears, as the sob that mingles with the groan of desire…! And you are two fortunate women, two of the elect…! Go your way…!

A Woman's Affair

Flee far from the crowd and retreat into yourselves. And your ecstasies, along with your loosened hair, shall combine in kisses, in embraces, in the perverse pleasures which grant a transient realisation of the ideal, and all shall be achieved through your twinned solitude... Go your way...!'

And he guided them towards the door. They were about to leave the bustle and the noisy crush when all at once, emerging from a shadowy corner, suddenly and unexpectedly, the Spanish lady leapt out at the departing group: 'No, this is too much...!' she cried, standing before them to bar the way. 'I'm a soul in hell! I've followed you through this joyful ball like some poor mad wretch, swallowing back my fury, biting my lip... A dozen times I nearly leapt on you, just wanting to annihilate you, strike you down there on the spot, lifeless, in front of me...!'

Dalsace tried to brush her aside, to come between them.

'Oh, if you understand everything, monsieur,' she continued, 'you'll understand what I'm suffering. Let me finish...! I don't wish to trouble these ladies long, two of the elect to that hellish and divine bliss. No, but...!'

She abruptly ripped off her mask, while Flossie and Annhine jumped back in alarm, clinging to each other, distraught and speechless.

The poor creature was majestic in her grief.

'What do I wish...? I wish that every time you kiss, every time you writhe together, and everywhere you go and every day and forever after, you find me there...! Me, me, the one you laughed at...! Me, the one your lies and disdain have killed...!' Shaking all over, she turned her gaze on Nhine. 'Yes, you! You lied to me, I was desperate as a wounded animal, I came to you humbly with my soul in anguish to beg sympathy for my passion and you laughed at me!' She turned on Flossie. 'You…! Ah, you…! The joys you taught me were so new and so intense I could have died! It's not your fault, or mine, alas…! I couldn't hold you! You have been the death of me, Flossie, and yet I cannot curse you, for I have loved you too much, but I want you to remember me for ever, whether you wish it or not, with no hope of ever forgetting.'

And suddenly, standing there erect before them and without a quiver, she plunged into her heart the sharp blade of a slim dagger she had been holding hidden under the black lace of her mantilla. She fell without a sigh, without a cry: she was dead.

Nhine whirled round, clutching a hand to her heart.

Deathly pale, her breathing stopped, she collapsed into the arms of a dumbfounded, horrified Dalsace, who lowered her to a bench. The crowd rushed over, cruel in its excitement and curiosity. There was tumult and chaos and the ball came to a halt amid shouts, hysterics and fainting fits. Trite and stupid rumours passed among the shocked and disarrayed groups who, in the grip of terror, rapidly left the building. The police were alerted; and by the morning no trace of the enormous commotion was any longer to be seen in the vast deserted rooms, apart from a few fading flowers still strewn on the floor and a bloodstain that lingered, dark red, impossible to erase, just inside the door.

The press seized on the drama, which drew lively commentary from several different standpoints. The families took steps, and the affair was suppressed as quickly as possible to avoid anyone being compromised.

XIII

The day after this terrible catastrophe, when Annhine regained consciousness after fainting and suffering a blackout that lasted nearly four hours, the first thing she became aware of was the presence of Henri and Altesse, leaning anxiously over her, waiting for her to return to life. Recovery of her senses came only slowly. She felt exhausted, shattered. She could just about remember that something unspeakable, dreadful had happened, right in front of her... but what it was she couldn't say, or even where she had been. What was it all about? She must have had a nightmare, some awful dream... She tried to smile. Lifting her head a little, she could see her bedroom more clearly, and all the lamps shining brightly. Was it still night-time then...? Then, by their light, she saw costumes scattered all around, gaudy theatrical clothes tricked out with a lot of embroidery and sequins. She fell back on the pillow,

A Woman's Affair

overwhelmed. Lights flashed before her eyes. She could feel her heart thudding as if it might burst. Oh, everything hurt, she felt so ill...! The thought she might be dying flitted into her mind, then, raising her arms and waving them agitatedly, she seemed to be trying to ward off invisible enemies.

'Oh...! Who's there...? Where am I...? What's happened...?'

'It's us, Nhine darling...' And they leaned over her more closely, concerned and reassuring at the same time. 'You've had a bad dream, poor little thing. Don't be frightened, it's all gone now. Everything is going to be all right and we'll be here with you.'

She hardly paid attention to their voices. There was a humming in her ears. Her breath came with difficulty.

'I can see you! Oh! Don't leave me...! Tesse...! Henri...! What happened to me?'

'Hush!' And Tesse placed a finger against her lips. 'Be quiet, darling, don't speak, I'll tell you. You had a severe shock and it was too much for you. Your heart stopped for a few moments. Ah, you gave us a real scare...! It was while you were dancing, at the ball... and then there was a hideous prank, a really naughty carnival prank that was played right in front of you.'

Tesse was managing the situation carefully, putting off until later the painful necessity of recalling the sad truth.

'Ah! Yes...!' Annhine's memory was returning now. 'So... it was all just a prank then...?'

'Why, yes...! A stupid piece of play-acting in any case. Nhinon, you're fragile, really quite fragile. We're going to help you get better, and as soon as you're on your feet again, we're taking you away, Henri and I. It's decided! We'll go and find some peace and quiet and some sunshine further south, in Italy... And very timely, because the nasty winter months are coming and they'll make this Paris lifestyle dangerous and unsustainable, so we'll get ahead of them a bit. Not Monte-Carlo... just a big factory, very unhealthy, and the types you get there, too high-society! No, we'll go to Florence, Rome, Venice, Naples. We'll cross to Palermo, then, when you're properly better, we'll sail to Malta, Gibraltar. We'll go to Spain, Barcelona, Seville, Cadiz... then Portugal, Lisbon, and we'll only come back to Paris in May. Henry will come back earlier, since he can't be away for six months... But the idea is to make this a voyage of rest and recuperation. We'll keep it very simple, just like two little Englishwomen on tour!'

'Yes... yes...' Annhine murmured. 'That's the thing... get away... forget everything!'

'Forget everything especially!'

She complained: 'I can't breathe...'

'It's all right, darling, there's an oxygen bottle. Here... Oh, what a lot of use it had last night...! Nothing else seemed to work. You're going to have to take much better care of yourself, my Nhine! We'll all help you!'

'Henri!'

Henri approached, glad to be summoned. He murmured kind words, holding her little hand in his own, squeezing it, full of affection.

Altesse went round the house and gave orders, busying herself.

'Make sure you hide those newspapers away! Madame mustn't be able to find out what happened!'

A Woman's Affair

Some flowers were delivered – a sad little spray, mauve, tied with a mournful black ribbon. As a symbol of hope, a tiny bow had been added, in green satin. Altesse seized the flowers and opened the envelope that was attached. She looked for the signature: 'That mad girl again…! Oh! No! Really…!'

The letter said:

> When I wander the streets, recalled to the grievous world of the everyday and especially just now, I have the impression that even the flowers are surprised to see me still living and they seem to ask me how it is that I can smile at times. They will never understand why, in spite of everything, I walk almost joyously through life. And so, making no reply, I send them towards the cause of my joy, towards my dear sister in dreaming. They will be with you an hour before I am – I shall call during the morning to hear how you are. Separated from you so suddenly and drastically yesterday, it is vital I speak with you – about a multitude of things!
> YOUR MOON-BEAM.

Tesse tore the missive into tiny pieces.

'Put these wherever you like. Madame is not to be disturbed by anything at all, and especially not by people. Tell anyone who asks she is not at home and will not be home for a long time. Admit nobody but the doctor.'

Appropriately, it was the doctor who next called. He examined the patient.

'Yes, that's definitely what it is…' He nodded his head.

'Overwork, acute agitation of the nerves. Oh dear, a broken leg would have been much easier! The organs are all sound. You should take her away quickly, without question. In twenty-four hours from now she will be well enough to travel, if nothing happens to complicate matters in the meantime. Get away as far as you can and come back as late as possible. Rest, calm, good hygiene, some gentle distraction. As little reading and letter-writing as possible, plenty of walking, rest for the head and exercise for the body. It will pass as it came, slowly but surely. There is nothing physically wrong with you, my child, yet this is more difficult than anything else. You must be careful. I prefer not to hide things from you: your recovery depends on your will to recover.'

As he left, he repeated the same themes: 'She is not at all well, in fact I should say she is seriously ill, but her youth will save her, with the help of your own close care. Act quickly... Here is a note, a sort of certificate for the Prefecture if one is called for. Oh dear, what a sad business! The whole of Paris is full of it, it's the only thing anyone's talking about...! Keep the shutters closed so that people think she's gone away already. It will spare her a great many tiresome and harmful formalities. She places too much stress on herself, she needs to let herself live, or she'll die of it. But she'll never be robust: her head drains all the vitality out of her. Still, she's in good hands, she'll soon be in better spirits.'

'We're going to prepare our trunks for the journey, Nhinette,' said Altesse, coming back into her room. 'Right away. I'm making a start today...'

'Anything you like, anything, but don't leave me!'

'And tomorrow evening we'll be off. You mustn't see

anyone, and you mustn't talk too much, even to me. Once we're on our way, you'll be able to do as you please.'

'Oh, I feel so tired, so tired!'

And she closed her eyes, dozing off. The smell of ether drifted from a phial and her head swam. She was overcome with torpor. Tesse left her sleeping and took care of everything.

The next day, all three set off on their travels, stimulating and restorative new scenery their goal, forgetfulness and health their quest. The journey would take them far away… to other places… to all that was unknown and mysterious in the marvellous and healing cities of Italy…

XIV

They set off like travellers making the Grand Tour, following the Rhine, making speedily for Switzerland, whose breathless heights they passed through before leaving the icy snowbound peaks in their wake and heading down towards Munich, from where they moved on to visit Italy.

Venice detained them longer than the other towns, for they wanted to try to taste for themselves the splendour and melancholy of its history, which grips every new arrival in the ancient city of the Doges and the great courtesans, and where the flavour still lingers of a world that no longer exists.

The friend of Annhine was obliged at this point to curtail his role as attentive escort and return to Paris, entrusting his mistress to the loving solicitude of Altesse.

They found lodgings in a very old palazzo on the Grand Canal, between the dead water and one of the town's few gardens, sad and bare at this season. The great stone staircase wound down to the sombre depths of the lagoon where, each morning, silently gliding gondolas came to collect them, waking them gently to the day without bringing them back to mundane reality too abruptly, respectfully preserving their dreamlike illusions, carrying them soundlessly through Venice...

Venice, rising from the waves like Venus! A vast ruin, like a city-sized palace once magnificent and now abandoned, its remains nevertheless splendid: streets which seemed as if they might once have been stone-flagged vestibules, now lost beneath the invading and slowly destructive waves... Outlines of old churches, convent walls, bell-towers. And ah, those mysterious reflections of the bridges in the water, those tiny squares where narrow streets led off in every direction, redolent of adventures and cut-throats!

Then, one day, Nhine said: 'When we get home in the evenings and I go out into the garden, where everything's still and quiet in the moonlight, and the vines and orange trees look silvery and peaceful, I breathe a sigh of relief. Outside, I live too much in the fabled past, as if I was half-remembering for myself things that happened long ago, a mysterious and obscure time. It's Venice's setting, all these buildings, they create an atmosphere I find attractive and also quite disturbing. Did you see that big ship at the Lido, Tesse, white all over like a swan, with its pale green keel and gilded portholes? It's the *Hohenzollern*, the Emperor of Germany's yacht. Well, for me, it becomes something else. The crewmen, all very fair and specially chosen for their beauty, put me in mind of great nobles in disguise. And the sun beats down on them, lighting up my illusion! Venice shimmering! Venice become magical, turned to gold...! A fairy story of love and blood, of rose-tinted wine, of enchanted waters that roll in their depths century after century of legend... Then time moves on, the sun slowly disappears looking like a great ball of flame sliding into the crimson waves, setting fire to the horizon all around, flooding with its splendours worlds unknown and inaccessible to us... After that, nothing left of it at all...! I turn my head and it has gone dark. The slap of oars in the water, the gondoliers' hoarse songs, voices calling, dull sounds, with no echo... then I don't know whether I'm living or dreaming... I feel scared... I want light, brightness, I need crowds... and I squeeze your hand, Tesse, to ask for help, needing the sound of your voice to shake me out of this morbid impression.'

'And all of that is bad for you, harmful because you're too sensitive and still frail,' Altesse replied. 'We should leave here as fast as we can!'

They departed for Naples, fell in love with Salerno, Amalfi, Sorrento.

'This is the land of the gods,' Nhine declared. 'This is my Town and my Homeland! I recognise it, I seem to have lived here before; and all the time I've spent in the mire of our overripe civilisation, and the wounds and scars it's given me, all that has been just a long and painful detour, and I know I can find my way back!'

'Your ideas are too extravagant, Nhine. Tell them to pipe down, and look at the living things around us instead, enjoy them. What pretty flowers they have here, for one thing: could there be a more perfect white? And the scent! These white carnations, these wild strawberries, so pure... so fragile...!'

A Woman's Affair

And yet so desecrated by the grubby fingers of these Neapolitan street-vendors, Annhine thought grievingly, no longer able to open her heart to such things. Tesse carried her off to visit some of the museums, and Pompeii.

'Look, Nhinon, these statues can't talk, but they're telling me something about you. See? They've got your thin hips, their slenderness in the nude is just like your own... in fact she's you, Nhine, the Venus with the Bracelet...'

But Nhine was no longer taking any interest in real things. She was permanently lost inside her head, thinking, searching... Her thoughts were turned to another nude figure, sister of her own. She was telling herself that in this setting of sunlight and life and ever-changing scenery one could inhabit a delicious tale of romance, one could act out, in a state of nakedness, all those pleasures that were so strange to her, so unknown and so desired...! Yes, desired, for now she ardently *wanted* to see Flossie again. Languishing and already afflicted by the illness that was undermining her, she was without defences, and even reaching out eagerly towards that perverse idea which had been the starting point for the upheaval that ensued. It was latent, germinating inside her in the loneliness of this total – and very abrupt – separation from the bustling life of pleasure which had been her natural habitat until now. She didn't think it out. With no strength left, she merely let herself go. She *wanted* to know, she burned for the knowledge. It was like a book that she badly wanted to finish: she had flicked through the first few pages without going any further, and it was this initial chapter with its cruelly tempting delights that had so powerfully attracted her to a world outside the everyday norms. She didn't want to miss out, she *wanted* to experience the sweetness and the sharpness of those forbidden, unhealthy sensations, even though it would mean stepping like a criminal into the realm of the unnatural. Like a person in pain, she could not rid herself of the idea, her thoughts constantly revolved round it. In spite of Tesse's efforts, in spite of her watchful concern, she was preoccupied... distant... precariously balanced all the time on the edge of her own understanding... filled with longing, with curiosity...! No news... nothing... not a word... no sign of the disturbing vision which had left such a deep impression on her...! Where can she be? What can have happened to her after all these upsets...? That terrible drama...! It still made her shake all over. In truth, she preferred not to know anything about it. The mere idea of revisiting those final hours, the whirling, masked hordes, that awful farce of the jealous woman falling lifeless by her own hand, was enough to cause her heart to surge out of control, as it had done then; but what about Her, the sweet, the impossibly blond child...?

She was going to take a risk, it couldn't be helped. Why not, after all? What harm was there in it...? In a day or two's time it would be the first day of the new year, an occasion when even people who know each other only distantly exchange greetings, send their best wishes. That was the thing to do, she'd write: a card showing a frosty landscape, then on the back, a line, a greeting: *I wish you all the joys of soul and senses*, that was all... Her name: Nhinon, then she would address the thing to Paris, to the Hôtel de Bade, for Miss Florence Bradfford. There, it was very simple, hardly anything, a politeness she was owed after all... she wasn't doing any harm. She wouldn't mention it to the others, though. Some things are too delicate for anyone else to understand. She secretly slipped the little envelope into a pile of dull missives due to be sent to the post office. Hardly had it gone, however, than she wanted to take it back again. Then she waited, in anxiety, for the result. Would there be any reply...? And what then...? Or else...? She remained on edge for three days, then, among various other items, a telegram brought her this simple response: *Then give me them!* Signed: Moon-Beam. So then she relaxed, and resolved to take it no further. What for...? What would be the good...? No, it was better to leave it at that.

Altesse received a grievous blow. Bad news arrived from Paris. The lover of whom she was so fond, Raoul de la Douanne, was getting married. The matter was decided, the date fixed. His family had taken advantage of his friend's absence to force the sacrifice on him. Being a man without fortune, the liaison with this beautiful courtesan he so adored had showered him with petty injuries and insults, arising from envy, jealousy of his happiness, the base natures and wicked tongues of people who are perfectly happy for a man to sell himself lovelessly to a thin-lipped snob out to acquire a male or a name, and yet narrow their lips in whispers and shrug contemptuous shoulders faced with the simplicity of feeling produced by the meeting of two hearts. On top of that, the calculated coolness of his companions, the threatened withdrawal of a meagre pension allowed him by two bigoted old aunts, and also the reproaches of his conscience which chided him for enjoying the luxuries of a lifestyle such as Altesse's. Raoul gave way, took the first name on the list of marriageable young ladies put before him, the way one chooses a dish from a menu, and he wrote to Altesse the classic letter: It had to be done... life, the future, so many difficulties, honour... The last word made her lips twitch ironically. Honour, they knew all about that, these people...! But there it was. He would love her all his life. He would never be able to forget her... Then, later, he would send her a souvenir, a present he begged her to accept. A present...! With the other woman's money...! Ah, yes, the famous honour! One is, after all, a gentleman; one knows that love has to be paid for. Then as if that wasn't enough, he asked her – *he* asked *her* – to help him have the courage: his suffering was appalling, life stretched before him like a desert, of regrets, of memories, she must lend him her hand even in this, to help him make this step: yes, a note to say farewell – and, who knows, *au revoir* – an encouragement to do his duty...! Altesse's face went very hot, her temples burned. Her eyes stared without seeing, misted over, then her heart ceased beating, an intense cold seized her. She jumped abruptly to her feet to shake off the dizziness, looking around with an expression that was both vague and wild, as if she wanted to clutch at something that was escaping her. The letter fell to the floor and Nhine, who was just coming in, recognised the writing. Surprised to see Altesse standing in such a strange attitude, she questioned her gently, tenderly, kind words rising from her heart to her lips for her friend, her big sister in distress. Without needing any explanation, she had grasped the situation. Altesse frowned, cold, aloof, her lips set and expression hard, trying to ward off Nhine's all-enveloping tenderness, then all of a sudden her tears flowed, and Nhine's mingled with them.

'Don't cry, my darling, you mustn't. It's right for me to suffer... weak little me, so fragile, so bruised, but not you, so beautiful, so splendid, so strong! Ah, no...!'

A Woman's Affair

They would continue their voyage, they would make it endless. Italy, they'd had enough of it, and of Venice as well with its cruel silences that left you listening too much to yourself. They'd go to Spain, it was jollier, livelier, all red and yellow and gold, and black hair and fiery eyes, castanets and bullfighters, then they'd push on as far as Portugal... Yes, that was it, and Tesse would forget. Everything is forgotten in the end.

Altesse shuddered violently, her great blue eyes darkened, she held Nhine tightly, murmured some strange halting words that Nhine couldn't catch, then never again pronounced the name of Raoul. Annhine set to with vigour, making arrangements and hastening all manner of preparations. They left, and crossed the south of France without stopping, to avoid the noisy hordes of interlopers who swarm every winter on the sunny shores of the Riviera, and, a few days later, they arrived in Barcelona. From there, they travelled on to Madrid, new country for them, still primitive, where everything stands out astonishingly white against the filth of the streets and their teeming, dusty liveliness.

Nhine felt alert yet tense, her head brimming with a thousand schemes, a thousand desires. She needed animation, noise, she wanted to distract Altesse from her sorrows and racked her brain to invent diversions, finding it a strain on her nerves in moments of weariness, going all the same, fearing on her own account as well as her friend's the loneliness of the night-time, inactivity, silence, those isolated hours when the mind is apt to wander. She was all too familiar with them, those periods of speculation, of gentle sadness when, with the complicity of night's softly falling shades, it is easy to drift quickly away into the remotest depths of the imagination, the dream world, where the spirit wanders, questing, frantic, sick with weariness and despair.

One evening, leaning at their balcony, shoulder to shoulder, she asked: 'Altesse, tell me what you're really feeling, now. All this going out and being busy here, in an exotic setting, so to speak: do you think it's done you some good? Tell me how you are, Tesse, darling, if you can…'

And Annhine cajoled and coaxed, as kindly as she could, a little uncertain still, and drawn by the deep look in Altesse's eyes.

Altesse smiled at the delicate face turned towards her.

'Nothing cheerful, my pretty. I don't know if I ought…'

Then, making an effort, suddenly resolved to open her heart, she continued: 'You see, I know how sweet and generous you're being, but I can't adapt and resign myself the way you mean me to. I can't tell you all the things that have been going on inside me. In spite of all the prejudice and bias and baseness of our social rules, you could say my existence was like a beautiful fruit, all scarlet and gold, unblemished, superb in colour and shape. A worm has crept into this rare and unique perfection. It was flawless, unbruised, and now a worm, a pitiless worm is threatening to corrupt the whole thing, to destroy it entirely. A black veil has suddenly been cast over my life and my heart. You see, Annhine, life has given me everything: health, fortune, intelligence, beauty and above all the gift of knowing how to make use of them. I have the soul and the pride of a courtesan in the best sense of the word: I am not petty, I do not hide behind a mask of hypocrisy, I do not cower in fear. The men who have loved me have gone on their way happy, more complete, I have shown them the path to follow. I may not be made for loves that last, but I do at least make deep and loyal friendships. I have all that. He, Raoul, was weaker, less gifted, perhaps just less confident, who knows? I started a love affair that became a passion.' Her pale hand clung for a moment to Annhine's shoulder, standing out against the soft blue of her dressing gown. 'I do not want to change any of the things that made me what I am, you understand, nor do I want to retreat, go back to him. I could win him back, make him mine again, break his career, ruin his plans, his hopes, carry him off somewhere far away, it would be easy. I despise that sort of thing. What's done is done. Except there is a certain bitterness in my heart, Nhine, because that man owed me everything, and his present happiness is being built on the ruins of mine. No, you see, now I've glimpsed the evil side of life, it has nothing left to offer me. It's over, it's all over...'

Her emotion was breaking through, her voice rising. She managed to contain herself, and went on: 'But then there's you, Nhine, you whom I love. You have an imagination that is a little wild and inclined to chase fantasies. It needs to be led gently back towards the simple view of things, and I want to help you do that. You need to assure your livelihood, compile your fortune, so that you can be independent and choose the men or women who are to enhance your life without the need to sell yourself. Fortune, Nhinon, for us, modern courtesans, means emancipation, superiority, the right to anything and everything, including respect, if we value it! Everything can be bought...! The courtesan gives or sells herself without needing to shelter behind conventional forms or the purchase

A Woman's Affair

of a name. Like Aspasia and Imperia, whom I often quote at you, Altesse and Annhine stand proud, idols at whose feet every man lays his offering and his homage: be it his talent, his fortune, his mind, his wit. This one brings an illustrious name and a coat of arms, that one a heart, another his riches; but all come to us and we must make each one of them happy. Nhine, we are priestesses at the highest of altars, that altar of Love, king of the World!'

Excited and stirred by her own words, Altesse had become magnificent. Nhine looked at her, then took her hands.

'In that case, darling, you won't be sad any more? You won't just stare... stare into the distance, the way you sometimes do?'

Altesse smiled: 'Oh, that? That's different! I have a terrible failing, Nhine: pride...! And I have been injured! I felt a pin being driven slowly, cruelly into my heart. A pin is a trivial thing, and yet my life will trickle away, drop by drop, through that tiny wound...! What do I want? Oh, I've thought all that out, never fear! When you no longer need me, I shall retire as far away as I can, to a convent in Italy, at Fiesole, where they take in rich and unattached women, disillusioned women who seek peace and oblivion. Just those things, not to take up the rituals of piety, because I don't have any faith, having neither Fear nor Hope, nor anything to ask for. I shall fade away there, in a perfect setting of sunny blue skies, hearing without understanding voices murmuring unknown words in a strange language. They will bear away my memories like frail dead leaves swept away by the wind. I shall mould for myself a soul, a very plain sort of soul, very peaceful, slow, and readied... for what...? I've no idea! That's my absolute and definitive dream. That's my goal, it's everything I want: Peace...! Peace, with no disturbances and no illusions. The first time fate throws a stone in my path I'll end my life. A page I don't like the look of looms, ironical, before my eyes – I throw the book away without turning it.'

Seeing Annhine's woebegone expression, she reached out and pulled her warmly to her heart.

'Don't give it a thought, darling, don't give it a thought... That's for later, when I'm sure you're strong and healthy again!'

'Be quiet, Tesse, everything you say affects me so strongly! Because I know you, once you've made your mind up... Ah, but no, you've a long way to go before you're finished, my little golden woman! You have me, my Tesse, my big sister!'

And Nhine leaned closer: 'And anyway, let's not talk like this any more, it's better. You're still here, one of us, the crazy and the profane. So laugh, and show us the way!'

'Will you follow, if I do?'

Nhine, turning thoughtful, made no answer. She was asking herself the same question, not daring to delve too deep into the crevices of her tortured soul. She tried to find a response: 'To look at you, no one would know that you were suffering inside. I'm the only one to see it, because I know you very well, and even then...! Hardly at all, just from the occasional little thing. You don't change, Tesse. How do you find me? I think I'm getting better, I'm gaining strength, I'm more myself...'

She turned in a slow circle, submitting herself with mischievous grace to Altesse's inspection.

'You, little one...? Well... No, not quite. At the moment,

all this travel fatigue, changing diets, different air... you're not as pale, that's true, your eyes are bright... too bright for my liking... features a little drawn... You laugh at nothing, nervous laughter... you cry easily, you stamp your foot, you're always impatient... and yet...' She lowered her head, considering... 'And yet, you're gaining a bit of weight, certainly... your shoulders are stronger, your breasts firmer... overall, you are getting better, yes... As soon as we return to a calm and regular existence, you will feel the full benefit of the cure. That's the point of this trip: lots of stimulation and no looking back.'

Annhine slipped off the pale silk dressing gown and contemplated her bosom, which was now a little rounder, smooth and white. She smiled, satisfied, then drew her shoulders back.

'Tesse, it's true, I have developed my charms! Look, my chemise is straining, too tight... There's a distinct curve, feel, it would fill your hand... Feel it, darling, go on, feel it...!'

With a stroking gesture, Altesse's hand traced the delicious contour of the offered breast. Nhine gave a cry and closed her eyes, then there burst from her a kind of shrill, staccato laugh that wouldn't stop. She seized her friend's hand and pulled her brutally against her, holding her crushingly tight; her head fell back, stiff and rigid; her eyes stared... and still came the laughter, while her body shook violently from head to foot. She swayed and almost fell to the ground. Altesse held her up with one arm, trying to break free, but the child's grip on the hand that she clasped against her taut skin was so hard she could only sway towards the floor with her. Then Nhine seemed to regain a glimmer of awareness and made as if to right herself, but she toppled and fell, landing on her back; and the fit became truly terrible: cries, groans, kicking out to right and left at empty air, her skull ringing on the tiled floor, hair flying, her neck jerking convulsively, her clenched fists striking the air above her then turning to pummel her own body. She ripped the delicate lace still protecting her frail, bare, convulsing form, then she seemed suddenly to feel heavy, her eyes closed, her teeth made grinding noises as if trying to bite something, and she collapsed, overwhelmed, breathing in gasps, with difficulty... Finally, tears came, bringing respite; she wept very gently, without stopping, and almost without a sound... then the tears turned into wild sobs, the cries began again. Altesse had called Ernesta: together they were able to carry Nhine to her bed, take off her clothes, persuade her to lie down. The coolness of the sheets and the ether's penetrating smell calmed her a little. She fell asleep as she was, shattered, still only semi-conscious, her face buried in a golden tangle of hair, holding tight to the little flask under her nostrils. Altesse bathed her temples and had a bed made up next to hers so that she could stay at her side. It was agreed they would tell her nothing of all this, but they would contact the doctor in Paris. In the first light of day, when Altesse woke, she saw Nhine sitting up in the middle of the bed, a look of bewilderment on her face.

'Goodness, what happened...? I vaguely remember... I feel so well this morning! What was wrong with me, Tesse, darling...? An attack of nerves, wasn't it? How ridiculous; and you've been looking after me, my guardian angel, you slept here, next to me, that's so kind, come here and let me kiss you... come here...!'

A Woman's Affair

She put her arms round her friend's neck and clung almost frenziedly to her lips, hugging her against her shoulder, holding her in a powerful, feverish embrace: 'Do you know...?' She whispered in her ear. 'I've been too good, I think. I've behaved myself properly for a long time. I dream at night, you understand? Yes, and I dream things when I'm wide awake too... I'm going to have to do something to relieve my feelings. Listen: you know, yesterday morning in the restaurant, I saw someone I like the look of. Oh, a real beauty!'

'What?' said Altesse, taken aback. 'Nhine, what are you saying?'

She sat on the edge of the bed and looked at her searchingly. Nhine, a little disconcerted, took her hands and continued: 'Yes, I saw a beautiful boy. You know, Tesse, one of those matt-complexioned Spaniards with velvet eyes and a mouth you want to bite and reveal his dazzling white teeth! He was very smart-looking, I assure you.' She didn't dare look up and she twisted her trembling fingers in Altesse's. 'Yes, I felt something stir inside me, desire, recklessness! The way he looked at me made me light-headed. He never stopped making eyes at me... I thought about it all day after that. He must be a gentleman, he had long white hands, elegant wrists and ankles.'

'My Nhine, I don't recognise you any more.'

'Nor do I any more, I assure you, I don't recognise myself either!'

She grew bold, jumped from the bed and ran barefoot across the room.

'But I want him, I want him! I want a taste of Spanish love! Come on, get dressed, let's go out!' She rang for Ernesta.

A Woman's Affair

'A blouse, a skirt and Princess, I'm going into town. Make up my bed with white linen, everything white and very beautiful. Valenciennes lace, blue ribbons, all sorts of scented silks... It'll be fun, just think, Tesse, roaming the streets in search of a man you want, a stranger, like a prostitute, well, like a street-walker in fact. I don't care any more...! Quick, come with me! No? You don't want to...? Silly! No one knows us here! Good day to you, then, I'm off. There must have been hypnotic powers in the look he gave me! You know, I'm sure he's waiting for me out there, under the arcades, where the shops are... Stand at the window anyway, you can watch me! See you later! Make sure my bedroom looks really pretty! I'll be back... or rather we'll be back soon!'

She ran from the room, swinging the door behind her with such gusto it slammed loudly. Altesse put on a dressing gown and went out on the balcony. She spotted Annhine below, leaving the building, crossing the road, walking fast. Her little hand, glove only half pulled on, held up her skirt, causing it to cling to her slender limbs; her heels clicked smartly on the uneven and dirty cobbles. She waved to Tesse and called Princess, who was trailing behind, happily distracted. At the corner of the street she hesitated for a moment, then carried on straight ahead. She walked pertly, nose in the air, eyes full of amusement, provocative and pretty, looking round on all sides, searching, hoping. All at once she blushed, then turned pale, her heart thumped in her chest. Yes, it was him, just along there, coming out of the perfume shop... She approached, excited and anxious, almost lost her nerve, then she made her mind up and bravely entered the shop. She asked for some eau de Cologne, explaining herself with considerable difficulty because the shopkeeper spoke no French, then cautiously emerged into the street and called, softly: 'Monsieur...! Monsieur...!'

The man looked round: yes, he was turning back, walking towards the shop-front, sizing Annhine up. He stopped in front of her. Her self-assurance deserted her, she felt panic. He smiled. She couldn't speak, horrified at her boldness. He offered her his arm, without a word. She took it, and indicated the hotel in the distance, sending a look of triumph towards the window where the silhouette of Altesse could still be seen.

He said, with a heavy accent: 'You are French?'

'Yes, and you?'

'Me, I Spanish. You vairry pretty! You are long time here?'

'No. But hush...! Here we are, this is where I'm staying. Follow me, I'll show you the way.'

She entered ahead of him, preceded by Princess who ran towards their apartment. Outside the door, she turned and put a finger to her lips. Then she went in slowly, making no sound, walking on tip-toe. At the same moment Tesse entered her own room and closed the communicating door; she had seen them arrive. She heard light footsteps, then other heavier ones... whispers, laughter, exclamations... kisses. Between stifled gasps and hoarse cries, the bed creaked, then there was a long silence and the whole thing started again... splashing sounds of water being poured, snatches of voices speaking, a sort of conversation.

'Farewell!' Annhine's enfeebled little voice was saying. 'We are leaving this afternoon, I shall not see you again. Farewell, handsome stranger...! We must go our separate ways...!'

Two minutes of silence, in which Tesse could just make out the muffled noises of someone leaving, with great care... and then Nhine called: 'Tesse...! Tesse...!'

Altesse went through, very curious: 'Well?'

Annhine, in some embarrassment, was hiding under the sheets.

'Well, it's done, so there we are...! Oh, what a horrible experience, Tesse!' She pulled a face. 'He wasn't very nice after all...! Common, and with most unpleasant underwear, a lawyer here in Madrid, Luiz de something or other. I enjoyed it, the capturing him part, or getting him up here rather. Now I merely feel sick...! What am I to do...? Oh, don't come near me! Don't give me a hug, whatever you do!'

'Do you want your bath?' Tesse asked. 'It will help you calm down.'

'You're right.' Nhine rang. 'Ernesta, order my bath, I'll want a massage, and set out some clean linen, quickly, quickly... Then, what do you say, Tesse, shall we go on somewhere else? I don't mind where, Lisbon, for instance, it's not too far. The overnight sleeper leaves at seven this evening, I think, we've got enough time.'

'Anything you like,' said Altesse, going over to the mantelpiece. 'But, here...' She picked up some scraps of paper lying there. 'What's this, tell me...?'

Nhine glanced up: 'This...? What do you mean, this?'

'Look, this...!' She waved two bank notes, a hundred pesetas each.

'No...! Two bank notes?'

'Yes, two notes, just dropped here!'

'Oh, it's too funny! It was him!' And Annhine burst out

laughing. 'Poor man, he wanted to pay me! Oh, it's too funny for words! He's paid me two hundred francs…! You've got to laugh, Tesse! Mind you, two hundred francs, your friend Annhine de Lys, it's not very flattering! I'd rather have paid him something myself!'

'No, it's all fine, it's very amusing, I promise you,' Tesse said. 'Don't take offence. When you think about it, what you gave him wasn't worth any more than that.'

'It wasn't worth that even…!'

'It was a lot to him, perhaps.'

'So, what we call Love isn't worth anything?'

'Or else it's worth everything! It depends on the feeling behind our actions.'

'I deplore his generosity,' said Annhine. 'It makes my sudden whim all the more vulgar.'

'Nhinette, you who have everything you can possibly desire, today you sold yourself for two hundred francs!'

'Don't let's mention it again… I'm ashamed…!'

'You must never be ashamed of anything.'

'I'm going to scrub my soiled body clean, Tesse… I'll see you later… And then let's pack!'

XV

They reached Lisbon the following morning and took lodgings near the station, in the Avenida Palace. Although to outward appearances she seemed well, on the inside Annhine was suffering. She wrote to her doctor, explaining, at length, her febrile state. Then without waiting for a reply she asked for the hotel doctor who came and prescribed for her a course of sedatives, sleeping draughts and showers, along with a few days of calm and bed-rest.

Altesse hardly ever went out and scarcely even left her side; they lived in their spacious apartment which was splendidly situated, overlooking the grand boulevard which, between the hours of five and seven, is as full of bustle as our own avenue des Acacias. One day Altesse ran in from the balcony and called to her friend: 'Nhine! It's the king...! The king! Quick, get up, come and see! He's going to pass right under our windows!'

Nhine lost no time scrambling from her bed and pulling on a long travelling coat made of a very pale wool stuff, lined in mauve. She leaned on the rail to watch the royal carriage. Behind came the leading nobles, the king's brother, the company of courtiers. Our two friends were seen and pointed out... Clever plots were hatched which provided them with some interesting diversions. Furtive invitations after dark, clandestine rendez-vous at the palace brought them some amusement and made them, for a while, fond of Lisbon. They looked in antique shops, they were able to attend two or three bullfights, less cruel than the Spanish version, a real massacre that had left them horrified. Altesse lived for her friend and Nhine seemed to forget, to some degree, Paris and her secret aspirations. She never mentioned Flossie and gave herself over to the simple joys of living for pleasure, sought after and in demand on every side, triumphant in her beauty and fêted by all. But she was wasting physically day by day. A nervous trembling would seize her for no apparent reason; it became so severe she could no longer hold a glass in her hand. If a door was closed firmly enough for her to hear it at all, she started; the least sound made her jump. She spoke very loudly, very fast; she couldn't keep still. Her nostrils quivered, her enlarged eyes shone with too much brilliance, like those of morphine addicts. She felt ready for anything, stronger and livelier than ever, then at other times she would remain motionless for hours on end, staring at the same point in space with a frozen smile that twisted her vacant, bloodless face. Nothing, one would have thought at such moments, could touch her... At other moments she seemed somnolent, eyes closed in thought, and she stayed in bed for several days, weak, overcome, unable to move. Among the people around her was a particular man to whom she had taken an instant and irrational dislike. His name was José de Souza Mialho... She couldn't bear the sight of him; as soon as he appeared among the crowd of her admirers, she would be overcome with rage and fury and heap abuse on his head. He would respond in kind, with a thousand impertinences, and any contact between them became an endless skirmish. One afternoon when Altesse was coming back from her walk, she found Nhine panting in this man's arms. He had come while she was alone. She had grabbed him and pulled him towards her without a word and she had given herself to him in a sort of manic fury. For three days she had a wild affair with him and then refused to see him ever again, and never offered a word of explanation to anybody. She tried to save herself, pull herself together, find normality again, but couldn't do it. Her imagination distorted life's smallest details, she attached significance to the most trivial of upsets, everything was finely sifted and analysed. She received a letter from Flossie which reached her after many detours. She recognised the large and slightly tortuous handwriting; she destroyed the letter without reading it, fearing a sudden relapse, a subtle magnet that would attract her again. She was frantic, quaking, in a fever...

One day, one of those sad days when the sun seems reluctant to rise, when the clouds hang low and heavy like wet cotton wool and the silence adds its oppressive note of morbidness and languor, she could bear it no longer; and while Tesse had gone to try her luck at the casino in Mont Estoril – two hours from Lisbon – she wrote to Flossie the following letter of farewell... Yes, she wished it might be a farewell, an irrevocable farewell from the agitated depths of a soul possessed, as she believed, by the soul of the intrusive child. Wanting to be alone, she shut herself away, after sending Ernesta out shopping, then, yielding to the need to confide that was wearing her down, she made this confession.

> To you who were my blond delight, my Flossie, to you who were because you had to be, and who ceased to be because you were; inevitably, by natural law. Poor little Prometheuses we tried to be: but suddenly, fatally, implacably subjugated! Subjugated, yes... and ironically brought to the point where we ourselves desired our human enslavement... where all that is born *must* die... even You and I, especially We! Only your hair will never be subjugated, enslaved, a rebel ever victorious! Your hair will always be a beam of moonlight... growing paler with the passing of time but even more morbid, moonlike, until the grave.
>
> I write these wandering words in memory of your hair and to bid it farewell. The moon was sulking yesterday, like You, like Me, like Us...! Invisible in the darkness, but there were plenty of stars in the sky and gas-lamps glowing out in the countryside... stupid, imbecilic little things, like clowns from some burlesque show trying to imitate the splendour of the astral bodies... And from a distance, through the myopia and incapacity of our dim intelligence, many of us took them for stars indeed, those simple flames lit by the hand of man, flames that wobble in

a puff of wind and go out altogether for little more, a quavering, sickly light, utilitarian and silly!

The moon was sulking yesterday, and I was out in the countryside driving along the banks of the Tagus in the saddening solitude of those shores, drawn on by five mad and beribboned little mules. In front of me, two people were in conversation, devising plans for happy days to come. Happy...! Ah, ah, ah...! As if there could exist on earth any happiness for someone who knows, who understands...! And I... I was seated at the back, alone, isolated... and I turned my head away so as not to see them, I blocked my ears so as not to hear them... and I let my gaze fall on the road behind. The moon was still sulking, invisible, but the white veil, the Milky Way, illuminated the sky, and I thought of you, Moon-Beam, of your pale, fine hair... Why? Because your fancy, mine, that Fancy that flies on fleet and brilliant wings, like a beautiful bird of the isles, alighted one day on a fragile flower, the union of our two souls; and because it was sweet, at such a distance, to think of it, beneath the lovely ethereal vault of darkest sapphire.

The roads behind were sad! I said to them privately, and to you too: I shall never see you again, my beautiful shady ways, my anguished paths, my ill-lit crossings, my trees lost in the distance... never again!

An abrupt departure, a sudden setting-off... of a fantasy. And the mules bore me away with a joyful jingle of bells, and the road went dark behind me, disappearing as I looked back into my past. And I thought of You, my Little Blue Flower whom I shall never see again and whose scent was such sweet inebriation. And the trees flashed past, I seemed not to be moving, it was the countryside that moved around me... as well as You, as well as Me. Is it You who have gone...? Or have I...? Or We? And the trees ran past, the low mountains retreated, a few white houses fled away, all so swift, and all of them returned the message: 'No, no, You are the one passing us by, You are the Wanderer! We, and the Sky and the Stars are the Impassive, the Stable, the Unchangeable, the Faithless! We cast our charms over you this night; and then we shall cast them over others. If you ever come back, you will find us again, more lovely or more ugly, but us, always us, lovely or ugly according to the Idea you harbour, the Fantasy or Whim which follows you and surrounds you, which leads you on and cows you and commands you! You will find us like this, ugly or lovely, always the same: Stable and Faithless...!' And I was pleasurably overwhelmed by a sweet and heady sadness that made me as one with You who were my fairest, my Flossie... I almost wept. Was it You...? Was it Me...? And my tears gave me a pleasure more intense than the laughter and merriment of the two persons in front of me: the son of a king and a beloved friend who turned in their seats at times desiring to share with me their joy. No, leave me to my dreams, all is well with me, I am not alone, no, I am with a soul who soothes and understands me! And the road fled past...! And I let my eyes fall on the ground beneath us. Then, horror! Disillusion...!

I saw stones, rocks, mud, grass trampled and crushed, flowers grey with dust, rubbish strewn about, the ground marked by footprints and rutted by wheels. 'Raise your eyes...' my cruel and tender inner voice told me – the voice which, at its whim, at yours, at mine, either tortures or consoles me. 'Raise your eyes from the squalid earth of your memory. You must always keep your gaze fixed aloft, remember this, and then you will be glad you can regret the Roads Already Travelled! Dreams sail on high and are never abased! Keep your gaze on them; the Earth is your enemy. Ah! The earth...! You tread it underfoot, soil it, sow it and make it sprout; one day, in vengeance, it will cover you, suffocate you, and, victorious, fold you into its moist black tilth. Therefore, raise your eyes, contemplate the stars and pass on your way... you will think with fondness of the paths once trodden... of You who were my fairest, of Me, of Us!'

And the human Grain, for it is human, Grain – which means tender and beneficent according to the dictionary's ironic definition but not according to my disillusioned heart – and the Grain we sow, which grows as we command and falls with a cry beneath our scythes, whose dried sheaves, after being cruelly ground, feed us, see how good they are, beneficent and loyal, not very human at all, wouldn't you say, this Grain...! The Grain surrounded me like a vast sea, leaning, bent, beaten down by the power of the Wind... and I fled, Flossie, you who were mine...! The barking of dogs, the clatter of the carriage under an echoing archway, two border sentries with questioning stares, a sudden halt... and here I am again a long way from You, a very long way... Farewell to Men... to Him... to All of Them!

I have tried to set down as much as I can of all the things that have gone through my mind in these moments of communion across the space between us so that I can send them to you and... perhaps?... bring some sort of pleasure... to whom? To You? To Me? To Us!

ANNHINE

P.S. – I forgot to tell you that while I was staring down at the earth, the night the moon was sulking, driving through the dirt and dust of that road, I thought I saw the body of a woman sprawled across a pile of stones, naked, frail, defenceless. This body resembled mine, the one you desire... and the people passing by hurled insults at it, violated it, defiled it as much as they defiled the road, with rubbish, with spittle, with kisses, with bites, with stains, with blows, with malicious words and bruises. The stones were more – less – human, since that is the word decreed by usage, we might as well use it! Whoever wanted me had me. No one could see my blemishes, for the moon was sulking, invisible, and I was rotting in my own slime, without the strength to get up, to flee! Vainly, I tried to reach out and stop the few passers-by who looked as if they might be willing to help; every one of them pushed me away and turned their backs. Everybody pounced on me, attacked me, men and beasts, and it carried on for centuries…!

I wanted to hide inside your great head of hair, because you came by as well, but you went on past, after dropping flower petals over my eyelids and my forehead, a unique act of pity. My gaze will never fall again on what is obscene, iniquitous; my brow, in the same way, will remain pure, perfumed by the fragrance of the pale petals your hand scattered over me, in abundance. And if they were to fade? Would you come back to scatter more…? No! Flee! Go your way! Fly on your angel's wings. The dews of heaven will have compassion and keep them fresh and fragrant for me. So let no one come, then, to disturb me in my torpor, in the sweetness of my dream. I see nothing. Like the ostrich, considered foolish by everybody, but highly regarded by me – and imitated – I see nothing and therefore I fear nothing! I imagine myself as a flower, beyond any risk of being plucked, because you have draped my eyes and my thoughts.

No more useless efforts! Let my flesh rot, disintegrating, as well as my once admired figure! My true beauty is safe, and beyond the reach, henceforth, of the lust of men!

So here then, my flowing pen tracing my flowing thoughts, is this… for You, for Me… for what was Us!
ANNHINE

A Woman's Affair

'It sounds a bit mad, this letter,' she murmured as she read it over, 'but Flossie will understand me. She's the only person in the world whose ideas are a perfect match for mine, and this is all true! I lived every moment of it during yesterday's drive.'

She dispatched the bulky envelope, then concentrated hard on not thinking about it again. She did not have to wait long for a reply; it arrived five or six days later and Nhine found an excuse for shutting herself away so that she could read the following:

> Adored woman, your letter is a light that crowns my hopes with a halo. I can scarcely imagine the riot of the senses you must have put your poor soul through to make it turn to me like that. It seems so sad and disgusted with the unworthy things your life has to offer that it wants to abandon the present and fly back to things that have been: to You, to Me, to Us...! It is sweet to feel the brush of your wings, but a sweetness tainted with fears. Shall I ever be able to find sufficient enticement for that vagabond spirit, or, hungry for the intangible and fantastical, will she just fly ever further away...? No! Am I right? I have the feeling that you will come back to me, disillusioned and bruised as you are, whole as before and that my immense love will teach me the skills I need to keep you. Oh, darling! I dream of the hours I shall spend with you...! The hours! The lifetimes! The eternities...! You truly are the sister of my soul, and nothing can break or untie that knot. We are united in the mystery of the Infinite!

A Woman's Affair

I have found you again. You tried to flee me but it was in vain because you *must* return to me and be mine. Everything will urge you, an invisible force, coming to my aid, will draw you to me. Your mind is already on its way back and to assuage my impatience, in the meantime, I have my memories! My hopes too...! You don't know how closely I cling to the memory of our short time together. I clutch it to me like a child whose toy is about to be snatched away! I even hold dear that tragic episode which, by precipitating your departure, put such an abrupt end to the first chapter of our love. Let your thoughts dwell on what it means: see Jane's voluntary death in its context, a place where everyone, except her, was wearing a mask. She staked her life on a feeling, a grand and noble feeling in that it elevated her above the instinct for self-preservation that most people consider much stronger. She saw everything that gave her pleasure and made life worth living reduced to ashes, and we must admire her for no longer wishing to tread an earth which had become for her barren and devoid of hope. How much better to put an end to one's life in time, rather than to witness the burial of the best part of oneself and not have the courage to go down with it. Not to have acted, for her, would have been to take the coward's part. Dear departed little soul, my life will be a long prayer of thanksgiving to her, for I have inherited from her a note that was missing from the harmony of my love, a heightened sensitivity. Through her end, I am learning to live in a better way, to suffer for you better. Go, travel! You may be far away, you may be by my side, my heart will never leave you, were you to drag me down to the depths of hell or lift me to heights inaccessible! There has already been enough time since your letter for your thoughts to have moved on or changed in a hundred different ways, but even now, in spite of the fact that four days have put their barrier of hours between the woman who wrote to me and the woman who forgets me, I sense you are thinking of me, I feel your presence all around me... Imagination...! What a gift for those who have lost the treasured reality and have to be content with its echo! – How do you interpret my silences? I like to think that you have felt me with you wherever you went... when I couldn't sleep at nights, I was following you! Helped by my own memories of travelling, I was with you, in Italy especially. It's the saddest thing I know, a country that calls itself, in mockery of its past splendour, *la Bella Italia*! And do you mean to say you travelled to the land of ruins to seek the rest and joy you needed? Would I be wrong to imagine you felt uneasy there, on edge, isolated? I don't know how many times I have thought: 'When she is standing beneath the lofty dome of some dead church filled with the breath of dead people, or somewhere where the bones of the once great crumble to dust and mingle in the twilight of another age which is already drawing to its close, perhaps she will feel the need for something warm, gentle, alive, something that is hers, a voice in the silence, as if there were, amid all this muteness and absence, some mysterious vibration that she recognised and loved. Or else, if she were to look upwards, through one of those rare windows that open on infinity, her weariness might bring her to detach herself from the terrestrial sphere, escape all physical bonds, forget those banal words and brutish gestures, and her soul will call to mine. And then, an unsuspected poetry will enter her soul, soothe and rock her to the measure of her desires, beyond the prose of everyday life.'

No scene representing the gothic, the medieval, is complete without, somewhere, the outline of a page-boy. Let me be there beside you, where you are now, curled in ecstasy at your feet, let me be your companion through the mystic nights that seem to swoon for Love...! Nhine, there is a sort of Love you do not know, a Love with as many modulations as the shifting decors of its setting! You have had only lovers who are excited by their desire, not by atmosphere or ambiance. For them you have been a woman – the female sex – and not the lover born of dreams! Let me go out in search of all that you have fruitlessly spent on them – spent of yourself. I will go out and gather up from the highways your lost illusions, my love will bring them back to life, and you, your joys restored, will make a crown of them for me...! Nhine...! Let me love you! Call me! Come! The very chaste friendship that you want would be the culmination of my wildest desires if it were a real and concrete thing. But you hunger after Impossible Things: Voice without Sound, Rays without Sun, Art without Inspiration, Beauty without Form! If I did not know you so well, all this might be more attainable, but I have understood you and loved you. For me you have become the essence of every fragrance, my life's one and only purpose! Your unique personality obsesses me, and I will cry with all my strength: I love you...! May you only hear me! The others will hurt you more and more! Go, travel! Reject me! Listen to them! What do I care, you are mine for all eternity and I dedicate my life to you, and I will wait for you.

FLOSSIE

'She is very sure of me,' Annhine said to herself.

The idea angered her, she tossed her head, then tore the envelope into a thousand pieces, in a nervous frenzy as if she wanted to erase whatever impalpable power it was that so frightened and attracted her.

'It's ridiculous, what does it add up to in the end? But it's very sweet, too. She writes so beautifully, for a foreigner. The sophistication of her thoughts, the fineness of her sensitivities! She charms and corrupts me at the same time... No, there's no doubt: she interests me too much...! I don't want this...! I don't want this!'

Altesse swept into the room with news on her lips, then stopped short, suddenly uncertain, finding Nhine miles away, lost in thought; and at the sight of the letter open on the table, she guessed it all. She asked no questions, waiting... Then, to put an end to an embarrassing and awkward silence, she pretended not to have seen anything and said: 'Nhinette darling, come and look, they're going off to round up the bulls for tomorrow's corrida, the green-bonnets[2] are lining up in a sort of procession, and there's a band.'

While Altesse was opening the window, Nhine quickly hid the letter from Flossie in the leaves of her blotter.

They leaned their elbows on the balcony.

'Shall we go tomorrow?'

'Certainly,' Tesse said. 'We must have one of the best boxes, near the king's.'

Annhine had no real desire to see the bullfight, but she thought it might be a distraction for Altesse, who, for her part, wanted Nhine to throw herself into this noisy reality to drag her away from her gloomy introspections. They exchanged glances, which made them understand each other.

Nhine was first to speak: 'Will you enjoy it? Will it make you forget for a while, being in all that crowd and din?'

Tesse replied: 'Nobody knows better than I do how to be alone in a crowd.'

'Well, I find the whole thing just bores me and gets on my nerves,' Nhine continued.

'So?'

'So?'

'Whatever you like.'

Annhine didn't dare confess it, but she wanted to go back to Paris, to Flossie, to the chimeras and wonders of an unknown world she wanted to penetrate, whatever the price of

---

2 These are people, enthusiasts, who, after the running of the bull, rush at the animal and hang on to it by the horns. They wear green bonnets.

despair that might follow. On her side, Altesse was dying to see her own home again, her circle, to contemplate, at close and bitter quarters, the ruin of her former joys and pleasures, the scene, now desolate, of so many happy times. They each told themselves these things during the long silence that ensued. Nhine turned her head to look at Altesse, whose gaze was fixed on some empty distance.

She called softly to her: 'Tesse!'

Altesse shivered and said in a toneless voice: 'What?'

'Do you want to...?'

'What?'

'Leave?'

'Where to...? Here or elsewhere, what's the difference?'

'No! Leave... go back... there!'

'There?'

'There! You know what I mean. *There*...! Home!'

'Ah! Yes... if you want to, Nhinon, if you want to and if it will make you feel better. As far as I'm concerned...!'

She shrugged her shoulders in a gesture of indifference.

'Oh, me, you know...!' Annhine assumed an air of complete disinterest. 'There's nothing I feel the need to go back for, I was thinking of you... I think it might be healthy for you to be home... There's a gap in your life and you feel it keenly, there's no disputing it... It seems to me you'll fill it more easily in Paris than you will by flitting from one country full of hot passions to another!'

Altesse shook her head sadly, then went on, willing to be persuaded: 'Do you think so? As you wish! But what about our friends, our new conquests...?'

'It's a very good thing to leave while you'll still be missed.

A Woman's Affair

I'd go without a second thought. And you…?'

'Oh! Me…! Well, when do you want to go?'

'As soon as possible… don't you think?'

'Straight away, if you don't see any difficulty?'

'That's what I was thinking too. The Southern Express leaves tonight.'

'Tonight, then.'

XVI

As they were borne away by the train, pleased with their decision, a whole host of ideas for a better future occupied their minds and smoothed their journey. They had been glad to escape from their usual lives; they felt glad to be returning to them. Altesse could see hers improving, without quite knowing how: a happiness of some sort would appear on the horizon, a healthy change or a diversion from her sadness, a whole parade of ill-defined but genuine hopes. She could imagine an unexpected encounter with the man she loved, the possibility of going back: in spite of her resistance he would beseech her, beg her for a meeting, one of those charged occasions where the two people, forgetting their stern resolve, fall into one another's arms. Ah! What was she thinking? Absolutely not! Her will power was ferocious, unrelenting. She could remember how, once, when she was fifteen, a woman cousin of hers had caused her some deep offence, hurt her badly. Tesse had cut this woman from her life, even though they were very close, and from that day, despite her letters of humble entreaty, despite her sitting on a public bench outside their house for days and nights on end, in tears, waiting for the forgiveness she sought, Tesse had never wavered, never for a moment wished to repair the rift. Then, one morning, she had been informed that the cousin had died and Tesse had driven to the cemetery to make quite sure the woman was there... in the ground... Well, in the same way it would be a relief to her to ensure that her own former happiness was as definitively buried! Perhaps she would find a letter saying that everything had been broken off at the last minute, he could not live without her, something along those lines, she didn't exactly know what, but she was going back to Paris with a notion, slow-developing and painful, almost a certainty, that some great and salutary upheaval lay in wait. The awakening from a deeply troubling dream, it might be, which leaves one shattered and bruised, certainly, but freed, all the same, from its appalling and oppressive grip.

Annhine closed her eyes and gave herself over to the enchanting fantasy which by now completely possessed her. She was annoyed with herself for having resisted the delights towards which she was travelling today. She shivered in anticipation at the thought of the excesses, whatever they might be, that she meant to lend herself to without reserve. This restful journey provided her with the ideal opportunity to feed her desire, and she could see in her mind's eye Flossie's penetrating gaze reaching deep into her soul, she trembled already in the fierce embrace of those white arms, she could imagine her whole being, body and soul, entwined with Flossie's, abandoned, yielding. She swooned with each kiss from her lips, then the child's soft voice murmured words of endearment, exciting words, urgent words, imploring and grateful. It was more than she could bear, she almost fainted away, overwhelmed, annihilated in a wave of irresistible desires and exquisite caresses. All control lost, she gave a loud cry. Altesse got up and came to sit beside her.

'What is it, Nhine...? What is it...? A nightmare?'

Alarmed by the sight of Annhine writhing and twitching, she anxiously patted her hands, then dabbed at her forehead with eau de Cologne.

'It's nothing... nothing...' Annhine struggled to sit up straight, her face bathed in perspiration. 'I'm so happy to be going back...' And she broke into peals of loud, nervous laughter and couldn't stop. 'I... I...'

'Calm down,' said Tesse, who feared a repetition of what had happened before.

She opened the window. A cold and startling rush of air came in, along with a powerful smell of coal.

'Oh! That's horrible! You can shut it again. Don't worry, it's not what you think... I'm over it now...'

And, after a final gasp, Annhine slumped back against the head-rest, her face suddenly pale. Inside her head she was thinking: "I must get a grip on myself, I don't want our plans spoiled by some mishap..." Then, aloud: 'Good evening, Tesse, how about you, are you feeling well, and pleased too?'

'Yes, my Nhine, pleased with anything that makes you happy especially.'

"If she only knew," Nhine said to herself, "if she only

suspected all the things I have in mind..."

The next morning they had to be up very early. The congestion of people and goods at the frontier, a biting cold that made them shiver, a clearer appreciation of their situation, all these plunged them into a fit of gloom and brought them closer to a disappointing and unappealing reality.

They made a show of looking after the little dog, seeing to the luggage, forcing themselves to ignore their discomfort, not allowing themselves to acknowledge the feelings of regret, the sort of fright that had come over them: they were subdued and resigned.

'Here we are in France, Tesse, home soon... Home...!'

'Yes, tomorrow...' And Tesse sighed in spite of herself. 'Tomorrow we'll be in Paris. It's cold, it's dark, it feels desolate...'

'Paris must be very sad...'

'Very sad, indeed...'

'Oh, that little station early in the morning, it was awful...!' Nhine coughed.

'I'm positively freezing, aren't you?'

'Me...?'

Altesse spoke out with resolution: 'I'm wondering if it will be good for your health, this sudden return in such damp weather, to a Paris with no sun. You're coughing! I've had an idea: Arcachon is quite close... Do you know Arcachon?'

And when Annhine shook her head: 'Quick then, let's wire ahead. We'll continue as far as Bordeaux, then we can branch off from there. My darling, it's a wonderful part of the country, especially at this time of year! What, you don't know Arcachon? But you must know it, Nhine! Oh, you'll be able to breathe properly there! The ocean, golden sands, trees, pine forests with their healthy stimulating scent, delightful villas, magnificent hotels, blue skies, warm and cheerful, it's marvellous! Why didn't we think of it earlier? We'll stop there... for a while... Would you like that?'

Yes, wait a while longer... not go back...! They instinctively feared it. Yes... stop, it didn't matter where... anywhere it was good to live! One more sunlit diversion... a delay, yes, yes...

And Nhine accepted.

At Arcachon, they rented a villa, a small chalet a short distance out of town, on the slopes of the hill, in the fresh air, among the woods, a very healthy spot, warmed by the mid-day sun and furnished with those odd little English pieces, white and cheerful, and above all comfortable. Nhine took on the pleasurable task of beautifying the house: they went down into town for a whole day and explored every shop, coming away with parcels of silk stuffs, blue or pink, laces, ribbons, strangely shaped decorative vases, a flowered china dinner service, fine glassware.

'Let's stay here a long time, Tesse, my angel, my guardian angel,' she said. 'You'll love it, just see. Your room will have pink everywhere, to line the windows and for your bed curtains. And in mine it will be blue, blue, everything blue. When I die, listen, Tesse, you must have my coffin lined with blue satin. Swear...'

'Idiot...!'

She had to give her word.

'I prefer cremation, it's cleaner.'

'Well, I wouldn't dare! How will you manage in the Valley

of Jehoshaphat, darling, searching round for your scattered ashes?'

'What about you, Nhinon the beautiful, with all those little worms?'

They argued. People turned round, thinking Annhine must be one of those people who came here for their tuberculosis, no doubt. She remarked as much to Tesse, who teased her for looking too healthy.

'Look, for example, there's one, outside the watchmaker's. Oh, the poor boy...! Look, Nhine!'

Nhine turned and recognised Robert Régis, a friend of hers, who waved and came over to meet her. She held out her hand, kindly and polite, but astonished: 'Hallo, Robert. What are you doing here? Still suffering a little?'

'A little,' he said, 'but I shan't be out of sorts much longer, I think, I'm feeling better. And you, Annhine? Who or what can have brought you to this place?'

'Me...? Us...? Nothing... Ah, let me introduce you: M. Robert Régis, lawyer; Mme Altesse, my friend...'

'Madame!'

He bowed to Altesse, who smiled at him.

'We came here on a whim, a mere whim,' she said. 'As simple as that.'

'Well, I wish I could say as much,' he sighed. 'But I don't want to keep you. Will you let me accompany you a little way? You're at the Grand-Hôtel, I expect?'

'No...!' And Nhine waved vaguely in the direction of the hillside. 'We live up there, very high...'

'Neighbours, then, because I've taken a place some way back from the sea as well... I'd like to offer you some flowers...'

A Woman's Affair

They went into the florist's. He chose two bunches of roses and offered one to Nhine, then the other to Tesse, kissing her fingers. Altesse looked at him, pained at the signs of the implacable and deadly disease discernible in his pinched, translucent features, his feverish eyes. The petals of a white rose, drooping over his hand, barely stood out against the sick man's bloodless skin. When they stepped out of the shop again, a faint breeze made him cough. He had to stop for a moment.

'I can't go with you any further,' he said regretfully. 'It's time for my doctor's appointment. Later, when I come back up from town, I'll call in on you, if that suits you: perhaps I may be in the happy position of being able to offer you my services in some way. Do make use of me.'

'We will,' Altesse said. 'We're counting on you already, dear monsieur. Come in to say good night... and incidentally, as a start, can you let us have your doctor's address?'

'With pleasure, for he's a delightful man, M. de Gastier, enormously talented, and in addition, a man of the world, thoroughly charming. He left Paris because of his mother, who had a very weak chest, and he came to establish himself here, to give her the best chance of a long life. He's a man of great heart and most refined feeling. He owns that fine château you can just make out from here, can you see it? It would be very useful to know him. I'll tell him about you when I see him today, let him know you're here...'

He took from his pocket a dark wallet bearing his initials in gold and searched for one of his cards. He wrote his address on it, added the doctor's name then handed it to Annhine. These mild exertions brought the red to his cheeks. When he had gone on his way, she said: 'That's Régis, a nice boy, still very young, and very rich. He was the beautiful Mme Trakir's lover for a long time.'

'Ah! Yes, I remember,' said Tesse.

'Poor man, and what a state I find him in now…! He's a friend of Henri's. You haven't ever seen him at my house because he devoted all his time and energy to his lady and her many demands. He's a cerebral type, highly-strung, and she simply wore him out. Henri told me a little bit about it. I hardly recognise him. The way he looked at you though! He must still be in love with her, you resemble her in some ways, the beautiful Trakir.'

'I find this Régis interesting,' Tesse replied. 'I knew nothing of his story, but I might have guessed. But he will live, he'll get his strength back, his illness isn't very serious physically: it's his morale that's under attack. He's a loving sort. He needs to find a woman, an emotional attachment to get involved in, to make him forget, and then he'll revive. In fact…' she became thoughtful, 'that's something I could do. It would be good. Get close to the boy, play at being in love with him, bring him back to life, save him. It would be a noble sacrifice, a goal to achieve beyond my own concerns. I like him very much, it won't be at all difficult for me to manage it… Shall I try?'

Nhine pulled a face.

'No, but think, darling, a man with T.B.!'

'He's so handsome, Nhinon, so sad and interesting with his pallid complexion and great deep eyes full of shadow and mystery, he's already knocking at the door to eternity. I will do this, yes… I'll do it.'

'Well, I like strength,' Nhine declared.

They returned home. Annhine's enthusiasm had evaporated, she felt tired, too tired to stay on her feet. She went to bed without saying a word, taking no notice of anything. Altesse found herself all alone amongst piles of parcels, with no interest in unwrapping them, when Robert Régis called.

'I'm worried,' she said. 'Nhine isn't feeling well. I'd like to send for the doctor, he could at least reassure me.'

'I'll go,' Robert replied. 'I have a carriage outside, I'll bring him back.'

'Thank you…'

And Tesse gave him a soft look as she squeezed his hand.

Half an hour later he returned with the doctor. Altesse advised him of the situation and, apologising to Régis, who took his leave, knocked on Annhine's door. Receiving no response, she entered the room and found her friend in tears. Annhine's tears were one of her most appealing features, for her face did not fold in creases and her eyes remained wide open, growing ever larger as the pearls sprang from their rims and spilled slowly down her cheeks.

'What's the matter, little one?'

'I don't know, I don't know…!'

And, noticing the doctor, Nhine hid her face.

'This is M. de Gastier who's come to make his little invalid's acquaintance. You have come at the right moment, doctor, I think,' Tesse said. 'Her nerves are very upset.'

Nhine sat up, wiped her eyes and docilely surrendered to a minute examination. She described her ailment calmly and without extravagant phrases. He smiled and was friendly. He was interested, and charmed by the alluring beauty of this pretty creature. She was staring closely at this robust young man, healthy and strong, as he questioned her, and something strange, abnormal then happened inside her. She felt an overpowering need to give herself, to be taken, taken roughly, ravished; her hands tightened into fists, a violent, unexpected desire coursed through her, delivering her up to this incarnation of the male she suddenly found so close to her. Her ears buzzed, her mouth turned dry, she could barely answer his questions. She let herself fall back against the bedhead and made a sign that Altesse didn't understand... then she opened her dress and, pointing to her heart, complained: 'Here, doctor, you see... I sometimes have pains... as if I'd been stung.'

While he was leaning over her, she shuddered and, unable to stop herself, caught the doctor's head in her hands and drew it towards her. Astonished, he raised his eyes and met the look in hers, then, abruptly, pressed his lips to her lips. The kiss was spontaneous, lengthy and beyond explanation, a kiss that became an exchange of souls, and he took her, as she was, unthinking, unreasoning, in a fiery burst of passion. The day was drawing to its close, darkness became their accomplice, stealing into the big bedroom and veiling all around them. Now, they talked together like two lovers. She snuggled against him, appeased, her eyes bright, her emotions profoundly stirred. He supported her in his arms, happy, thinking he was dreaming. Altesse, coming back into the room, joined them. Then protestations were exchanged, confessions made, and endless plans devised. He would cure Nhine, yes, he understood her completely, this little thing, so feminine, so fragile, so full of soul! She, immediately, at first sight, at their first exchange of impressions, had decided she was his, totally, without restriction. She wanted to know about his life, tell him about her own. He, similarly, had fallen for her straight away. He was mad for her. He wanted her to live with him, decided on the spot he would invent a pretext – a journey he had to go on – to allow him to take leave from his duties and devote himself wholly to her. Tesse refused to go with them. She was so pleased to feel her Nhine joyful again she wanted to let her savour her happiness in undisturbed privacy.

'I shall stay here, darling. You can come and see me from time to time. Go, enjoy this chance of happiness that's come your way, so sweet just now. I have my romance as well…!'

After two days, Annhine came to see her on a delicious warm evening, beneath a clear, motionless, glittering sky, having driven over by carriage with him, her Max… And the tremor in her voice when she pronounced that name! Her happiness was increasing and becoming more complete with each day… but she missed her Tesse… yes.

'Liar…!' And Tesse wagged a finger at her. 'But I too have my idyll!'

Just then, Régis appeared in the conservatory doorway… He looked so pale and spectral, an effect the probing moonbeams only served to emphasise, that he produced in Annhine's nervous mind a surge of morbid terror and a wave of sadness.

'I don't wish to trouble you,' he said, and he disappeared.

A week went past with no communication between the two friends, then one morning Nhine arrived and stood at the window, framed in sunlight.

'It's me!' she called. 'Tesse…! Robert…!'

There was no response. A heavy silence reigned in

the house. Her throat tightened. Could they have left? she wondered anxiously... Finally the servant came to let her in.

Madame was at home, yes, in her bedroom, she was still asleep.

Reassured, Nhine climbed the stairs very quietly and cautiously opened the sleeper's door. The room was flooded with light, for the shutters were still open and the curtains had not been drawn, but Altesse saw none of this, heard nothing: she lay stiffly on her bed, her eyes closed, her eyelids swollen and red, as if she had been crying, her face drained and looking naked amid the great sheaves of her undone hair, all white against the rusty gold of her tawny mane, white in the dazzling gold of the sun, white as a dead woman... white... inert... lifeless... Annhine nearly fainted to the floor. A terrible suspicion flashed through her mind. She came closer, calling: 'Tesse...! Tesse...!'

Altesse opened her eyes, as if in a panic, tried to move but couldn't. Little by little she came to her senses, like one departed who is slowly, painfully, restored to life, looking all round, searching in herself the reason for this deep slumber, recalling with difficulty her deadened memories... At last she said, in unhappy tones: 'Is that you...? You...! Oh, don't leave me! Don't leave me ever again!'

'No, my Tesse, no...! And in fact, I was coming over to ask your advice. Max is abandoning me today for the first time, he has to attend to his patients, attend to other people instead of me...! In short, real life has got me in its hold again. And it makes me wretched, and I don't want to be wretched. This morning when I woke up I found I was alone.' Her voice trembled, she had to make an effort not to collapse in tears.

'Then I felt in such anguish… such anguish that I thought of you, Altesse, my darling. I came to ask your advice, you're the only person I can turn to…! I think I'm going mad. I find you here, like a lifeless body, like a castaway, all alone, when I thought you were with…'

'Oh, Nhinon…!' And Tesse covered herself, pulling up the fine silk sheets. 'I tried, I wanted to… After forty-eight hours of it, I just fell back into my terrible void… incapable. No! It's all over. I've reached the end, you see, nothing works for me. Ah! Don't create situations where such miseries are even possible! Run away…! Leave…! Cut your own hand off if it will save the rest. Put a stop to it the moment it causes pain.' She was becoming overexcited. 'Let's get away from here, the time's come…! For you too! And for me!'

Annhine caught her frenzied mood.

'You're right, let's go, let's leave them! We should fear the pleasure as much as we do the pain. Yes… I'm going to have my things brought over… he isn't due back until dinner time this evening… we should leave quickly, we can take the first train. Ernesta will follow us with the luggage. It's Paris we need. I'll send a letter, write him a farewell. When it comes to suffering, I'd rather suffer for my freedom than suffer for my enslavement. And you must write too, prepare him for the break-up.'

'Me…? That's done already: after a horrible crisis, yesterday evening, we separated. I wasn't able to play my role to the end. He's clever, he realised what I was doing, and I was only making his affliction worse by adding my own. Instead of doing him some good I was actually doing him harm. For his own sake, I have to let it go, because my charitable charade was not a success, it had already begun to affect him. As for me, it doesn't matter, everything remains the same, but you, I'm certainly taking you away! Oh, I won't let you lose your way...'

'I'll write that letter,' Annhine said, her mind made up. 'You do whatever is necessary. Ah, yes...! It's being together that will make us strong!'

'Yes, provided there are no lies between us,' Tesse asserted gravely.

Nhine looked away awkwardly, in some confusion, then sat down at the table and wrote a long letter. When she had finished, she passed it to her friend.

'Here, read this,' she said simply, tears welling in her eyes.

Altesse had meanwhile been attending to the urgent practical details. Then she read:

My sweet and beloved lover, this is to bid you farewell. I have to stop seeing you, and yet I love you!

You see, we have just been living a dream together, the sweetest, most lovely of dreams. We should not wait for the moment of awakening, but keep it as a beautiful memory, as I shall always remember it!

Filled with the gladness of living, handsome with all that life-force you radiate, your voice ringing, your eyes clear and laughing, a joyous man, there you were, striding through the sunny garden of the perfect life with its delightful lawns and lofty trees through which might be glimpsed, like a hope, a patch of blue sky! And who should find herself in your path but me, a poor sickly little fairy, so tall, so fragile, so pale...! Bruised by life, wounded by her contacts with men, crushed by the brutality of things, she was drifting away for ever, feet barely brushing the ground, away to worlds beyond the distant mists...

Ah, that first tentative exchange of looks, of thoughts, then that sudden passion which bound your strength to my weakness, that intoxication which filled our two souls, that sensuality which precipitated us instantly into each other's arms...! Because, far from playing the flirt with you, my love, I responded without hesitation to that kindling of the heart and senses which brooks no argument and will not put off until another day the happiness on offer...! And so I wanted to live...! And I was transformed...!

Yes... it was a dream, a late winter made summer, a passion so warm and so sudden that everything in us and around us seemed to beat in unison! Those delicious walks along narrow, secluded lanes, far from prying eyes, hand in hand, when I lived only for the look in your eyes, the kiss on your lips! Then, when we were apart, waiting for the moment when we would be together, then your return, our embraces, our caresses, and finally that marvellously tender peace when I felt you still beside me in my misty dreams all through the night, the long silent night...! And later, those few days we spent in your magnificent home, far from the sounds of the masses, far from everyone! Close by those old gothic ruins, their towers reflected in the water, the dark mysterious water guarded by its grey-feathered, red-beaked swans, majestic, sad swans. Ah, who will tell us the secret of those thick walls, of those drawbridges, of the huge ancient stones covered in inscriptions, of those faded paintings, of those age-old trees, last vestiges of a past that has disappeared into the night of time...? Then that park surrounding it, those flowers, those gardens, and finally you own corner, your home... and we two, alone, in love, and cut off from the world. Who, too, will tell us the secret of our hearts? Oh, what a wealth of happiness you have given me, Max, my sweet beloved. I had forgotten it all, my resentment, my sufferings. Your love let me be born again, I was transfigured, happy, glad to be alive!

And it is to avoid the stupid and eternally-repeated mistake of lovers, the lovers who pursue their happiness to its conclusion, to satiety, to bitter tears, to betrayal, that I *want* to interrupt this dream of love – which we have found so sweet – before reality looms fatally before us, before it arrives to remind us what we have been, what we are and what we must be!

Enough... It would be a crime to go any further! Like you, I hold inside me an ineradicable memory, so sweet, so full of poetry and enchantment that the memory is sufficient in itself to give me the strength to say to you this:

Farewell, Max, my sweet and beloved lover, and

because I adore you!
NHINON

'That's good,' Tesse approved.

"Poor little thing, how she loves him. It's time I took her away... This letter: h'mm! Under the surface, it's an appeal for help. He'll come running... No, but anyway, it won't reach him before this evening, by then we'll already be long gone. Difficult for him to leave, so many connections tying him down here, a man's natural selfishness, there's every chance he won't follow us. He'll take her at her word, without reading between the lines. It will be fine as it is."

She sealed the letter and gave the caretaker her orders, herself wrote a consolatory note for Robert, then they left as if in flight... fleeing love, fleeing joy, fleeing pain, without looking backwards, as if wanting to take flight from themselves, fearful of any abiding memory.

XVII

After a few days, an indeterminate but all-enveloping and disquieting sense of apathy settled over Annhine. Her return to the company of her friends, to her customary activities amongst her very charming surroundings had afforded her a measure of enjoyment, a sort of fevered pleasure for a brief week, then she had fallen back into her sad lassitude, worn out, more discouraged than ever, with no goal to aim towards, she told herself, nothing to live for.

She had been happy to renew contact with Henri, with his affection for her. She wished she could have loved him, she wished she could have transferred to him the feelings that were weighing her down, the strange, unspecified torment that gripped her, was slowly killing her. Her overstretched nerves accentuated her suffering and drove her into his arms with such wild and inexplicable passion that he was at first delighted, and then very frightened. He tried his best to calm her, resisting her ardours out of simple goodness of soul, talking to her gently, tenderly, fearing that gratification of such excesses would only harm her, exhaustion would set in and make her genuinely ill. She looked so well, she really did, coming back to Paris in such a splendid state of health, so fresh, so rosy, bright-eyed, full of life and joy. She really must make sure she stayed like that, it would be a shame to ruin such an excellent outcome. If she loved him – for he took this expansive fervour as an expression of love – she would understand. So then Nhine went out a great deal, rushing hither and thither, visiting her friends, harassing tradesmen and suppliers, ordering this, tearing up that. She was capriciousness itself, turning everything upside down, trying to divert her mind by any means available. She changed her perfume, chose a particularly penetrating one, strong enough to make one's head spin. Blue became a hateful colour, she wanted nothing but pink. Her undergarments were pink and white, pink ribbons now decorated her linen, she had all her little blue ribbons thrown away. Her bedroom struck her as insipid and affected; she wanted something much more severe, with lofty sculptures and ancient tapestries. They had to hunt down old wood-carvings, she visited all the antique dealers, rhapsodised over renaissance stained glass windows that would complete the transformation. She changed everything, even the ceiling, to which she had dark-stained ornamental beams fixed; then she decided she had to have a large four-poster bed, with a frieze made from old and faded silks. This manic activity only finally subsided when her doctor found for her a skull, which she placed on a table at her bedside. The macabre object rested on a cushion of dark green velvet which made its bony contours and the pallor of its old ivory stand out all the more vividly. For some time, after it was all finished and when she was at home, she decked herself out in grand dresses, long and straight, heavy with embroidery, in wide-sleeved robes worked with precious stones, adorned herself with antique jewellery: extraordinary pendant earrings studded with baroque sapphires, finely wrought belts sown with strange pearls, byzantine necklaces, enormous rings consisting of a single ruby, or a huge beryl, their bizarre gold mountings dulled by time and turning green. She wore a little Venetian bonnet over her hair, threaded with gold, pearls and turquoises; then she wanted ornaments, of improbable subjects and fantastical shapes. She had to have frogs, mythical animals, chimeras, dragons, yellow and black cats, crocodiles… she placed them everywhere: on consoles, all round her bed, on the tops of furniture, on the floor, in front of the fireplace, on the tables, under chairs. Then she dreamed up extravagant stories, and wanted to try writing. In a sentimental hour she composed a rather pretty little piece which she dedicated to Tesse. It turned out not too bad at all. She wrote of flowers, *fragile and fragrant, which we cruelly strip from their mother plants and allow to die, a banal bouquet in some shuttered chamber, yet which still charm us, even to the end, by the delicacy of their forms and the sweetness of their scent.* Dogs, *faithful and devoted, whom we neglect, treat harshly and even beat, who then humbly turn to us once more and lick the hand that strikes them* and finally men, *whom we adore, for whom we make sacrifices, to whom we give our souls and our whole being and who pitilessly break the heart that has dedicated itself to them.* She sighed heavily and thought of

A Woman's Affair

Max de Gastier. That particular man had quickly forgotten her: a brief note expressing sadness, with a few words of farewell; a present, an unimaginative brooch, nondescript and very expensive, as a reward for her love... Another one who had failed to understand her! She was upset with him for having accepted their separation so easily, she imagined herself to be deeply unhappy and wept bitterly, then thought how she might console herself... that was the answer... now it was her turn to make others suffer... that would be her revenge! Flossie was no longer even mentioned, she never thought about her. Once, in rue Royale, she thought she had spotted a particularly pale head of blond hair... so she had leaned momentarily out of the coupé, and then sat down again, pursuing another idea... No... Her mind was wholly in Arcachon, thinking about Max. That impassioned entanglement had suddenly come apart, in such an abrupt fashion! She needed something new, something that would take her interest in a different direction.

One morning when she was walking along the avenue des Acacias, Tesse introduced a young man to her, Maurice de Sommières. Annhine studied him surreptitiously, then, finding him nice, allowed him to accompany them. They made banal conversation, which Annhine's friendly manner and Maurice's turn of wit transformed into a delightful flirtation. They pleased each other immediately and made no attempt to hide it. He was very young, hardly eighteen. He had often heard people speak of Annhine, he followed her comings and goings, at a distance, loved knowing what she was up to. He had heard about her lengthy travels and thought he could guess at the reasons. At which point he stopped, blushing, embarrassed at having said too much. She teased him, questioned him. He quoted some lines by the poet then on everyone's lips, cleverly and aptly, then he requested permission to call at her house.

'Certainly...! When?'

'I am very restricted, madame, my family still treats me as if I were a young child, but as soon as I can escape it will be to rush to your side. At five o'clock, one of these evenings, if that suits you, I will try my luck, my happy fortune...'

He kissed her hand and disappeared, his emotions in turmoil, carrying away in his heart a whole world of deluded desires and high hopes. "I'll go and see her tomorrow, tonight," he told himself; then a child's pride intervened: "No, I mustn't come running, she'd think I was too fond of her and would laugh at me; I won't appear until the day after tomorrow." He told himself many sensible things, battling his instincts. Three days afterwards, Nhine returned very late; a visiting card was handed to her, belonging to young Sommières, who had called in her absence. He had wanted to wait for her, had left, then come back. In the end he had gone away, very downcast and sad, saying he would come back another day, soon, whenever it might be possible. Annhine was left out of countenance... it was a shame!

The next morning it was snowing. No one would be going to the Bois de Boulogne in this kind of weather. Good...! She insisted on being driven there as soon as possible, wrapping herself in an ermine jacket that matched the white cotton wool silently and stealthily covering all outside. She'd love it, walking in the new snow...! She put on a hat, also in ermine, her little feet were protected by dainty snow-boots, a clinging skirt in black wool, which she lifted saucily, revealing a lower part of the leg both shapely and nimble. She trotted rapidly along the bright deserted paths, nose to the wind, pink from the chilly breeze that plucked at her cheeks, her face animated, her eyes sparkling, with Princess following in her wake, covered in a fur coat matching her mistress's. Suddenly she noticed a solitary man on horseback coming towards her. She recognised Maurice.

'This is funny,' she said to him with a smile as he rode up and greeted her. 'There are only two people in the park this morning, and it has to be us!'

'A stroke of fortune I give thanks for,' he replied. 'But don't stand still, you'll catch cold. Let's walk on, I'll follow you slowly.'

'I'm wearing angora wool,' she said, 'I'm afraid of nothing. This is very rash on your part, though!'

'Inspired, you should say. Sunday is my day off, my holiday, as with little children. Something told me I would run into you, yes it did, in spite of the snow, in spite of... No, you'll make fun of me...!'

'You're too nice for that,' she told him, turning round with a graceful little gesture to send him a smile. 'And in truth,' she said, wagging her finger in reproof, 'you don't believe it for a minute!'

He asked her urgently: 'Tomorrow...? Tell me, will I find you at home tomorrow around five...?'

'Why such an awkward time of day? Everybody is out then, doing things, the park, dress-fittings... Come earlier!'

'Impossible, alas! I'm working...' He hesitated. 'I'm preparing for my exams...'

She laughed at his woebegone expression, the tremor in his voice: 'In that case...later?'

'The thing is... I have to go home...'

He was thoroughly disconcerted, his face ever more desolate.

'You have pretty blue eyes,' she suddenly said. 'Yes... I shall be at home tomorrow. Now, we should go back. Go on ahead so that I can admire you, my handsome cavalier!'

He looked at her, face glowing, happy. He felt a man, powerful, he would have defied the whole world. To kiss her finger tips he bent so low in the saddle he almost unseated himself, then he rode away. In the middle of the main avenue he turned to look back at her one more time. Following on behind, she waved a hand in farewell. In that short moment of inattention, a phaeton appeared on the scene, bearing down on horse and rider at great speed. There was no time to avoid a collision. The horse reared up and took a blow to the hindquarters that caused its two knees to buckle. Maurice righted the animal by sheer strength and pulled it hastily over to the left. The phaeton rushed on its headlong way, leaving him alone once more. After a glance to reassure himself his horse had received no real damage, he rode back towards Annhine, who had followed the unfolding of his minor accident with visible alarm. She was still very pale, leaning against a tree for support. She tried to laugh but her lips trembled, she was unable to speak.

'You don't know how much pleasure it gives me to see you were frightened,' he said as he drew level.

She straightened up, not prepared to let the remark pass.

'Out of humanity for the horse,' she threw back at him. 'Until tomorrow, you great clumsy thing!'

She climbed back into her coupé, forgetting all about

Princess. Maurice hurried after the carriage shouting: 'Your dog! Your little dog!'

She clapped her hand to her forehead and rang the bell. The coachman halted. She opened the door and called Princess.

'That's the first time I've ever forgotten her, and it's your fault...'

She drove away, fussing over her darling, her sweetie, her little pet... Oh, she begged her pardon, yes! Poor Lolotte! She'd been left behind and forgotten... in the park... in the snow! Like a poor person's little dog... a tramp's! Oh! Princess would never forgive her for it, no she wouldn't! Princess, harbouring no grudge, let herself be hugged, and darted her tongue right and left, licking her mistress's hair, her ears, even her veil and her furs.

During the rest of the day, Annhine's thoughts returned to the morning's outing many times: "To think I forgot my Princess, it's too awful!"

In the evening she went to the Folies-Bergère with Altesse and some friends. Towards eleven she wanted to leave, feeling weak, tired, tense. She left their box ahead of the others and caught sight of Maurice, waiting anxiously behind the little door. She almost didn't recognise him, so prettily turned out in evening dress... a real cherub... looking even younger. She held out her hand, remarking briefly on his appearance. He stammered in confusion and watched her move away surrounded by a joyful troupe of friends. "What's the little man doing here, if he's as strictly supervised as he says?"

'I can't imagine your family happily sending you off to the Folies-Bergère,' she said when receiving him the next day.

'Well, yes, in fact,' he replied. 'They let me go to see the wrestling bouts, which are the most fascinating spectacle. I saw you, so I quickly hid behind your box, on the chance of catching your eye or getting a smile, if you came out, or even hoping for a word, which is what happened. I dreamed about it all night...!'

She pulled a face.

'And if I hadn't been there?'

'Then a rather ordinary evening, but the memory of that morning, so bright and crisp in the snow, left such a warm impression, and then the things you said... every word... I've thought about it so much, don't laugh at me!'

His voice changed. It became tender, and suddenly quite childish...

'You told me I had pretty blue eyes... so I looked at myself... several times, like this, watch!'

He covered the lower half of his face with the palm of his hand so that only the eyes and forehead showed...

'And I discovered something that really excited me...! Can't you see? Honestly, it's very noticeable, to my way of thinking at least...! Look at me carefully... carefully... don't you notice anything?'

Annhine studied him, searching for the answer to the riddle but failing to find it. In the end, he took her hand and led her across the room.

'Come and look in the mirror. You must see it. Do the same as me.'

She copied him, masking half her face.

'Well, don't you see anything?'

'No, or rather... yes...' She dropped her hand, discouraged. 'No, I prefer to confess I don't get it at all!'

'What?' he cried, indignant. 'You don't think I resemble you...? The eyes...? Just the eyes, I mean,' he added, embarrassed.

She burst out laughing, then said: 'Goodness me, it's true...! You're right, it hadn't occurred to me, that's all! Do it again! Yes... it's true... there is something... Yes, the shape is the same, and the colour's the same, and almost the same expression of sadness behind them too. I do beg your pardon.'

He felt better and kissed her hands, full of joy now.

'How happy I am, Annhine...! I have your eyes, your pretty eyes!' He stared at her, enraptured. 'You're so beautiful,' he murmured. 'No one else can remotely compare with you. So alluring...! I'm so pleased to have your eyes, Annhine! I'll look at myself all the time when I'm away from you.'

She sat down by the window. The fading light of day coming through the glass framed her delicate profile in a soft, pale, almost mystical nimbus. In her long dress of white satin, very loose, hand-painted with wisteria falling in purple swags, its wide slit sleeves revealing her bare arms and spreading like wings, and her hair bunched high on the gracefully silhouetted head, it was as if some unreal vision was slowly detaching itself from a stained glass window, so ethereal and misty that any change in the light, any sudden sound of voices might make it disappear from view and break the intense charm of this silent dusk.

The effect on Maurice was so powerful he came and knelt at her side, staring at her without daring to speak. Then he began to whisper words to her, in disjointed fashion, very simple words, often the same ones over and again, almost religiously, words which one might say, or sing, or dream in the first flush of love.

Annhine listened, tender, reflective; there was something compelling about this child kneeling at her feet, offering his adoration so prayerfully, so fervently. He asked her permission to go now, he wished to take his leave while still under the spell of this voluptuous vision. As he got to his feet, his hand brushed Nhine's forehead, unintentionally and entirely chastely.

She shuddered, and called to him: 'Maurice?'

He answered: 'Nhine?'

'Maurice,' she said in a voice that made him stop in his tracks, 'you're completely unlike any other man. I feel it so strongly, I think I want to fall in love with you… Is that terrible?'

'Is it terrible…!'

Emboldened by her thrilling words he turned and took her in his arms. His response was a long, ardent, endless, almost ferocious kiss. Annhine returned it with abandon, happy, moved, full of desire…

And the two of them plunged into a love affair of unparalleled joys and exceptional happiness, free of all clouds.

They met everywhere: in the Bois de Boulogne, memorable scene of their first encounter; then, at five, Nhine would return home to see if her little man, her Momo, would come, as if by chance, after an exam or between two lectures; then, before dinner, to say goodnight… Very early in the mornings, at an hour when everyone was still sleeping, he would arrive at her house and it would be he who woke Nhine; he gave her her bath, she got up in his presence: he adored this time, when he had her all to himself, a pretty lady at her toilet, dressing before his eyes. Oh, yes, how totally she was his, in the mornings. In the evenings, his hours were sad ones. As his mother was no longer alive – she had succumbed to a sort of consumption whilst still young – and as two of his little sisters had not survived, victims of the same disease in the springtime of their lives, and since he too was himself delicate, his father kept him very close, watching over him with extreme care, seldom giving him permission to go out, staying with him himself or entrusting him to a private tutor in whom he had confidence. And so, over those long evenings spent apart, Maurice grew fretful. Anxious and jealous, he thought about Annhine all the time and imagined her in all manner of hurtful settings. He pictured her, wearing her finest dresses and jewellery, laughing and surrounded by friends, going to theatres and suppers where anyone could admire her, enjoy the spectacle of her beauty... Then, on other occasions, he saw her at home, in the unsettling décor which so cleverly emphasised her own exquisite frailty – not alone: another man was there, whispering to her, loving her, possessing her...! His head throbbed with terrible rages, he was in pain, his sanity was at risk, and these visions plagued him relentlessly through whole nights without sleep. In the morning he would leave as early as he could, wanting to know, imagining he could catch them out by arriving before the agreed time... The blood drained from his face when, on the doorstep, ringing the bell, he believed he could hear the sound of muffled, hurried footsteps and he felt a rage of desperation at any delay. Then, as soon as he saw a smiling Annhine, opening her arms and offering him her lips, he forgot everything and, intoxicated, overcome, he let himself be carried away on the waves of his vast happiness.

XVIII

One evening when she had no entertainment in prospect and was feeling more bored than usual, Annhine telephoned Tesse.

'My darling, what are you up to…? Whatever can you be doing?'

Still grieving for her loss, hurt by the cruel disappointment, Altesse had shut herself away, wanting to hide her troubles from everyone, except her friend. She answered: 'Nothing, Nhinette. I'm at home, on my own, with my memories. And you?'

'Me? Nothing either. Which is why, tonight, I thought it would be a good idea if we went out and did something different together. What would you say to going slumming in Montmartre or somewhere?'

'What did you say…? Slumming?'

'Yes, it's the only appropriate word for what I have in

mind. Will you come with me?'

'Yes, definitely! Come and pick me up in a quarter of an hour.'

'Right. Get ready.'

A long quarter of an hour later, an impatient Altesse was about to telephone her friend when Aline, her chambermaid, announced Mlle Louisette, from the Lewis fashion house. The sharp retort that sprang to Tesse's lips – 'Are you mad? You know very well I'm not seeing anyone' – was checked by a guffaw of laughter and the sound of whispering and shuffling. Then Annhine appeared, an Annhine transformed, unrecognisable, who, unable to keep a straight face, had somewhat spoiled her own surprise. But yes, Nhine it was, this fluffy black-haired girl, dressed like a factory worker, a factory worker from earlier days it should be said, since the least of them nowadays know all they need to rival our most elegant women... She had a little black skirt, shortened and dipping a bit on one side, and a beige jacket over a simple little white blouse, fastened by three mother-of-pearl buttons with a pink ribbon at the neck, a little straw hat perched jauntily on a head that looked completely different under its dark locks but very sweet all the same. She hitched the skirt to her knees, put her best leg forward and held the pose.

'Aren't I smart, Tesse? Aren't I just the thing? My black stockings, coarse silk, my little patent leathers, very High-Life! And since we'll be going on the wooden horses and cats and rabbits, I've put this silver chain round my ankle to excite the elderly gentlemen.'

And, imitating la Goulue, she raised her leg high in the air, arched her little foot and waved it enticingly. Tesse examined her with amusement.

'A most comical effect, yes. You look like some ravishing little errand girl. Black suits you, it makes your eyes seem darker, you look like a real brunette.'

'I put extra rouge on my lips, painted my cheeks and darkened my eyebrows, that's why I'm a bit late, I wanted it to be perfect! You'd never have recognised me in the street, would you?'

'Never,' Tesse said. 'Where are we going?'

'A long way, the other side of Place de la République. Quick, darling, let's go. We'll leave the carriage a little way off and go on foot for the fun of it, like common people. We'll play the part, put ourselves into character as two little working girls out on the spree. You need a short cape to go over your shoulders, you old beige one, and a boater as well. It's Easter in three of four days, you can go out in a straw hat. There...! Smart...! Put some powder on your hair to make it looser, then coil it on top. Take your jewellery off. I'll allow you one big gold brooch, that's all. You'll do very well like that. Let's go...!'

An hour later they were in the thick of things, arm in arm, having a wonderful time. Annhine was full of exuberance, laughing at everything and everyone. Within a few minutes of arriving, she had made a conquest, in the shape of an old man who followed them round everywhere, wanting to buy them drinks. They tried all the games. The wheel of fortune proving unfortunate, they ran to the merry-go-rounds, meaning to go on the animal rides.

'No, look, there's the new ride, automobiles.'

She jumped on to the seat of a tricycle, Tesse sat in the

trailer behind, and they whirled round, breathless and grinning.

'Feeling sick, Tesse?'

'No, I'm having terrific fun!'

'Me too!'

After five or six circuits, they were ready to dismount, but the proprietor came over and offered to let them stay on and enjoy as many free rides as they liked. They looked so good flying round, a pair of pretty birds like them, they were bringing him in loads of customers. They consulted each other, then, deciding it was uncommon to be treated to so much fun for nothing, they stayed on. When they left they were followed by a crowd of men who'd had their eye on them. Altesse was a little frightened: might they have been recognised? They didn't look nice sort of people! She gripped Nhine's arm tightly, while Nhine, in great humour, smiled at everyone, talked at the top of her voice, wanting to make herself part of this rowdy crowd as convincingly as possible. A young man wearing a worker's blue blouse and cap, a labourer no doubt, accosted her more boldly: 'You ain't half bad!' he told her, nudging her forcefully with his elbow.

She looked him up and down: 'You're not bad yourself!'

'D'you fancy a drink?'

'Who could refuse…?'

They sat down in a café.

'What'll you have?'

'Cherry brandy, and you?'

Tesse was lost for words.

'Me too,' she stuttered, 'same as you, Nhi… Louise,' she corrected herself on receiving a vigorous kick from Annhine.

'What are you called?'

A Woman's Affair

They exchanged names. He was André Denis, he worked in a big candle factory at Levallois. Nhine had hypnotised him, it was a thunderbolt. He'd never seen a kid like her... What about her...?

She lied boldly: her name was Louise Aubin and she made fashion accessories in rue Royale. Madame was a very nice lady – she indicated Altesse – who had always been especially kind to her – she indicated her dress – yes, Madame gave her her old togs, her old hats, so tonight she'd been really glad to do her a favour in return by bringing her along to enjoy herself in a place she wouldn't normally go to; it would take her out of herself, give her a bit of fun. She flashed her eyes at Denis, showed interest in his affairs, paid back his compliments: he was a handsome man too, lord, yes... ever so clean and nicely turned out, everything a girl likes to see, he was...! The fellow puffed out with pride: 'Oh, yes! I take care of myself, I do... you've got to!' Eight francs a day he was earning, right now. Free of ties, no women... if she wanted, the kid, they could see how they got on? They could meet up in the evenings, after work. He got dinner at his lodgings... what about her? She did too, but she was free quite early, quarter past eight, every day, except Saturdays, because on Sundays – she put on the expression of a busy and serious person – on Sundays there's so many pieces of work to deliver!

'And how old are you?'

'Guess!'

He studied her, then, without flattery: 'Twenty?'

She protested: 'Oh! No...! Only nineteen!'

He apologised: it was the same thing...! It was all that dark hair, brunettes always looked more.

'Oh, it doesn't matter... And you?'

'Me...? Twenty-seven...'

'Your future's all ahead of you!'

Ah, nothing mattered any more, he was hooked!

The women stood up.

'We must be going.'

He begged: 'Oh! No, not yet!'

'Yes, yes, we get up early.'

Then he asked if he could go with them. Impossible, Madame had a carriage... and then, he mustn't get the wrong idea, she was a good girl!

'Good...? You mean...?'

Definitely, and she meant to stay that way. Marriage was what she wanted, there!

His enthusiasm only increased: in that case they could see each other a lot, they could get to know each other... 'Why not?'

Yes...! Goodbye...!

No, she must let him come and wait for her tomorrow, when her workshop let her out. She agreed, as a nice girl: 'All right, come tomorrow.' But now he must go, it wouldn't be right to compromise them in front of Madame's coachman.

So they separated. Altesse was aching with laughter. Annhine had thrown herself so whole-heartedly into her character's imagined reality that she almost felt obliged to scold her.

'Behave yourself, for heaven's sake, you'll get us arrested!'

The carriage was some distance away. They were accosted again. This time it was a band of young revellers. She spun them the same line. The young men wanted to take them for supper at Les Halles. One of them, getting carried away, took Annhine by the arm and insisted, whilst the other two latched on to Tesse. To preserve the peace they accepted. The youths conducted them as far as their carriage.

'Madame's carriage...!' Nhine sighed. 'When will I ever have one like that...?'

'Soon, if you want, pretty baby,' her companion said. 'Start modestly, small streams turn into big rivers!'

The men hailed a cab. They would follow behind and meet up at Baratte's. They were about to set off when Nhine's admirer, scenting a trick, darted over, caught her foot and pulled off one of her shoes: 'You can't run away now!'

And he brandished the gleaming trophy triumphantly on the top of his cane.

'Really...? Well, just you see!' Nhine growled as the carriage moved off. She leant forwards and called to the coachman: 'Emile, get away, quick, quick! Keep making detours to throw them off, then drop Madame at her house first, and home after that.'

She fell back on the cushions, worn out, but delighted nevertheless with the fun she'd had that evening! It was entertaining, to say the least, and far from ordinary. And how many new lovers had they collected?

'You see, Tesse, we could have covered all our living costs! I'll believe I'm pretty for a whole three months now!'

'Yes,' Altesse said, 'that was a real success. In the sort of world we inhabit, so many of the men look at the horses first, then the clothes, and only then at the women, which is why you see so many ugly ducklings living the high life. Men seem to be inevitably stupid, all blindly following each other like Panurge's sheep.'

'That's what I tell myself every time I run into Jane Dubois,' Nhine replied.

Tesse continued: 'The worker, the man of the people, his tastes are sincere and natural. You can strut about in your richest, showiest finery but if you're ugly, over-painted or the wrong shape, they'll tell you so without a second thought: "What a fright..! Clear off, eh, hag, bag, shrew...!" While Prince X or Count Z will bow their noses to the ground before madame Hideous herself if she's had the luck to become some royal lover's luxury. If he spots a pretty little shop girl dressed however plainly, he'll happily call out after her, "Blimey, what a looker...!" or something like that, and send her a big smacking kiss.'

'I love the people,' Nhine said.

'They're brutal, maybe, but they're always frank.'

'And here I am with one shoe! It's the funniest thing...! Goodbye, darling, this is your house. Sleep well. I'll try to find us another thing to do. Did you enjoy it?'

Tesse hugged her.

'I'm very touched by the affection you show me, dearest heart. Ah, I do love you! Right, see you soon...!'

As she entered her own house, Annhine thought she must be hallucinating: she found Maurice in the hallway; it was he who had opened the door to her. He was in a state of high emotion, shaking, and ashamed too. He was very fearful of making her angry, but he hadn't been able to restrain his urge to see her tonight.

'A whole night, think of it...! Don't be cross with me,

A Woman's Affair

Nhine, I escaped from the house, I planned it so carefully, and anyway, too bad, I don't care what might happen tomorrow, do you see? Are you glad I came…? Oh, I was so scared! Your maid was very reassuring though, she promised you'd be pleased to find your Momo here, and you'd be coming back alone.'

He carried her off in his arms, towards her boudoir. She was delighted, although a little embarrassed to be discovered wearing such clothes.

'What do I look like dressed like this…? A madwoman! Momo, tell me, do I look like a madwoman?'

He embraced her happily: 'I knew beforehand, my Nhine, Ernesta warned me.'

She crossed into the bedroom, unfastening her clothes. She described her evening, very cheerfully, leaving nothing out: 'So you see, Momo, I lost my shoe, but I retained my innocence, as it says in the song. Oh, but honestly…! If I'd known you were waiting for me, my Momo, my darling, my dear little love…!'

He laughed at her good humour, still dazzled by pulling off his own daring coup as the dashing lover, and feeling uplifted by the sweet intimacy that the late hour made more precious still. It was their first night together. It was a night without rest, without pause. They made love frantically, in a state of near delirium, their hearts as enraptured as their senses, each taking the other in a fury, giving themselves ardently, with abandon. Dawn found them in each other's arms, languid, heavy-limbed, all energy spent. They closed their eyes, as if not wishing to see daylight come, after such a beautiful night… and sleep captured them gently, insensibly, stirring together the vague dream and the heavenly reality of their love!

Towards noon, Ernesta permitted herself a tap on the door. Annhine slept on, but Maurice quickly fled, extricating himself from his beloved's embrace, because for him the hour had become dangerously late. By chance and good fortune, his cleverly prepared disappearance had passed unnoticed at home. He told his mistress so with considerable satisfaction when, at around five that evening, he met her in the Bois on an out-of-the-way path where he often waited for her. They made plans to repeat the joyous adventure as soon as possible and were walking along, smiling at one another, exchanging melting looks, very weary, when Anhhine suddenly gave a start, bumping against Maurice.

'What is it…? What's the matter…?' he said, worried.

She had already recovered.

'Nothing,' she said. 'A shiver. Let's go back, I need to rest some more. I'm shutting my door to everyone, except for you, my love. Come when you can, I love you and I'll be waiting for you.'

He saw her back to her carriage.

"It's her, it really is her this time," Nhine was thinking as she drove back along the main avenue. "I recognised her plainly enough, hiding among the trees. The way she stared at me…! Her eyes carried all sorts of messages, reproachful, but timid and gentle, and hopes, wild hopes… Ah! No! I am strong now, she won't draw me in again, the two of us are over, miss Flossie, in spite of how sweet we were together, in spite of everything I find so seductive about you…"

This encounter had nevertheless left its impression on her, for she thought about it all evening. Towards ten, when she had just gone to bed, Ernesta brought her a letter.

'There are some flowers too, madame, some beautiful red lilies.'

"I expected as much," thought Nhine. "It's her."

'Put the flowers downstairs, in the big drawing room, I don't want them anywhere near me... ah, no, it's black magic, they're a spell.'

Her first thought was that she wouldn't look at the letter either, and she made as if to tear it up without even opening it, but then, being alone – and, oh, she was finding her solitude a terrible thing! – she hoped she might find diversion in the bizarre prose of this odd child.

> Perhaps life is telling me it is worthwhile: from now on I shall listen, since you have come back...! Back to me...? For good...? For ill...? I don't know, but I have wooed Fate with sufficient devotion for her now to plead my cause with Beauty, which can surely not act inhumanely to one who lives through her alone. What I am saying has the modest virtue of being true: I was wandering like a sleepwalker in a wood peopled by ghosts at that soothing hour of dusk when everything takes on a different form. The sky, growing bored, was losing its colour. Suddenly the setting sun darted its final glance through the Acacias, those bored, restlessly rustling trees. Turning my head I saw you and everything in me suddenly woke up in the magical springtime of your gaze. Why did you walk on...? Why did my eyes stray from yours...? What a disappointment, you were not alone! You were quietly

talking to a person at your side, worse than a person: a man! Every torment that Sappho describes, I felt them all in that cruel moment of rude awakening, just when my dream told me there was still Life! Ah, if dream had matched life, the ensuing happiness would have been too much, too much, for everything here on earth must have a limit. Only suffering has been given complete freedom, and it has taken advantage, acting like an immortal goddess! It makes a mockery of my hopes and casts trails of doubt behind every step I take…! Nhine, disperse this dismal procession, send me a word, a word of summons. Take a step yourself – towards me…! Let me come to you…! I want to live a dream of love in your arms, on your lips…! Those rosy petals, how passionately I treasure them: I shall make my mouth the jewel-case where they are kept! And the long kiss I give you will so silence all complaints and protestations that you will never be able to cloud my ecstasy with some too earth-bound word! But from now till then, what a long wait…! What does it matter – am I not yours for all eternity? Nevertheless, call me, darling, quickly… call me! The beating of my heart will speak to you better than any prayer. Feel me…! Throw yourself open to the love that flows so warmly from your
FLOSSIE

"I shan't answer! No…!"

She went to sleep in a state of firm resolve, then, by morning, had changed her mind. "Why not, after all? Poor thing, she's very nice. There are memories we share, memories that shouldn't be forgotten, that bind us. She hasn't done me any harm, all in all. Yes, I ought to answer, but call her? No...! For her as much as for me, our friendship came to nothing, but that's no reason to be dishonest about it... Yes, that's the thing, a note, just a brief note, because there's nothing in common between our two lives, hers and mine... mine especially!"

She thought about all the things that had happened and had put a further distance between them since their idyll had been so fatally interrupted... "Yes, that's what I'll tell her, so that she understands we are not made, the two of us, for a happy union!" As was her habit, she allowed herself to get carried away and ended up saying more than she had intended.

> Thank me for not calling you towards the Outer Form that masks the Inner Me. It thinks of you and is hardly ever apart from you and takes joy in being with you. The rest can give you nothing and teach you nothing, any more than it can tremble for you. So what purpose is served by seeing each other again? The You that once was is something that, for me, cannot return...
>
> Why did your lips utter words that cannot be taken back, or forgotten? Why does the sweetness of your Being reside solely and sovereignly in your astonishing head of hair? I wanted your silky blondness to be a nest, I wanted being with you to be a source of rest, tenderness, a touch of velvet, tranquillity, clarity, a warm bath of forgetfulness and regeneration; instead of that, you plunged me even

deeper into my dark places and my bitterness. Fate was fatal to us…

Your hair, Floss, and the charm of your mind, your bewitching way with words, the wonder of your thinking, yes, but never again your lips, never again the smallest contact between our bodies. Through all that may happen, and for always – if your wishes are the same as mine – this union which no one can take away from us, and no one can understand perhaps, will give me – and you – the true joys, joys that no other people could aspire to… Why do you focus on the things so close to me, the things that surround me? Why descend to these lower levels? Lift up your eyes and listen to your senses: I am here, with you, and I will be so for ever. Would you not see me as I am…? Flossie…? Would you not hear me…? Would you not understand me…?

ANNHINE

As she wrote this letter, her heart began to warm to this way of seeing Flossie and she began to find pleasure in imagining the kind of relationship that might bring them together. "It's true," she reasoned, half convinced, "a friendship at one remove, very pure, very exclusive and life-long: that would be good, it would be gentle and consoling. There's no getting away from it, love is brutish, love doesn't last. If she wants, if she accepts, she will be my friend in this special way, a mysterious and tender little friend."

She had her letter sent and waited for Maurice. When he missed his usual time, she had her coachman drive her to the park. On returning, she found nothing, no message from him, no one had come. She began to feel uneasy. To dispel the sensation of waiting, she telephoned her dressmaker and ordered some new lines to be sent round, along with a sales assistant. The day seemed slow and featureless. She asked for Altesse, who, as chance would have it, had just gone out. Towards five o'clock, she was handed a letter from Maurice, very cold, very dry, and dictated by his father no doubt. It felt like it. Their secret had been discovered, their little intrigue; he had been obliged to leave suddenly; by the time she received his farewell, he would already be in England, but... later he would come back to her – a flicker of rebellion – when he was at last his own master!

Once she had got over her initial stupefaction, she laughed thinly: later...! Love doesn't wait around...! It was altogether too much, really too bad...! Tears of rage welled in her eyes. She was being robbed of the one thing that could have saved her. Her throat tightened, her expression hardened, then eased, merely sad. Maybe he was right after all, the father; any parent would have done the same, but it was hard! Ah, men...! That youngster had no blood in him, he should have resisted, fought, come back to her anyway... Perhaps he would come back. Yes, yes, he would, out of the question to think otherwise. She would soon be getting more letters, written in secret, in haste, with new details saying how they could carry on corresponding. He couldn't live without her, couldn't forget her just like that...!

Nothing came.

XIX

Her thoughts had turned once more to Flossie; her every thought, her whole mind... By the end of this long and ceaseless struggle against herself, in defence of her most basic principles and her natural instincts as a woman, she was at a morally low ebb. Every attempt at resistance foundered, inadequate, futile. On a number of occasions Flossie had been seen in the vicinity of Annhine's house, lingering, watching; thus it was that one evening when Annhine was again mournfully and sadly alone, she thought she caught a glimpse of her in a cab, just there, opposite her windows. Cautiously, she crept forward to stand at the Juliet balcony of the big drawing room. Peering hard, she recognised her: that was surely Flossie, that was her outline, blond and finely drawn, trying to conceal itself in the darkness of the closed cab. She waved an arm in summons. The little pale head leaned forwards, hesitant, as if fearful of making a mistake, of misunderstanding: "Was that really for me…?"

Nhine called out: 'Come over!'

So then Flossie jumped resolutely down from the cab. It was dark, the broad street was deserted save for a few rare passers-by. She approached the window and held out her hands. Annhine held out hers.

'Hold on tight…!' the child said, and, bracing her foot on the stone pediment, climbed swiftly and nimbly over the iron balustrade and dropped lightly into the room next to Nhine. 'First obstacle overcome…!' she said, and threw herself into her arms.

'Don't speak,' Nhine said. 'This is a reawakening, this is a renewal, nothing in the past has ever happened, nothing, I will do anything you want. I have sent you the call, and I come back to you more bruised than ever, discouraged, destroyed. I've done everything I can to forget you, I thought I'd achieved my aim; and now that you have me again, look at the state I'm in, I'm crippled!'

'My Nhine, my sweet Madonna,' Flossie murmured, contemplating her ecstatically, touching her fingers lightly to her cheeks, running them down her arms, barely skimming them as if afraid any real contact might injure her. 'I understand you, I can sense all the things you're not saying… There's nothing we have to do except to savour the joy of seeing each other again, and of imagining the future opening before us. I knew, I felt deep down, that you would call me to you again.'

The evening of sweet harmony that followed redeemed old causes of bitterness. Each opened her heart to its deepest, most vulnerable places. The lesbian wept and emerged from her tears feeling purified, made chaste, seeking now a tenderness that was mystical, a union of souls; whilst the courtesan was seared by the rehearsal of her own distress and despair, of each slow death of some part of herself, a slide towards evil.

'More soiled, more ruined, but wholly yours, with no strength left, to do as you please with...!'

'My love will bring you back to life...'

And there were more outpourings, more moments of tenderness and ever fewer constraints.

Leaning back against Flossie's shoulder, and silent now, Annhine, very pale, seemed like a flower plucked and given up in offering. Her languid, expressive eyes said: "I place myself in your hands, but I am so weak, treat me well, Floss, or else kill me...! Make me die of ecstasy beneath your caresses." And Flossie: "How my love for her kindles my desire, how my desire kindles my love! But what I want is nothing that invokes the beast in us, the earth-bound! Ah! Saving her...! Making her want to live again first...! Making her smile! That's what she needs so badly! When the time is right, I will take her, for she will give herself, she is doing so already."

A fever rose in her: "To possess her, ah...! To hold her naked in my arms, driven to frenzy by my kisses...! My kisses which will be a dazzling rain of fire, sparked by the electricity coursing through our young bodies! For us, excess will only be a beginning, for the desire for moderation is as foreign to me as the moderation of desire!" This idea frightened her as much as it enchanted her: "But could such excess put her life in danger...? Kill her...! Kill the angel who gives herself to me, too weak to resist, so weak, so sweet! Oh! No... I could never...!" A voice coming from the darkness, from her heart, from all around, an unreal voice, told her with grave implacability: "Never...!"

And meanwhile, Nhine continued slowly: "Take me in your arms, then, Flossie; would you reject me...? Warm me, console me, I feel as if I'm going to cry. I could have held it in, said nothing, but I find it good to let my heart speak out to yours, whose own voice is so dear to me!" Aloud, she murmured to Flossie: 'You will become my companion, won't you? I choose you. You will find a way into my soul, you will plant faith there, belief, love..."

'If you, my sovereign, wish it, then I shall be capable of doing anything. Like Prometheus, I shall go and steal fire from the gods to see you happy; but you are not as helpless as you think...'

Nhine sighed: 'I know. It is difficult to believe in a fire when, instead of magnificent flames, all that's left is black and shapeless debris. That's what the passions in my life, joyous or painful, have been like, intense but brief. I have sometimes lived centuries in a few hours. That's what I feel, my head is so empty and my heart so sad.'

'The language of sadness is a form of tender music to me, and I will suffer for you, by loving you more the more you wound me: it will be a way of softening, for both of us, all the harm that has been done to you, my darling Nhine. In the olden days they used to assuage the gods' anger by sacrificing a spotless lamb. I shall be wise and subtle at the same time, refusing to let the enervating breath of Desire trouble me, and although attracted by the exciting scent of these flowers of life, I shall turn away, resisting, because I know that beneath it hides the serpent of destruction.'

'You're making a mistake, Flossie, we aren't forming a

gracious group at the foot of the cross. Think of Marguerite in *Faust* or Elisabeth from *Tannhäuser*... You have to pay, and make your way alone, carrying your grief with you.'

'No, let me believe, in good faith, that I have not entered your life too late, and for us it is not "Like ships that pass in the night."'[3]

They withdrew to the darkest corner of the boudoir and remained there for a long time, making endless and inconclusive plans, very happy... Then they suddenly fell silent and their tears came again, their breath mingled, they trembled in one another's arms, their souls joined. Florence's eyes dilated and an almost ferocious expression of exaltation flickered once more at the corners of her vivid red mouth, the redness of repressed fervour and violence. When they parted their parting involved no separation, for they were too close to each other in spirit for any physical act to disturb their sense of oneness.

---

[3] Longfellow, *Tales of a Wayside Inn* (1874), 'The Theologian's Tale: Elizabeth'.

XX

It was a day of delicious spring weather, a bright sun, gently warm, playing through the fine, pale green lacework of the trees, whose buds were just beginning to open.

Flossie – a Flossie in high spirits, since they had over the last few days exhausted the well of sad confidences – was lying propped up on the pillows of the great bed, seeking to excuse herself for arriving so late whilst at the same time raising to her lips the hands of Annhine, who was gently scolding her. Two elderly ladies, friends of the family, had arrived just as she was about to leave. How cross she'd been with these well-intentioned guard dogs who had blocked her path with a show of friendliness, the sweet path that led to her Nhinon's door, a path garlanded with hopes that guided her from darkness to light.

'You are truly lyrical today, Floss…'

And Nhine got up from the bed.

'We do the best we can, you see? I didn't dare be rude to those poor old ladies, that's the result of being well brought up, a habit worth losing. In the meantime, I shall have to call on your mercy... and your lips. I am more to be pitied than punished.'

Annhine couldn't help laughing at the way Flossie seemed to be taking the whole thing very seriously.

'Very comical,' she said, 'or no, very mad rather! I never know with you where the joking ends... I have a plan.'

'Which is?'

'To lunch here, at twelve, then go out, set off for Saint-Germain and spend all day in the forest.'

'Yes, let's do that. Turn our backs on town, the noise and the people, and flee among the nymphs. We shall take fright, like those startled little creatures, and hide ourselves beneath the leafy canopy, admire resurgent nature, enraptured, recline on mossy banks, sheltered by sun-kissed fronds, our eyes half closed, eluding the bold gaze of woodland creatures.'

'You are too poetic for the morning, Flossie!'

Annhine laughed, teased her, walking up and down selecting clothes to match the radiant weather outside. After lunch they telephoned for the carriage, ordering a wide and comfortable landau suitable for a page who knelt at his lady's feet. They set out in the middle of the day, passed through the Bois de Boulogne, happy to be alone and enjoying the fresh spring air all around them.

When they reached Le Vésinet with its shaded parks they wanted to walk, and got down from the carriage. Then Nhine said: 'No, let's drive on as fast as we can to the forest at Saint-Germain.'

Once they were re-embarked, she said inquiringly: 'Tell me, Flossie, my sweetheart, tell me something... tell me about you... I want to know if you have had lots of lovers, women I mean, and who was the first, and how did it happen, and why. I'm wondering how the idea can have developed in so young a mind, it's a perversion that doesn't seem natural to someone of your tender years, unless it's instinctive, because it's a vice that usually only appeals to women who've grown tired of other things.'

Flossie answered: 'Some women stray down all manner of paths before finding the true one, others have a guardian angel to show them the way, and once they have found a paradise that reflects their own individuality, they stay there. For me, always preferring what is pretty, tender, delicate and fragile, how could I not have loved women, those flowers of light, those flowers that have souls and so many other exquisite things too? The caressing music of a word can draw a response like the quivering strings of a lyre. The harmony of a caress can draw in response words of ecstasy. Describe the shape and colour of all the flowers that have blossomed in the garden of my heart...? Darling, it's not possible...! Your beauty is a fragrance that dispels from my memory anything that isn't connected to you. I can see very dimly, as if through a dream, a cloud of red hair, a living flame that inspired me and showed me what love was. She was called Eva, the mother of my desires, the initiator of my first true joys. I believe she has since died or got married, yes, married, which comes to the same thing. But before, well before that, when I was eight, I remember feeling vague desires.'

'Eight...!' Nhine started. 'You were throttling snakes in your cradle, like Hercules!'

'A sacrilegious woman, you are, Nhinon, blind and deaf; but I shall make you see and hear! I have no more to say...'

'Yes, yes, please, go on.'

'No!'

'Yes, I want to hear...'

'My cousin was pretty, I could forget to go to sleep, just watching her at night. She said her prayers in the evening and I would have liked to know what she desired so that I could beg heaven for it on her behalf. Only I didn't dare ask her, I'm too timid...'

She looked at Annhine who was laughing under her hand.

'You wouldn't suspect it, but it's true nevertheless... We were travelling and she took a photograph with her everywhere, the portrait of a horrible man in a red plush frame. Once I saw her secretly kissing it and I thought: "What a shame...!" and I felt it so keenly and so powerfully that I cried. Then she came over and took me on her lap, telling me she understood my misery, probably caused by a recent scene with my governess who had been unjust towards me. I let her believe what she liked, privately glad that she hadn't guessed my secret.'

'Flossie, you turn everything upside down. When I hear you talk, it seems to me that the things that have no importance in the world's eyes are in fact the ones that do matter. My life – and what I ought to do with it – appears far off and of no interest at all. I'm like a thousand-stringed instrument only one of whose strings has ever been used, and that one is now broken! Any impulse to poetry has had its wings clipped and my existence seems to me today stale, flat and unprofitable, since the best in me has not flowered. What has been cultivated instead is the brute beast, the idler. I have been much desired; I wonder if I have ever been truly loved.'

'We're here,' Flossie interrupted.

The carriage stopped.

'In that case we can go for a long walk and take as much time as we want. The sun's beginning to go down, it will be delightful.'

They were soon in the depths of the forest, unseen by any eye. They walked on, holding hands, in such a perfect harmony of ideas and intimacy of sensations that talk was for a long time unnecessary.

Then Flossie, first to break the silence, said on the way back: 'Who knows, we might have found a magic stream in those woods, little sister to the great river Lethe which brings oblivion to suffering souls. Then I could make you more wholly mine, we would begin life again, together, our old memories washed away. Oh, I'd love it if we never had to go back...! If I could keep you here, all mine, far away from everyone else. What sweet enchantment: this dusk with its dark mystery all around us, Nhine walking at my side, held safe by my protective arm, wrapped in my loving care...!'

Annhine felt all restraint slipping away, touched to the depths of her soul. The harsh lights on the road which ran round the forest, leading towards Henri IV's hunting lodge, recalled them abruptly to reality.

'We have to find somewhere for dinner, Flossie...'

'Have to, have to, it's always have to...!'

Then, suddenly light-hearted: 'I want to be your little husband, taking you out to dinner at the local inn!'

She put on a deep voice and commanded the waiter to bring the menu.

'You see, it is essential that I eat well, little wife. I get up early and I go to bed late. The Stock Exchange is very wearing, but I have to work in order to earn the means to satisfy your many whims... Nhine, I think I'm a man with a beard, whose eyes light up at the sight of oysters, and whose rumpled shirt front is about to get very stained. I wear a heavy gold chain from which hangs the watch my grandfather had and when I open it, there's a miniature of you, which I show off so proudly to my fellow brokers with the words: "That's my wife...!" How nice it is for husband and wife to dine together like this.'

Turning round in her seat, Flossie jumped and gave a startled look: 'I was so caught up with my character it was a surprise to find myself quite different in that mirror. Look, Nhine, I'm just a woman. Put your head close to mine, we make a pretty couple like that, better I think... and we won't have any children either!'

They laughed, pleased with the idea, then, dinner finished, linked arms and left. Out in the evening air, there were soft whispers, kisses, stifled exclamations, suggestions of shy caresses... and Flossie's pretty blond hair came undone.

Darkness slowly fell without their noticing, but they suddenly became aware it had turned chilly. They asked for the carriage to take them back to Paris and set off. Flossie took care to see that Nhine was warmly wrapped.

'I'll spread the rug over both of us. Pull your cloak tight.' She wanted to remove Nhine's hat and pull her hood up instead. 'It's especially pretty like that, no, please, let me... It's a shame to leave this solitude behind, but what a lovely way to go home, the two of us together, huddled up close, alone... in the inky night.'

'No,' Annhine said, 'Look!'

And looking up, they saw the moon slipping slowly from behind the clouds, full and gleaming.

'It will light our way.'

'Ah, and may it fill your senses with its magical powers, the Subtle One, and how I pity the poor creatures so bent towards the earth they cannot possess it...! Unpin your hair... Ah, Nhine, what a forest of light! If I didn't believe that one day you'd be mine, do you know what I'd do? I would coil these tresses like this round your pretty neck and imperceptibly tighten them until you were strangled. They would choke you so fondly you'd die almost without knowing... Then, when you were well and truly dead, I would unwind these silken cords and I would weave them together with a silver beam of the fateful Ashtaroth, which would lift you, thus bound, towards your native realm... So then my love, having nothing more to keep it here below, would unfold its wings and I would follow you. The pale children of the pale planet will come and melt before your lifeless beauty and will lend me their lucid counsel so that I might bring you back to life. I shall bring together my body's opaline fires and your deathly whiteness, there will be an initiation: I shall show you how fingers stroke their languishing caress on pallid brows. And little by little your flesh will resume its pearly shimmer and shining through it will be seen the warm glow of your soul, awakened, enraptured. The virgins of the moon will gather, attracted by the spell of our mystical love, to offer you the throne of their morbid realm. You will glide, sovereign priestess, slow and supple, and I shall kneel at your naked feet whose dazzling matter will be nothing less than the same limpid crystal of which the shining sphere is made...!'

Then, contemplating the moon, which seemed to be looking down on them, she spoke to it: 'Paradise of grieving souls, of gentle lesbians, of women misunderstood, of all women who wish to renounce the vile slavery of natural love, let us rise towards you, lose ourselves among your misty beams, pluck with pearly fingers your strange silvery lilies...! Let us embrace our most ephemeral desires, live out our dreams in all their beauty, caress with phantom kisses, with imperishable kisses, the lips of our wildest imaginings...!'

'I listen to you putting your caresses into words, and I listen to the caressing sound of your voice,' said Nhine, borne along by the charm of this double pleasure. 'I am completely hypnotised, but there is nothing phantom-like about your kisses...! They are definitely not the caresses of pale lovers from a luminous other-world, Flossie!'

'That is something to look forward to...!' said Flossie, her increasingly frenzied desires suddenly interrupted. 'My Nhine...! My sovereign, my fiancée...! Yes, my fiancée, if you will have it...? Your tremblings now are timid promises, promises that you will be mine, completely mine! I shall teach you to know another love, like a religion of the body, in which kisses are merely the prayers. When, in time, you want to be my flower, you will let me inhale you; and when our mood is on a higher plane, you will come and shine in my sky, spreading over me and filling my heart with a heavenly radiance that is both peaceful and divine, O my Star.'

'You intoxicate me, Flossie! The way you describe love

makes my head spin...! I have glimpses of such amazing joys...!'

Annhine had turned pale, her whole body tense. A sudden desire gripped her, powerful, domineering, its fire consuming her. She surrendered to her friend's embrace, quivering, longing for the boundless, brutal ecstasy that would finally calm her tortured nerves, appease her pent-up ardour. They arrived at her door.

'Are you coming...? Yes, come in... Ah! Don't let's put it off any longer, since my soul has understood your soul and my lips want yours...!'

And Flossie followed her.

At the sight of her bedroom and her unmade bed, all the painful memories suddenly overwhelmed her: 'No, not yet, not here, not like this, I want to stay as your fiancée... Go away... go home, leave, quickly, if you really do understand me.'

Almost piously and without trying to hide the tears that sprang to her eyes, the child withdrew.

Annhine stood for some moments where she was, motionless, panting, then, when she found herself alone in the darkness of the bedroom, she abruptly broke into sobs and rolled, like an animal, face down on the carpet, biting on its tassels to prevent herself from shouting out, knocking her head violently against the furniture, seized by a sudden fit, a stream of words stuttering from her lips, none comprehensible but the repeated name of Flossie.

'Go away... no, come back, take me... Oh, no! Oh, no...! I don't want to...! Ah...!'

A strangled sound caught in her throat and she fell back, inert, like a discarded bundle.

A Woman's Affair

When she regained consciousness, she was in her bed. Ernesta was watching over her. She closed her eyes, not fully understanding what had happened, her strength ebbing away, like Narcissus in despair. She could hold out no longer against the tyranny of such an imperious, incendiary desire, burning her veins and parching her lips, reducing her, inescapably, to dust and ashes.

XXI

She woke up the next day very weary, feeling hollow inside, barely able to focus her eyes. She felt perfectly calm, but found it hard to think clearly, her ideas somehow trailing off. She had nothing to say, not even questioning her maid, nothing was of any importance or interest. She got up, hardly knowing what she was doing, and spent a long time getting ready. Sitting dreamily in her bath, she nearly fell asleep. Ernesta had to remind her repeatedly that time was getting on. She came to her senses with a start. Then she stood in front of the mirror, naked, and examined herself: not, as one might have supposed, in order to practise striking the pretty poses she was known and admired for. It was a game which Annhine did sometimes enjoy. She would reach her arms out full stretch in front of her, bring the palms together so that her body made a single lissom shape, and appear to dive forwards with the joyful cry:

A Woman's Affair

"The swimmer...!"; or else, arching her back gracefully and leaning forward, fingers splayed and pressed to her pouting lips, it would be The Kiss; and then dozens of other tableaux along similar lines... Correggio's Venus, for example. No, it was a different matter altogether on this sad morning. Pale, exhausted, shoulders drooping, body slumped, eyes ringed with mauve, she examined herself with curiosity and almost with concern. There was nothing humorous about what she saw now...! No...! It was the end of April, meaning it was rather more than a month since... yes, in fact it would soon be two months... All those changes of climate, her anaemia, the general frailty of her nerves, all those things coming together could easily interrupt the recurrence of that natural cycle which brought one regular reassurance and renewed the blood. Her brow furrowed, her teeth clenched, the colour drained from her face. She glanced down. It seemed to her a slight bulge was already detectable there... yes, you could tell, there was a faint rounding in the impeccable flat smoothness of her belly... Ah, it was too bad...!

'Oh...! The saucy creature...! The saucy thing...!'

And the little face of Miss Florence, amazed, appeared in the opening of the door.

Without interrupting her investigations, Annhine called her. Her voice was dry and hard.

'Come over here, Flossie. Come here...! Look...!'

The child approached, troubled. Seeing the expression of alarm and fright on her face, Annhine spoke more gently: 'Oh, my darling, we're paying for the peace of the last few days with a terrible awakening. I hadn't told you anything before, but I can't keep my suspicions to myself any longer. It's been nearly seven weeks already since… oh, you know what I mean! It's dreadful…! It would be dreadful,' she corrected, seeing Flossie turn horribly pale.

The young woman began to tremble all over; then, unable to contain her rage, she burst out, almost beside herself with dismay: 'Ah, my lovely Nhine…! My beautiful Nhine…! What are you telling me? I know exactly what you mean, nature is bending you to its horrible law! Yet they know exactly what they're doing too, men, the snakes. One of them has left his poison in you…! What sacrilege…! To make a reproductive machine out of such fragile perfection, desecrate the altar to my desires, which were so much more refined than theirs, the cowards…! Daring to spoil such flowers! Oh, I'm furious with them, with those brutes, for all the damage they do, wherever they go, unfailingly, knowingly, cruelly!'

'Ah, Floss! This will kill me! It's so unexpected. It's the worst possible thing that could happen, and I'm powerless to do anything about it.'

'What can we do, darling, what can we do? Tell me… what if we could find a way to abort this seed that's growing in you, because it's a cursed seed, you know…! No good could come of an unwanted being, of a conception caused by the sort of diabolical chance that shames true love! There are barren wives who spend their whole lives praying to be mothers, women who long to give a child everything it's entitled to demand. And we're supposed to respect nature when it commits these clumsy blunders! Oh, you're a monster, a blind, pitiless wild beast, there's no guiding hand of god in your scheme of things…! To satisfy his male needs, man sacrifices absolutely every human feeling…! For the sake of a minute's

A Woman's Affair

selfish pleasure he willingly risks causing infinite misery...!'

'It's true,' Annhine replied, downcast. 'And the woman he's chosen for the purpose, he claims to love her! And then he nearly always absolves himself of all responsibility towards them both. He's the one who's made the laws, he can run away...'

'They abandon, very honourably, a woman and a child, then they go round shouting: it's unnatural, it's repugnant, women loving women! All the imbeciles – there are millions! – who listen to them repeat the refrain without thinking and the whole world rings with injustice and inhumanity. Beauty has to go into hiding to avoid punishment and lesbians keep their heads down as if their sweet union were a crime, because it's a crime to have an opinion that diverges from the mass's! One has to submit and learn to silence, to conceal a thing that is sublime and beyond ordinary understanding!'

In her enthusiastic vehemence, Flossie was losing track of the original point at issue. A stifled sigh from Annhine reminded her of the poignant sorrows of reality. She went over to her friend: 'But I want to help you... I want to...'

'No...! Don't say anything more about it, Floss...! Do you see, if it's there, well, I shall have to make the best of it. If it's there...!' She began to cry. 'I'm scared, you see, I'm scared...! Of everything, of the suffering to come... and of life afterwards!'

'Let me see what I can find out, darling. I know some doctors...'

'No...!'

An anxious Nhine was trying to order her thoughts and recognise her feelings in the chaos of her troubled brain.

A Woman's Affair

"Let's see, Maurice is eighteen... I can't admit a thing like this to a minor. It must be his nevertheless... but there's a law standing in my way, unbending and unjust. Henri, unlikely, and then would he believe it anyway...? All the same, he's the one I have to tell." She felt slightly reassured. "He claims he loves me: he'll be proud, he'll listen to me, why would he doubt me? The others..." She waved a hand in contempt. "The others don't count, it's been too long!" A thought made her hesitate, however... "But...? Ah, no! No! That's too far off even to be a memory any more!"

Feeling more at ease, she dressed, pulling on a long dressing gown in fine white wool, very loose and floating, which she held at the waist with a belt of blue enamel. She had a telephone message sent to Henri saying she needed to see him immediately, it was absolutely essential he came to her house at once, on a serious matter.

'Darling, I'm going to have to send you away. I need to think out how to parry the blow, as they say. See, I'm myself again.'

'No, Nhine, no...!' Flossie begged. 'I don't want to leave you!'

'But my lover will be here!'

'Hide me somewhere, in a corner! Oh, don't force me to go like this, before I know you're going to be all right, that our future's safe.'

'You're sweet!'

And Annhine kissed her, touched.

She led her to one of the downstairs drawing rooms, installed her at a large table and gave her some books, some albums of pictures: 'As they say to little girls: be good...!

Look, I can laugh! Ah! Now I'm certain of a happy ending!'

Flossie gave a nod of the head that resisted interpretation and, her eyes seeing nothing, without turning the pages open in front of her, she set herself... sadly, profoundly... to reflect.

XXII

'Henri…?'

Nhinc hesitated, uncertain.

'Henri, you do love me, don't you…?'

Her lover, startled, took her in his arms and covered her in kisses, to which she offered no resistance. She asked him again: 'You do love me…? Really love me, tell me, Henri?'

'My funny little thing, why do you ask me that so seriously? You mean you're not sure?'

Trying to keep her composure, she played with her enamel belt, running her slender, nervous fingers over its metalled blue surface. Her voice wobbled as she replied: 'I want to be even more sure, I need to be, because… because…'

She suddenly confessed: 'You'll have to love me twice as much, now…!'

He was surprised. He asked: 'What…? What…? What do

you mean?'

'What I said: you'll have to love me twice as much... now.'

Taken aback, he stared at her without replying.

'Oh, you idiot... The fact is, I'm pregnant...! There, now do you understand?'

'Pregnant...?'

He abruptly let go of her and went pale. He tried to laugh: 'You're joking,' he said. 'Pregnant...! It's not possible!'

'Yes, didn't I just say so...? You think I'd make a joke of a thing like that? I'm pregnant...! I'm pregnant...! I'm pregnant...!'

She sat down at the furthest end of the chaise longue, repeating grimly and bitterly: 'I'm pregnant... and it's yours!'

He could think of nothing to say in reply, not yet sure whether to laugh at her or get angry. A thousand thoughts rushed through his mind, a sudden and inescapable series of worries, scandals. What a burden a child would be! What a stroke of bad luck...! Was it really his, for one thing? He didn't dare go too deeply into the question of Annhine's fidelity. And what about his own family...? His position in society...? Oh, the whole story was ridiculous. A hoax, of course it was, a joke, and a stupid one whatever else.

Nhine was watching him, staring at this man with clear-sighted and unconquerable disgust. She wanted to see it through to the end, and continued rapidly: 'Yes, I'm pregnant, my friend, and several months gone.' She was exaggerating now. 'I kept it from you at first, because I wanted to be sure, and that's what was making me ill. My doctor said so, and he agreed with me that I had to tell you. I'm pregnant, by you...!

Who else do you want it to have been, then...? You are my lover, my generous, adored lover, and I don't have affairs behind your back. Ah! No...! It would be criminal of me to deceive a man as good as you are,' – she articulated the words with precision – 'as open, as loyal, as sin-*cere*! The blow falls on us both, it can't be helped. I have no choice but to accept it, but you must take your share as well. So come on, make your mind up, like a brave man...!' She put on a honeyed tone. 'You'll be happy, won't you, very happy to have a baby with me, your darling's baby, your Nhinon's? A baby born out of our passionate love-making, yours as much as mine...!'

And, as he remained dumb: 'Don't you have anything to say? Your head's busy planning such nice things, I expect? Wonderful ideas for our future...?' He looked up at these words. 'Yes, that's what I said, our future, the happiness of the two of us who belong to you. Tell me, Henri, what will you do...? What do you want to do for the family that love has chosen for you, the family love has given you...?' Dumbfounded, he uttered not a word. 'You're silent...? Joy has overwhelmed you? Joy...! Say something then, speak to me, speak...!'

He lowered his head, discomfited, avoiding her gaze, stammering vague phrases: certainly, he would do what he could... he would see.

'Ah! No...! Ah! No...! I demand something be done now, straight away, something definite, if not for me, at least for him. What will you do...? There's no choice, you see, you have to do your duty!'

Embarrassed, he answered her: yes, of course...! That was what he intended, naturally... But... this child... did she want it as much as that...? He couldn't seriously see why...

A Woman's Affair

What good could it do her? Perhaps there might be a way of... God, yes... He knew of women who... that is... he had known some, lots... he'd had a mistress in high society, before her, and the same thing... Oh, it had all gone off fine, no difficulties, very secretly, no one had known a thing about it. In about the fifth month they'd gone to Brussels...

She yelled at him.

'Ah! It's unbelievable...! So they're all the same...! Cowards, all of them, wretches, criminals! He proposes I have an abortion...! An abortion...! An abortion...! From the bottomless pit of your selfishness the only piece of good advice you can come up with is: abort it! Because I, of course, I am no more than a machine for your pleasure, a device to give you a thrill. The machine's out of order? Right, you send it to Brussels or wherever to get itself repaired, and hope it'll come back in good condition, just as exciting and pretty as before. If not... well, there are others...!'

'Nhine...!'

He wanted to stop her. He protested feebly, trying to exonerate himself. But she, carried away by her fury, continued relentlessly: 'Abort it...! Me! Ah, ah...! I may be no more than a worthless whore, but in spite of all the terrifying and disgusting things I've done, I still had this unspoken little feeling lurking somewhere deep in my guts, a streak of something, hidden away, that could maybe have rescued me, set me straight, given me a reason for living... And a man of honour, so-called, whose position in life places him above all suspicion and should at least give him cover for his crimes...' She thrust the word in his face. 'Yes, that's what it is, a crime, do you hear...! This man proposes an abortion...!

He proposes to kill...! Murderer!' she shouted passionately. 'Wretch...! Go away...! Go away...! I'm throwing you out! I hate you...! Ah! I hated you already because I hated needing you! I knew all the time your supposed love was only grubby desire, and that is so base and demeaning! Your passion made me servile, submissive! You had me as if I was a luxury object, your satisfaction was my degradation, and that's the way it is, and that's the way it always will be...! That's the punishment the rest of us women are handed, the weak ones and the loving ones: trapped into this need for a man only to be ruthlessly abandoned afterwards...! And what of your wives...? Your wife is there to service your daily needs. Her job is to run your household, keep your family name alive, look after your children, your house, look after you in your illnesses...!' She laughed harshly. 'Vile illnesses caught far from home, far from them, and most of the time the dreary result of chance encounters...! As for us, ah...! As for us, your mistresses, what irony! You treat us like exhibits in a gallery, the same as you'd choose some piece or other because it was pretty and much-admired and available to the highest bidder...! And we give you our beauty, our youth, our flesh...! Ah! Our flesh, our lips, that's the most painful part of it...! And then, sometimes, our hearts...! But me...' She grabbed him by the collar, pulling him closer to spit her disgust directly in his face. 'When it comes to me... ah...! ah...! I won't have it any more! I rebel!' She let go of him and stood back. 'I'm sending you packing, but before I do I want to tell you – and oh, how I've been longing to! – that I've always known exactly what sort of man you are, right from the first day... that I've hated you, yes... that I've cheated on you...! The child you condemn, the child you want to have killed, it isn't yours! You'd no idea, but you were right when you rejected it! I've cheated on you everywhere, always, every time I had the chance, because I was looking for a genuine, purifying passion to wash me clean of your filth, because I wanted caresses that meant something and would obliterate yours! I've cheated on you constantly, again and again, out of sheer hatred! For us, it's our only way of taking revenge! You've been deceived, deceived, deceived…! Liar…! Cuckold…! Murderer…! I laughed at you, I used you, I made a fool of you, because I could tell you were a monster…! A man…!'

She leapt violently at him again. He tried to get away but she clung to him to hurl yet more insults.

'Ah! I'd have liked to ruin you, to do as much damage to you as I could!' A kind of delirium gripped her. 'Ah! Now I'd like to kill you, kill you… kill you…!' With a sudden twist, he wrenched himself free, absolutely horrified, and managed to get to the door.

She rushed after him, then stopped abruptly, the blazing fury in her wild eyes died, as if a veil had suddenly dropped over them, a dizzy spell rooted her to the spot, unable to move. She staggered, then a horrible pain bent her double. A dull, unintelligible cry escaped her lips.

'Oh, it hurts!' She collapsed into an armchair, head thrown back, overwhelmed by weakness and vertigo. 'Help, I'm going…! I'm going…!'

Her cries of fury, as well as the sounds of doors slamming and hasty departure, had alerted Florence and Ernesta, who came hurrying in to find Nhine groaning and writhing in the torments of pain. Dark shadows ringed her closed eyes and a thread of blood dribbled to the floor. Her movements ceased, but she was still breathing. Greatly alarmed, they carried her to bed, where they arranged her carefully with feet raised higher than head to stop the flow. A neighbouring doctor, hastily summoned, came round at once. She had indeed suffered a haemorrhage. He administered first aid, chloral hydrate, styptic dressings. By the time her own doctor arrived, Annhine, though still unconscious, weak, dreadfully pale, was saved. Altesse was there, at her side. In low voices, the three of them talked things over at length and Flossie told them of the morning's fears.

Pregnant...? Ah, no, that wasn't the case, alas! Her severe anaemia and nervous disorder were the sole causes of this setback, which was not uncommon in these sorts of illness. Today's accident was going to make her trouble worse... it would be long, difficult... but not, in the end, hopeless. The doctor broke off, listening: the telephone in constant use, people ringing at the door, the rumbling of carriages in the street, a general bustle and din. He lowered his voice: 'And then, as soon as she's fit to be moved, in twelve to fifteen days' time, you must take her away somewhere. Here, in the middle of all this noise, she'll never be able to get back on her feet. Any long journey would wear her out too, because this illness she has is already quite advanced in its course, complications are possible. Her anaemia is pronounced, her breathing much weakened, and her heartbeat is irregular, oh, a minor heart disorder, nothing organically wrong, but it amounts to a serious situation, given the poor state of her nerves, which are very disturbed, and her cast of mind, which makes her over-think things. It leaves her with little power of resistance. She needs a very personalised regime: showers, a diet, I'd advise serum injections and perhaps a few specialist treatments using electricity. It would be a good idea to settle her in a nursing home.'

And to their indignant exclamations he replied: 'But a nursing home isn't what you imagine, it's the wisest course.' His voice became commanding. 'And I would add, the only course! I know an excellent one in Passy; the care there is first class and the air good. In fact, last summer, I sent Mlle Marbaud from the Comédie-Française there, and she emerged transformed. You'll be able to come and see her, just you two and her family, because it would harm her recovery to be visited by crowds of acquaintances. She can take her chambermaid with her, it will be like being at home, and they'll make sure she follows my orders strictly. She'll have tranquillity, the ideal break from life, absolute rest, and she'll return refreshed, alert, sounder and stronger than ever.'

Altesse was convinced, and said: 'Yes, doctor, I understand you perfectly. She will go. As soon as you judge the time is right, I undertake to persuade her it's the only thing to do.'

Flossie remarked quietly: 'I find this very sad.'

'No, no, it's necessary. She has to. If you want the best for her, you must encourage her to go as well.'

'I will do,' the child said. '…And afterwards…?'

'Afterwards, you'll need to take her away somewhere for a while, as a distraction: the mountains, or a watering place.'

In the troubled little soul of the younger woman a battle raged between her sense of reason and her love for Nhine. Suddenly her features set decisively: 'Right, we'll do all of that…!' The doctor, surprised, looked at her more closely.

'But I don't believe, madame or mademoiselle, I've seen you here before. May I ask who you are then...? Are you a member of the family? Her sister, perhaps?'

Tesse said: 'No, she's a friend.'

'No,' the child said sharply, 'more than that. Annhine is everything to me, I adore her...!'

Altesse sent the doctor a glance that the doctor understood: 'Ah! That too would be fatal for the patient. I must keep you away from her.'

'Doctor!'

'But yes, if you love her you must be willing to do anything that helps her recovery.'

'But, doctor, I love her in a way you can't even suspect.'

'That's as may be. But her mind is disturbed and overactive and if it can't be calmed down she may lose it altogether. No, madame, I shall do my duty.'

And without wishing to stay and hear more, he left the room with Altesse, while Flossie slumped, very upset, murmuring to herself unhappily: 'Ah, these doctors in their bushy beards, brutes, all of them! They only consider the health of the body and ignore the health of the soul! But I'll be stronger than them, the weak resort to cunning, I'll foil their plots against us. They won't keep me away from her or from achieving my goal.'

Tesse returned. They looked at each other, mute, as in the aftermath of some disaster.

'Are you staying, miss...?'

'No! I'm leaving... Goodbye, madame. And will you, I hope, give me permission to come and find out how she is...?'

Her voice dried up, her lips quivered, she was about to

break into tears. Altesse was struck with pity, drew her close and said, simply: 'Poor little thing!'

In reply came a sob, and the child wept, huddled into Altesse's shoulder, for a long time. Altesse, in charity, and herself moved, offered words of encouragement and advice and forgot for a while her vague rancour against the woman whom, privately, she accused of exerting a harmful influence over her sick friend. They parted as friends, motivated by the same desire to overcome Annhine's frailty and the deadly illness that threatened to steal her from them.

As Henri did not appear, Tesse tried to discover the reason for his absence. She quickly understood. At the mere mention of her lover's name, Nhine became distressed, feverish, she mumbled incoherent, violent words of hatred that revealed the extent of her disillusion and disgust. Henri's name was never mentioned again. She readily accepted the idea of going into seclusion and soon came to think of it as desirable: the ill have these intuitions. She felt an increasing distaste for her own home and everything around her, wishing instead for a complete and radical change, with the idea of forgetting it all and in the hope of emerging completely reborn. She asked about Flossie and was told that the young woman had been obliged to leave, to return to her own country; they invented excuses: her family, who had suspicions and who had wanted to get her away from Paris. Annhine fell into a state of prostration from which nothing could lift her. After an initial outburst of anguish, she had submitted to all their arrangements, resigned, waiting for any sort of improvement or release. She remained in bed, not speaking, for days on end, inert, not even turning her head but staring constantly into the same dim corner of the room. Suddenly she called out: 'I can't breathe!' and in a panic, choking, struggled to sit up against the pillows. She pleaded, wild-eyed: 'I'm dying...! I'm dying...! Ah! Don't let me die...! Tesse...! Ernesta! Save me...! Save me...!'

Then she slumped back in a deep faint and lay for a long time unconscious. She suffered black-outs about three times a day. It was dreadful. Oh, she wanted the end to come... or else she would have undergone anything to be cured...! When she was in possession of her senses again, she took her medicines docilely, despairingly; tears ran down her cheeks. One day when the doctor stood over her she asked him plaintively: 'Can you tell me, doctor, what people feel when they're about to die?'

He answered her with feigned assurance: 'Oh, my child, you're nowhere near that point, your symptoms are nothing like serious enough.'

And when she insisted, with the obstinacy of the ill, he ventured: 'Well, your sight begins to get more and more clouded, you see dark patches, your vision becomes occluded... You haven't got that, have you?'

'No.'

'Then you've nothing to worry about.'

She pretended to go back to sleep and the next day she welcomed him with the remark: 'You know, doctor, those dark patches over the eyes you told me about yesterday, I had them...! I'd been having them for three days...! You shouldn't have told me. It's not true, anyway, because I haven't died and I'm feeling much better.'

When she was asked if there was anyone she would like to see: 'I want to give up the ghost in peace, by myself... leave me alone!'

Sometimes she called Altesse and held her hand, without speaking; then she buried her face in the pillows and lay motionless. Frequently, at night, she woke with a start, terrified, thrashing about and trying to beat off invisible enemies, a huge giant crushing her under its foot... here...! here...! – she pointed to her chest, struggling to breathe. Or else it was water that submerged her, cold and asphyxiating. She writhed in her sheets, calling out names no one recognised, strangers, lovers, former friends; spasms of fever made her shiver; then coiling snakes reduced her to terror; a cord tightened round her heart, strangling her... fire burned her, consuming her altogether... strange apparitions, foul and terrifying. She was bathed in sweat; blood rushed to her head, it felt her temples must burst; then she turned pale, an intense cold took hold of her, her teeth chattered. They gave her all the help and sustenance they could: sub-cutaneous injections, oxygen masks, a spoonful of meat jelly, a little milk, potions. In the first week of May an improvement was noticed. She seemed stronger, calmer. She was hungry, thirsty, wanted to talk, to know what was happening. The doctor therefore took his opportunity and moved her to rue de la Pompe and settled her in the nursing home. They would begin a course of hydrotherapy, very gradually and carefully, following each small improvement in her condition. While she was taken to the nursing home in a carriage, she fainted, her head falling against Altesse's shoulder. Her friend was struck by the changes that had come about in such a short time. In the harsh light of day, her drawn, emaciated face had the yellowish tint of an ivory figurine. The delicacy of her pinched features stood out all the more, as if

A Woman's Affair

strangely idealised. She came to and had to close her eyes, dazzled by the daylight, then put her head in her hands.

'I feel as if she's going away, you see,' she whispered.

At the clinic, the nurses thought at first it was a dead woman who was being delivered to them. She adapted quickly to the regime, finding the air of calm very beneficial. Altesse came every day and stayed all day long. Nhine remained silent and dreamed: a hundred extravagant plans took shape in her afflicted mind, distant travels, changes of lifestyle. Soon she felt stronger; as the heat of approaching summer revived the earth, so it filled her too with a sense of great well-being, the languid ease of a convalescent. She was able to get up and drag herself unaided as far as the chaise longue. One morning, she heard music in the courtyard and made the effort to go to the window and open it, her spirits lifting. Full of curiosity, she leant out. It was a strange-looking old man holding a monkey on the end of a rope. A long white beard made him look like a character from the old fairy tales. He had a pair of blue-tinted spectacles perched on the end of his nose and a jolly appearance. Beside him a very grubby woman in rags held a wooden bowl full of small coins and was selling song sheets. And then there was a child, singing a lament in a very fresh and penetrating little voice. Annhine had to lean against the wall several times to get to her purse and retrieve the handful of coins she wanted to throw down to them. She tried to throw them across the courtyard to fall at their feet and had to give up. Overcome by weakness, she grabbed the window sill for support, almost bent double, and tossed them limply out. The woman thanked her with a smile, then stared at her, muttering something.

A Woman's Affair

Annhine looked slowly about her. The beggar was still talking... who to, then...? Why, yes... she was talking to her! What an extraordinary thing! What did she want?

She called down, gesturing at herself: 'You mean me...?
'Yes!'
'Oh...!'

Her head swam, it was her, Flossie. She had made herself unrecognisable, in that get-up. She felt hot all over, but found the strength to smile.

'Ask,' the woman was saying, cupping her hands to make a loud-hailer, 'ask for a dress to be sent round from Callot's, and say you have to have an assistant here, for four o'clock!'

A wave in acknowledgement and Annhine withdrew into the safety of her room, shattered.

So, it was Flossie...! What a strange child...! Ah, now she at least was someone who could do her some good... They had lied to her, why...? That was very wrong! What force was it in Flossie that enabled her to overcome every obstacle like this, defeat all their tricks...? A new life... far, far away... she would leave them all, all the liars, the bad people! Flossie would carry her off, she would find a way to rescue her, then cure her! The sea... embarkation, the voyage... lands unknown... better lands...!

She played her role very naturally. She absolutely had to have a pretty blue dress, sky blue, very bright, in taffeta, with white embroidery. It was for her first excursion, for she would be able to go out soon, wouldn't she...? No, no, she would not leave it for later, she wanted to order it immediately, today, this morning or anyway this afternoon at four o'clock, she wanted it to be quite ready for the day when she would be allowed out for a drive. In the end she stamped her foot, wept, commanded and was obeyed.

XXIII

They were alone. Nhine had sent away the models and the fitters from the famous fashion house so that she could speak with Flossie, who had taken advantage of all the coming and going to slip in, wearing a brown wig and the plain and slightly worn costume of a neat and honest little working girl. She was clutching a sheaf of samples in various colours.

'I'm very weak,' Nhine murmured, 'and I'm worried someone might come.'

Flossie looked at her, overcome with emotion, and couldn't utter a word. Nhine had so many, many things to tell her she didn't know where to begin. Then it all poured out, her illness, her hopes, her desires: 'And you must help me get out of this, take me with you, somewhere far away… I shall come alive again, you will tell me lovely things. And I'll have nothing to do with any man again, ever, ever, finished!'

Flossie had recovered from her initial shock. She crossed to the door and turned the key twice, then ran back to Annhine, who was now laughing with malicious pleasure at the success of their clever stratagem. Her head, though, still felt quite dizzy from having seen so many people. She lay back on her chaise longue.

'Hold my hand, Floss, and talk to me.'

The tender, caressing voice of Flossie soothed her gently, like the lulling chant of religious devotions: 'Joys without end,' her friend concluded, 'for both of us.'

Then a sudden concern made her ask: 'Nhine, my darling, tell me, did you ever get the letters I sent, the flowers...? I came here several times a day, very early in the morning, in the evening, even at night. They wouldn't give me any news of you at all. I only knew you were getting better and would be leaving soon. Your door was barred, I was being shut out, I kept running up every time against the cruellest, strictest orders. Then I suddenly took fright... I was scared they'd take you away one day to some distant place and I wouldn't know where.'

Then, reproachfully: 'And nothing from you...! Not a word!'

Annhine lifted her pale thin hands and plaintively turned the palms up. She said, sadly: 'From me...! Ah, my poor darling, but I don't even have the strength left to hold a pen...! Ah! I really believed it was all over, yes... But now, happily, it's all in the past, that terrible dream...! So, you thought about me? A lot...? Often...?'

'I never stopped. And do you want to know what else I've done...? Here, read this!'

A Woman's Affair

She passed a letter across; Annhine shook her head and put a hand up to her lustreless eyes, which had darkened and sunk deeper into her face.

'Read...? Do you know, Floss, since the accident I haven't been able to read a line, but I shall try anyway. Show me...'

She took the sheet of paper and attempted to decipher it.

'*Time has... time has... time...* I can't...! I can't...! The writing just dances in front of me, it makes my head spin... I'll have to give up!'

And the paper slid off her knees.

'You poor angel!' Flossie said. 'My martyr, my madonna...! It's my letter to Willy, my fiancé. I'll read it to you, that won't tire you too much, will it?'

'No. Read, read, your voice does me good...'

Flossie sat on the floor, next to Nhine, and read out the following communication:

> Time has softened my anger, as proved by my writing to you once more: something about your last letter touched me. Yes, I am ready to take you back, my dearest Will, my little fiancé; but admit it, you deserved being cast into the darkness these last few months, because you failed to respect the thing I love. It isn't clear to me how you meant to spare me a disillusioning shock by giving me one, and the final scene in that house of shame revolted me in the extreme. Not so much because of your motive, I never analyse the finer points of such questions, but because you demonstrated a complete lack of sense. It is not acceptable for the person I have chosen to accompany

me through life to be so inferior in intelligence, so stupid, and your plan – to make my Beloved an object of disgust – was extraordinarily inept. Did you not know me well enough by then? Didn't you know that nothing could have turned me away from Annhine or broken the spell of enchantment her magnetic beauty continues to cast on me? I loved her, not just for what I could see, but for all the dreams she inspired, and when we feel that one weak mortal is the living embodiment of all our wildest fantasies, we must make her every possible allowance. You do for me! Why shouldn't I, for my part, be capable of showing the same sort of love to Nhine…? But in my usual headless way, I am straying from what I have to say to you. To come straight to the point: whether this seems possible to you or not, for the first time in my life I love someone with a love that is steady and unbreakable. When you come to know Nhine you will understand me better – in the meantime I must ask you to make no blasphemous observations, nor will I even allow you a smile. Take me seriously for a moment and listen to me carefully, for I need to speak to you frankly about something that might radically alter the lives of all three of us. Since it is not possible for me to marry Annhine, I agree to marry you, as had been arranged, and we then leave this place at once for some distant country, taking with us that frail and precious plant who will be our child. Setting love to one side, it seems to me more worthy of a civilisation that prides itself on its capacity for reasoning to work

A Woman's Affair

at preserving what exists already than to populate the earth with new creatures no one will know what to do with! At all events, holding the instinct for motherhood in horror as I do, I prefer to choose the people who matter to me rather than leave the job to chance or the clumsy Omnipotence that is... Nature!

It is rare that the thing that one most wishes should be possible and profitable at the same time. When this phenomenon is within the easy grasp of three people, therefore, it is incumbent on them to put it speedily into execution. So, if the accomplishment of your desires is still dear to you, cable me and arrive here as soon as possible to give me the independence I need. We shall announce our marriage for the end of the month. Malicious tongues will wag, but who cares...! People know me as an eccentric already, my marriage to you will be one of my more sensible fantasies, that's all. As for the rest, your millions will silence them: no one shows disrespect towards the rich! Come, and as quickly as you can, because Annhine is not well, she is sick in both body and soul, and she is in dire need of a change of circumstances. Let me also say that if you marry me you will perhaps be making the biggest mistake in your life, but it will not be irreparable, because the day you find another woman you can love and who can offer you the joys – if that is what they are – of hearth and home and family life which mean little to you today, I would give you back the freedom you are giving me and, on top of the divorce, you would have my blessing, because, fundamentally, I wish you to be happy! If you aren't happy with us, you will be with someone else, someone who can give you more than your friend Flossie ever can, or perhaps less, if you are to be believed when you say that you would not give up, for possession of all the women on earth, a single one of my soul-tingling caresses...! Come, and everything that is best in me will thrive. You can't imagine how grateful I will be to you for enabling me to be what I wish to be. All the higher certainties I am striving towards I shall find through you and I shall not be disappointed because you are my friend, my support and will be my companion on the long and sad journey of life towards better things, for the purity and infinite reach of my feeling for the one I love, the depth and sweetness of my friendship with you are enough to make me certain there is a realm beyond!

This present life can be a delicious foretaste if you help me cut this Gordian knot and solve the problems of material existence.

In the hope of very soon having the pleasure of bearing your name, I sign my own.

FLORENCE TEMPLE-BRADFFORD

Annhine, touched, said: 'It's good, it's very good! Thank you, Floss, and have you sent it...? When...?'

'A few days ago, I should receive a telegram any day now.'

'And was it true, then, really true, all those things you said...? Have you thought about it properly...? It's a bit mad, what we're intending to do!'

'Wise people will call it mad; and mad people will call it love!'

'Darling...!'

She fell silent, then, suddenly: 'It's getting late, when will you be coming back? And how...? You may have got in without being noticed but you'll surely be spotted on the way out. You'll have to think of some new trick. How funny you looked dressed like a beggar, my Floss, doesn't your wig change you!'

She spoke with difficulty, slowly, her words not at all clear, as if each one drained a little of the life left in her. She noticed it herself: 'Ah! I've hardly any strength...! Do you find me changed, very changed...? Be honest!'

And her inquiring stare held Flosssie's.

'I find you even more adorable like this, my pale angel, more other-worldly, more ethereal, you look like a saint, Nhine, a soul inspired.' Her voice took on the accents of a prayer. 'Oh, my fragile flower, you will, won't you, let me love you properly as I so long to do, and you will give me your heart...?'

Her thoughts turned practical: 'I must go. It's a cruel wench, but I can see the lights are being brought.'

'The lamps make me sad,' Annhine said. 'I don't want any, my eyes are so weak I have to close them; see, even a shaded little lamp like that dazzles me. Night-time... night-time is better for thinking, you can dream with your eyes open... Good then, keep your hopes high, and goodbye!'

'Darling, look after yourself carefully, you need to be a little more robust before we make our escape. What fun it will be, abducting you! Keep it in your thoughts, and work on making yourself stronger.'

Nhine could hardly keep herself straight in her chair; she made a vague gesture that might have been a kiss and murmured: 'I'll be waiting for you... until very soon!'

Flossie withdrew, damp-eyed. A great sadness enveloped her, pierced by gloomy presentiments. When the door swung shut behind her she thought she heard menace in the squeaking of the hinges and the scraping of the lock.

'So thin, and her skin so translucent, all her ardour gone, her pretty body ravaged, propped against those bright cushions... She's wasting away from some invisible affliction, her eyes are dull and the look in them is already melancholy and far away, withdrawn, not of this earth. Even her voice sounds faded, like an echo...! Is she going to stay with us...? Oh, I'm so frightened, and today the sense of my own uselessness is so strong... the uselessness of everything...! It's as if spring has come to an end and a flower is dying, its petals coming off and blowing away! That was its life, alas! Hers too...! Poor little thing! No, happy rather, I'm the wretched one, me, the survivor... Oh! Shall I have come so close to my happiness only to grasp at nothing!'

She refused to admit it to herself or believe it, willing herself to hope in the face of despair.

'No, she's young, so young, so young, she'll get over it, of course she will. A memory comes back to me: Mary Hampton, a childhood friend. She had anaemia and her case was so severe she was blind for three years. No one could understand what lay behind it, and today she's as strong as could be...! so strong...! All too strong, alas!'

A Woman's Affair

The image rose in her memory: Mary standing before her, fat and ruddy. Mary, seven or eight times a mother, breasts swollen, looking like a wet-nurse, a fertile matron, her stomach misshapen from repeated parturition, horrible to see, her gait awkward and heavy. This image, brutally natural, filled her with such disgust she wondered if she didn't prefer the other a hundred times over: the poignant impression of that little suffering figure, lying on her chaise longue as if sinking finally away, so thin, so white, so beautiful...! Which death should she weep over, then...? That of Form and Beauty, the unchanging and universally dominant religion...? Or the end of a radiant day that softly vanishes in the dying reflections of a lake's peaceful waters...?

Life...? Waiting and fearing! Hoping always for the realisation of the same dream, uselessly, perhaps...! Uselessly...!

XXIV

'A beautiful May day, Tesse...!'

Annhine stirred restlessly in her bed. She had not left it for a week, still too fragile, but on this bright morning when cheerful sunlight spurred lawns, hayfields and flowers to new growth, she seemed to be stronger, her cheeks had a trace of colour, her eyes gleamed...

'What pretty roses...! And white peonies... and some lilac! What a wonderful bouquet...! Thank you, my Tesse...!'

Her slender hands reached for the flowers; she smelled them with delight: 'What a heavenly scent!' Then she wanted to separate them stem by stem and arrange them in a vase.

'Bring me some fresh cool water...! They smell of summer, heat, green parks, leafy shade, lawns, ah... the countryside...! Darling, what do you think: I'm going to get up. I was waiting for you, to help me, the doctor has given his permission, and then in three days' time we'll leave for your house, at Ville-d'Avray, it'll be charming! There's nowhere else I'd rather be: all of Paris in easy reach and yet you're surrounded by green fields. I certainly won't be going to the park at Saint-Cloud for instance, it made me too sad last time. I remember, it was with Flossie... where is she, Flossie...? Gone...? No...! No...!' She shook her head. 'No more white lies, Tesse, I know the truth...!' She leant over to confess in her ear: 'I've seen her, she came here, yes, she did, and she promised me she'd come back, she's going to take me away, we're to get married, yes, to the same man, just you wait and see, I'll explain the whole thing to you afterwards, yes, my big sister, because you...' she waved her hands expansively, 'you, that's something sacred, you understand, that's part of me, only death can separate us! Tesse, I'm feeling much better... and so what shall we do...? Ah, yes! Summer with you, I'm not strong enough yet to travel very far, summer with you, then will come the big up-rooting, all three of us with that Willy, he'll do all right for himself, won't he, with all us women...! Oh, I'm in such good spirits, I'm excited, I'm happy, I'm going to eat a lot, I'm hungry, I want to be myself again very quickly, I want to get fat... And if he doesn't want to come with us, we shall live together all the same, we'll travel all the time, I'll go back to acting, you too, she can start as well, we'll put on something charming, a show no one's ever thought of before, unique, we'll be a troupe that travels the whole world, but we'll never, never visit countries where the cold bites deep, where it snows.'

'Darling, you'll tire yourself out, don't talk so much.'
'No, listen...'
She lowered her voice and carried on.

A Woman's Affair

'A beautiful yacht, a great big one, always on the move, no house, not anywhere, no country, wherever fancy takes us, our home will be the whole universe; or maybe instead: a gipsy caravan, something really splendid, properly fitted out, comfortable, smart, which we'll live in, here one day, somewhere else the next... in villages, in forests, always in the sun...! I don't know if you're like me, but I dream of a country where it's too hot... Come on, my stockings, my dressing gown...! Pink, everything pink...!' She looked at Tesse. 'You seem unsure, but I've been given permission, ask, Ernesta knows.'

Without too much difficulty she managed to roll her stockings on: 'Ah, my legs, my poor little legs...! My calves have shrunk to nothing...! Never mind, we'll put that right...! Look, it's funny!'

She poked at the flabby skin with her finger, making the slack flesh wobble.

'A few more nights of proper sleep, like these last three! Oh, such wonderful sleep...! I had dreams, though, what about...? What were they...? Ah, yes, they were about water... dark, at evening time... a big pond with beautiful water lilies... You wanted to pick them and I did too, we leant forward, we kept leaning forward... the flowers kept moving further away, out of reach, then, just as we were about to catch them, they weren't water lilies any more, they were a flight of gulls, all white and slowly unfolding their wings and flying up and away from us... and we followed them up into the air, and then... they turned back into flowers and plunged into the water to escape us, and it went on like that, on and on, oh, but it was pretty, so pretty, nature, the setting, it was perfect...! Everything bathed in unworldly light under a full moon. Flossie was there, just standing, happy to gaze at her reflection in the water while telling us we were silly to be giving ourselves so much trouble...'

Annhine was perspiring now, exhausted, out of breath; she had to stop.

'I'll keep my nightdress on, anyway, under my dress, because it would be too tiring to change out of it, too many arm-holes and sleeves... My dress, quick, quick...!'

'Calm down, Nhinette, there's no hurry!'

'Yes, yes, there is. I want...' Her little tousled head emerged from the satin sheath Ernesta slipped over her. 'There...!' She arranged the folds, shaking out the white chiffon so that it fell evenly round her. 'There...! At least I'll look like something...! I have an idea someone will be coming to see me... that I shall have a very nice visit...'

'Who from, darling?'

'Ah, that's the point...! Curious, are you...? You'll see...!' She was thinking of Flossie. 'I shan't tell you!'

'If you want to see someone, on the contrary say so, and we'll go and fetch them!'

'No, I mean yes, I do want to, but it's much nicer if they come of their own accord...' She found the idea amusing, wondering what scheme the young woman would devise this time to get to her. 'Tesse, I want to stand in front of the mirror, my legs are wobbly, I'm a bit dizzy... can you help me...?'

Supported by her friend on one side and Ernesta, whom she leant on, on the other, she slid, rather than walked, towards the wardrobe mirror.

'I don't look too bad, do I...? No need for any rouge,

nothing like that...! And my lips...? And my gums...?' Pulling a face, she opened her mouth. 'Well, honestly! If those are the lips of an anaemic, well...!' She stuck her tongue out. 'I am reborn! Glorious summer is come, darling...!' Her joy was infectious. 'Let go of me...!' She stood quite straight, without support, then swayed. 'No? Ah, all right... not all at once...! Ernesta is going to tidy the room now, take me out on to the balcony.' There was wisteria in flower and she plucked a number of heads to make adornments for her friend. 'I want to see where they should go for myself... just to discover if I still have taste! There, in your belt, then in your red hair. That's beautiful! Beau-ti-ful...! Now watch... what I want is roses, give me some... different colours...' She pinned them at her breast, then set one in her hair so that its petal brushed the middle of her forehead. 'It's cool, it's sweet, against my skin...'

She sang:

> *'Make every brow fresh flowers bear,*
> *Thread lilac blossom in their hair.'*

'Shall we have lunch beside your bed, darling?'

'No, no, out here, on a little table. It's so nice, so warm, I want to stay up! I'm going to have to get used to it...!'

'Aren't you afraid you'll...?'

'No, no!' She was laughing. 'You amuse me, my Tesse, don't you see the progress I've made? In fact, no, you're here all the time, it isn't so easy to tell, but you'll see, you'll see...!'

And a little later, as lunch was served, a joyful Nhine ate heartily. Tesse couldn't get over it, she had imagined outcomes that were very different and much sadder...! Nature, incomparably its own best cure...! Nhine was definitely not the same any more, she seemed much better! And surely, summer would see her fully restored, it was beyond doubt now. To think how readily – oh, she was going to drive such silly thoughts right out of her head from now on – how readily she believed a sad end was coming, so dark, so near: Annhine dying, succumbing to one of those appalling attacks, her own flight now without purpose, her flight to Italy, to peace, her voluntary renunciation of all worldly pleasure and pain. Ah, one should never lose hope!

The convalescent, with plenty more that she wished to say, started off once more: 'You see, Tesse, I'm going to sell everything. Here's what I'm thinking: a great big sale, one final burst of noise and fuss surrounding my name, then no more jewellery, no more smart town house, nothing left of the old life, I want to put it behind me for ever; and that will give me some money, quite a lot... What about you? Would you do the same, what do you think...? We shall realise our assets to buy our freedom! I shall change my name so that everyone will think I'm dead, because that's my idea, and when it's all over I'll write a letter of farewell, and I'll throw my clothes in the water, as if I'd meant to drown myself. They'll believe it was suicide, they'll never find my body, the body of Annhine de Lys, and little Anne-Marie – alas, I have no other name – little Anne-Marie will resume her life as a wanderer and vagabond...!'

Disturbed by the incoherence of these wild plans, Altesse watched her closely, fearing the onset of another bout of delirium, but Nhinon, still voluble, carried on: 'Why, yes... It will truly be a new life. Everything around me will be brand new, different, changed, myself included...! And if anyone ever comes up to me thinking he recognises me and calling me Nhinon, I'll tell you what I'll do to show him he's wrong...! I'll make the deception complete by talking with a lisp, I've always thought a slight lisp was rather adorable, it's childlike, it's sweet, don't you find...? And I'll say: "Oh, you're mistaking me for the beautiful de Lys, but isn't she dead...? I've often been told I look like her...!" I'll let my hair grow, very long, and I won't curl it any more; if necessary, I'll even change its colour...' She checked herself. 'Ah, no! I won't be able to do that, because... because... you don't know, Tesse, my angel, I haven't told you everything. In my worst moments of fear and suffering, when I thought I was dying... I tried to hide the anguish I really felt. Do you remember the other night, when I had an attack, you were all there round me, I could feel a great block of black marble pressing down on me and I was calling out for someone to lift it off, but you couldn't see anything; well, as a last resort, I asked God, because I believe in him, a God who is good, Tesse... Ah, yes, that's when you truly realise you believe, when you think you're dying and your final moments are coming... You must believe, Tesse, you too, because God exists, and I've had proof. Listen, I asked him to let me live, not to take me yet, and in such a horrible way; I'm only twenty-three years old and I have done so many bad things that I need to atone for...! So, I promised him three things, I made three vows: first, to give five thousand francs to the poor, I'll do it, Tesse, I'll sell my beautiful emerald ring, you know, it's worth more than that, you'd pay twice as much at any dealer's in rue de la Paix, then next, as the terrible pains were still continuing, I tried to think of promises that would cost me a lot to keep, so that the good Lord would take notice... and I swore never to tell a lie again, never, you hear...! So, I can't dye my hair, no, that would be lying, wouldn't it, and I can't wear make-up any more either, powders and paints are just hypocritical lies... Oh, I'm very scrupulous, I am...! And, in the end, I promised something else as well, as a thanksgiving, because the weight that was choking me had suddenly disappeared, my mind was becoming clear again, I'm still alive and I'm on the way to recovering! So, Tesse, think, all that, it's proof to me, within the limits of my meagre intelligence... that the good Lord does exist.'

'Darling, you'll wear yourself out, don't talk so much, you can tell me all this later.'

'No, I'm back to my old self again, so don't worry...! It's important that you know the third thing, don't you see? It's...' She lowered her voice, imparting a confidence. 'It's... about Flossie... I promised to do everything I can to bring her back to the path of duty, of nature. I promised to see that she and Willy are united in the way two people should be united. As for me, I shall always be their little friend, I shall live with them, but I swore to sacrifice everything to that union, you know, my dreams, those troubling instincts in me that were aroused by her own particular forms of desire, I promised to resist her and to convert her. That's what I said, and I'll do it, yes, because God has answered my prayer. If she loves me, she will listen to me, she will marry in good faith and she will have children, and they will be my own family, my work, my atonement, do you understand...?'

Altesse was very moved, she felt a constriction in her throat; to change the subject, she said: 'Have you seen these, Nhinon? We've got some lovely strawberries, sent to you by Georges, my old friend. Take a look, smell them, you really should. Sample one at least.'

Nhine reached for the little basket.

'It's much nicer to enjoy little fruits like this by smelling them and looking at them than by eating them... it's a different sort of pleasure, you know, the same with cherries too, and peaches, and lots of other things in life, it's a shame to destroy them, a shame...!'

Her voice lost its confidence, grew weaker, trailed off. Her features became strained and hollow, the colour in her cheeks vanished, giving way to a waxy pallor, livid, turning yellow in places.

'I feel tired now...' Her eyes closed. 'I want to sleep... I've got to lie down... Help me back to bed... I don't want any little strawberries just now... keep some for me, will you, for this afternoon... sleep... I want to...' She was almost inaudible. 'I want to...'

Then, when they had laid her, fully dressed, on the bed whose brilliantly white cambric cover was suffused with the pink of the sheets underneath...

'Thank you, thank... you... Good... night, Tesse...'

She called to her, a little more loudly: 'Tesse...!'

Altesse returned to the bedside: 'Kiss... me, dar... ling...'

Her voice was slow, thick... Tesse placed on her forehead the lightest of kisses, with all the tenderness that rose from her heart, but Nhine no longer had the strength to return it...

'Stay... here... will... you, Tes...se... Good... night

good...'

She did not finish, overtaken by a deep and kindly sleep that caught her unawares and suddenly defeated her; and there was the suggestion of the lightest of laughs that ripples and ceases, the momentary charm of a ray of light that turns iridescent and fades, the softness of a sigh of wind that glances past... slips away...

XXV

Towards the ninth hour of that same morning, Flossie was dreaming in the darkness of her shuttered bedroom, still balmy from the night's gentle heat. She was dreaming about the future which was about to take shape, in all likelihood, over the hours of the coming day. A few rays of sunlight thrust through the cracks in the shutters and the sounds of comings and goings could be heard inside the hotel. Feeling lazy, she remained where she was, but with her eyes open, focussed on nothing, dreaming, when she thought she heard the light sound of a tap on her door. She started and asked: 'What is it?'

'There's a telegram for Miss,' came the answer.

'Wait!'

She jumped out of bed. The slip of paper was passed through the gap in the half-opened door as she stretched out her arm to take it, impatient, keeping the rest of her person out of sight. She was almost naked, her body only half covered by a little jacket in mauve silk which, very thin, clung to her skin and traced her deliciously sinuous outline. Her cheeks coloured, her heart beat faster. She calmly climbed back into bed; it was more comfortable. She tore open the blue paper. It was from Will... ah! And this is what it said:

> Miss Florence Temple-Bradfford, Hôtel de Bade, Paris – from San Francisco.
>
> Thanks for calling me to be with you forever. Leaving in three days aboard *Columbia*, overjoyed. I am the man who loves you and understands you.
> WILLY BARRETT.

"Everything's fine," she thought. "Everything's wonderful! Hurrah!"

And with a brusque movement she threw aside the sheets and blankets, in a hurry to get up and run round to Annhine to announce the good news she had been so eagerly waiting for. Paying no heed to her flimsy attire – the great bushy mass of her tangled hair would at least cover her blushes – she opened the window and pushed back the shutters. It was a superb day. The brilliant sunlight dazzled her momentarily. She turned back into the room, rubbed her eyes with naively childish gestures, reread the telegram and executed a little dance, something between a jig and a cancan. She bumped into everything, her table of toiletries, which clinked cheerfully, the piles of papers scattered here and there, and almost every piece of furniture, then suddenly she stopped, one leg raised, her nose in the air:

how was she to get access to Nhine...? That was the snag...! She quickly dismissed her doubts: "Pooh! I'll find a way...!" She was content to leave it to fate to provide solutions to even the most worrying problems. "Let's get dressed and go out, something's sure to turn up and point me in the right direction...!" Getting dressed was not easily accomplished, or quickly, but finally, with the help of the chambermaid, whom she rang for energetically, not wishing to be held up, she nevertheless managed to get the job done. Breakfast...? She needn't bother about that! She could think about it later, later. It was a detail easily ignored: joy is sustaining in itself! As she went out – where...? She didn't exactly know, but anyway, off and away, her star would guide her, invisible though it was – as she went out she couldn't help smiling at the scene of sheer muddle left behind in her room.

It was a place of riotous disorder: books rose in towers from the floor, some here, others there, yet more lay open on various surfaces, and papers covered everything. A jumble of photographs caught the eye: on one table the deliciously youthful nudity of Mebbaï was on display, in a variety of poses; Naléry, clad in Greek drapery, held outstretched arms towards some invisible lover; Sarah, the divine Sarah, haughty and impassioned, swathed in brocade and gold, commanded with a cruel gesture the death of some dramatic hero or other; Mary Anderson, her great eyes looking into the distance, hands clasping her knees, appeared calmly confident in her beauty. The engraving of a portrait of Maud Gonne was stuck in a mirror, and there were others, still more: Myrhille de Neiges, as a svelte and lissom Florentine page, was gracefully entwined with a dreadful-looking girl from the ballet; Hading, very severe, her eyes piercing and head intent, seemed to be trying to hypnotise or petrify all of humanity with the proud, calculating stare of a tigress. Then some who had become friends, grandly dressed for a ball, invariably in white satin; Otero, in a fluster of tulle, wearing the prettiest diamonds in the world; Cavalieri, adopting a pose that profiled her unclad bosom; Germaine Gallois throwing her shoulders back, smiling, sure of the effect on the packed audience of her impeccable turnout and vanished charms. This mass of photographs had one goal: simply to allow Miss Flossie free possession of the image of her Beloved, which was everywhere. There were Nhinons of all sorts, Nhinons in all styles, Nhinons without number, and it was the strange girl's great joy to be thus surrounded by a whole range of these pretty reproductions which provided such satisfactory illustrations to her reveries. She loved to spend hours looking at them, paying no attention to the others, which – choosing nevertheless from the prettiest – she had gathered in large numbers to deceive her family, who saw in it no more than an innocent and understandable mania for collecting.

Before taking her chances in the street, Florence wanted to telephone to Passy to see if there had been any developments overnight. In this way she learned that Annhine was feeling much better, that she was out of bed, stronger, that there was hope for her, at last! She left the hotel radiant: "These are happy omens. Happy omens...!" she sang for joy inside. "But how to approach her and show her this...?" She turned over in her fingers the little twist of blue paper that contained the realisation of all their hopes...! Someone brushed past her, making her look round. It was a nun, going on her way lost in holy meditation no doubt and not noticing she was there. Inspiration...! How had she not thought of it before, dressing as a nun...! She asked the first person she met where one went to obtain costumes of a similar sort, disguises, as if it was for a ball. She was told of a shop in boulevard de Sebastopol. It was a long way, but what did that matter, it was worth travelling any distance if her efforts were crowned with success. Once she had found the place, difficulties arose, she had to wait, and then come back after lunch. Only towards three o'clock was everything agreed, organised and crudely run up. Then she trotted down the stairs from the dressmaker's, carrying her clothes in a little parcel under her arm, hailed a cab and had herself driven to rue de la Pompe. What was the matter with this carriage, they were hardly making any progress at all...! What a long time it was taking...! As they drew close, the fear of some unforeseen difficulty bore down on her, some obstacle. She felt a weight pressing her heart, something sinister, painful. She talked to herself rationally: no, no, all would go well, come along, the thing to do was to present herself confidently, boldly, say she had received orders from above... from whom...? Ah, yes, from whom...? Pooh, she'd think of something: from Tesse, from the doctor, she'd say the first name that occurred to her and say it with aplomb, an important message for Charlotte, the little nurse, that was it... phew, she breathed again, relieved. She commended herself to – I was going to make a mistake and say to all the saints in Paradise – no, it was to Sappho that she addressed a mental prayer, and with a firm step, but a modest one in keeping with her new incarnation, she crossed the great courtyard. Oh joy... the door was open...! The door from the entrance hall to the stairs... open as well...! The staircase itself, deserted...! No defences further on either, some sort of commotion on Annhine's floor, people hurriedly coming and going... there were whisperings, something afoot... What was this, then, what had... happened...? Doors were banging... a general state of confusion. Good, all the easier for her, then! She hurried on... a thought struck her, a fear: could she have left already...? That was her room, there, at the end of the corridor... At the threshold, the smell of wax, like in churches, a silence... but just here... only here... why? Oh...! What was all this...?

She stepped back, appalled: shutters tightly closed, mournful candle flames the only light, indistinct figures, on their knees. Her eyes widened but saw nothing, so sharp was her pang of affliction... why...? where did it come from...? So, then... that long shape, stretched out on the big bed, it was...! Her legs wobbled under her... she was forced into the room because someone was pushing her from behind, curious to get close.

She knelt, without thinking, at the feet of the deceased... yes... yes... Nhinon was dead... that was it...! Ah! She really must be dead, why else would someone now have crossed her arms like that and closed the eyes whose heavy lids no longer let through any light? A tide of indignation swirled through her, she could neither weep nor pray... she didn't want this... she didn't want this... she felt a violent churning inside her, she got to her feet, very rapidly, desperate to run... she couldn't see anything or anyone clearly; only the vision of Nhine, a distant, confused vision, Nhine lying amongst flowers, her pale little head on the cushions, inert, bloodless, as pretty as in sleep, a sleep that released her from suffering, softening her calm, pure features... the religious piety of her folded hands...

Her senses disordered by the keenness of her grief, she backed away, unaware of anyone else, and bumped into Altesse, who did not recognise her, Altesse, red-eyed, blowing her nose all the time, tears running down her face, lost amongst the many people filling the room.

Ah! Now she could make everything out clearly. With the stiff gait of an automaton she looked for the way out but couldn't find the door, for people were constantly coming in. Flowers were arriving... quantities of flowers; servants were being given orders, telephones could be heard ringing.

Suddenly she found herself outside, in the brightness of daylight... She heard a journalist asking for details and writing things down in his notebook. Horrible...! Her face tightened into a hard, angry glare... Her cab...? Ah, yes, there it was! The same dirty, mud-caked cab, its worn-out horse, its driver... and there she was, dressed as a nun...! What a vicious irony...! She quickly slammed the door and shouted: 'Take me away from here! Anywhere you like...!'

And when the coachman stubbornly wanted to know where: 'Back to where you picked me up!'

The same streets... the same things... and Nhine gone...! The end of life...! The end of joy...! The end of the Idyll...! All their pretty hopes turned to dust...!

She ripped Will's telegram into a thousand pieces and flung the fragments out, scattering them into the void where all their desires had vanished... Not a tear, not a cry! Nothing...!

She felt a savagery stirring inside her. She leaned forward and said very loudly to make sure the driver heard: 'No, take me to the main post office!'

Once in rue du Louvre, the good cabman had an unparalleled shock when, to his stupefaction, instead of the timid young sister of poverty he had been driving round Paris all afternoon, he saw stepping out of his cab a petite young miss, pink-cheeked, hair tossed in the wind, under a jauntily tilted boater.

He couldn't restrain a cry of astonishment.

Ignoring his bewilderment, Flossie paid him and handed him a parcel with instructions to return it to boulevard de Sebastopol.

He clattered off, not caring to bother himself further, thanking Flossie.

Her self-assurance having returned, she strode resolutely into the foyer.

The thing was beyond remedy, irreparable, putting a cruel end to everything!

She thought for a moment, then with a firm hand wrote out these words:

Mr Willy Barrett
San Francisco Club, San Francisco

Future now pointless. Do not come. Annhine is dead.

FLOSSIE

Dedalus Celebrating Women's Literature 2018–2028

In 2018 Dedalus began celebrating the centenary of women getting the vote in the UK with a programme of women's fiction. In 1918, Parliament passed an act granting the vote to women over the age of 30 who were householders, the wives of householders, occupiers of property with an annual rent of £5, and graduates of British universities. About 8.4 million women gained the vote. It was a big step forward but it was not until the Equal Franchise Act of 1928 that women over 21 were able to vote and women finally achieved the same voting rights as men. This act increased the number of women eligible to vote to 15 million. Dedalus' aim is to publish six titles each year, most of which will be translations from other European languages, for the next ten years as we commemorate this important milestone.

Titles published so far:

The Prepper Room by Karen Duve
Take Six: Six Portuguese Women Writers edited by Margaret Jull Costa
Take Six: Six Spanish Women Writers edited by Simon Deefholts & Kathryn Phillips-Miles
Slav Sisters: The Dedalus Book of Russian Women's Literature edited by Natasha Perova

Baltic Belles: The Dedalus Book of Estonian Women's Literature edited by Elle-Mari Talivee
The Madwoman of Serrano by Dina Salústio *Primordial Soup* by Christine Leunens
Cleopatra Goes to Prison by Claudia Durastanti
The Girl from the Sea and other stories by Sophia de Mello Breyner Andresen
The Price of Dreams by Margherita Giacobino
The Ridiculous Age by Margherita Giacobino
The Medusa Child by Sylvie Germain
Days of Anger by Sylvie Germain
Venice Noir by Isabella Panfido
Chasing the Dream by Liane de Pougy
A Woman's Affair by Liane de Pougy
La Madre (The Woman and the Priest) by Grazia Deledda
Fair Trade Heroin by Rachael McGill
Co-wives, Co-widows by Adrienne Yabouza
Catalogue of a Private Life by Najwa Bin Shatwan
Baltic Belles: The Dedalus Book of Latvian Women's Literature edited by Eva Eglaja
This was the Man (Lui) by Louise Colet
This Woman, This Man (Elle et Lui) by George Sand
The Queen of Darkness (and other stories) by Grazia Deledda
The Christmas Present (and other stories) by Grazia Deledda
Marianna Sirca by Grazia Deledda
Cry Baby by Ros Franey
Border Lines by Ros Franey
The Pearl Whisperer by Karin Erlandsson
The Bird Master by Karin Erlandsson
The Scaler of the Peaks by Karin Erlandsson

The Victor by Karin Erlandsson
My Father's House by Karmele Jaio
Edo's Souls by Stella Gaitano
Take Six: Six Balkan Women Writers edited by Will Firth
The Innocent Libertine by Colette
The Soldier's Hat by Colette
The Fire Within by Touhfat Mouhtare
Take Six: Six Estonian Women Writers edited by Elle-Mari Talivee
Take Six: Six Irish Women Writers edited by Tanya Farrelly

Forthcoming titles include:

Take Six: Six Catalan Women Writers edited by Peter Bush
Take Six: Six Latvian Women Writers edited by Eva Eglaja
Blue Yarn (A Personal & Social History of Knitting) by Karin Erlandsson
Revolver Christi by Anna Albinus
Take Six: Six Ukrainian Women Writers edited by Steve Komarnyckyj
Lucrezia Floriani by George Sand
Wild Iris by Ruth McKee
A Space Bounded by Shadows by Emine Sevgi Özdamar
Monsieur Venus by Raschilde

For more information contact Dedalus at:
info@dedalusbooks.com

www.dedalusbooks.com

Chasing the Dream by Liane de Pougy

'Pougy's debut novel, *Chasing the Dream* was published in 1898. Admirably pragmatic, Anderson describes it as "a kind of half-time report on her career to date". It opens with the heroine Josiane horizontal on a chaise longue in her negligee. Suddenly a stranger arrives—her old lover, Jean, who declares his undying love, then politely enquires what she has been up to. It is a long story, so Josiane proposes a correspondence in which she will relate the details. The letters that follow chart Josiane's ascent through the Parisian demimonde via assorted aristocrats, politicians and businessmen.'

Miranda France in *The Times Literary Supplement*

'*Chasing the Dream* is a light piece of entertainment, but it is cleverly done. Managing to indulge in the most typical romance-tropes but also upending many of the expectations one has from this kind of story, de Pougy shows a fine touch in this, her first novel.' M. A. Orthofer in *The Complete Review*

£9.99   ISBN 978 1 912868 49 0   172p   B. Format

The Price of Dreams by Margherita Giacobino

Margherita Giacobino's book is a fictionalised biography/autobiography of Patricia Highsmith, taking the form of diary entries supposedly written by her, interspersed with a third-person narrative. It focuses on her psychological and emotional life, with the emphasis on feelings, relationships and aspirations rather than facts, dates and events. A lesbian in an era when to be homosexual was to be reviled and discriminated against, and made to feel guilty and ashamed, Patricia Highsmith struggled with her sexual identity in this social context, and the book fruitfully explores how this might have contributed to her creative output.

The title is a reference to Patricia Highsmith's second novel *The Price of Salt*, a lesbian romance originally published under a pseudonym after it was rejected by the publisher of her first novel. It was not until 1990 that she agreed to its reissue under her own name, with the new title *Carol*.

'*The Price of Dreams* has captured something essential about Patricia Highsmith—a unique but altogether plausible version, whose voice so echoes the voices the woman created throughout her writing life. This is just an astonishing work—a revelation.' Dorothy Allison

£12.99   ISBN 978 1 910213 95 7   336p   B. Format